A Long Dark Rainbow

Also by the author

Pegasus to Paradise

A Long Dark Rainbow

Michael Tappenden

The Book Guild Ltd

First published in Great Britain in 2019 by
The Book Guild Ltd
9 Priory Business Park
Wistow Road, Kibworth
Leicestershire, LE8 0RX
Freephone: 0800 999 2982
www.bookguild.co.uk
Email: info@bookguild.co.uk
Twitter: @bookguild

Typeset in Adobe Garamond Pro

Printed and bound in the UK by TJ International, Padstow, Cornwall

ISBN 978 1912881 789

British Library Cataloguing in Publication Data.
A catalogue record for this book is available from the British Library.

For the unlearned, old age is winter
For the learned, it is the season of harvest
The Talmud

Prologue

─────

H IS IMAGINATION DRIFTED upwards and outwards, through the cold dankness of the November evening and he was suddenly floating high above himself, looking down at his lone car, now speeding like a sleek missile, along a technicolour Hollywood freeway, headlights red hot, engine panting, seeking out his warm, soft destination.

Rick and Ilsa. Harry and Sally maybe. Scarlett and er… Oh, what the hell was his name? You know. Big guy. Tash. American. Lots of teeth. Frankly my dear, I don't give a… shit! What was it? And Ben and Mrs Robinson of course… No… maybe not Ben.

Reluctantly, he returned to the darkness of the old Volvo; to its drone and musty smell, wipers complaining as they were asked to sweep away spots of threatening rain. He shuffled uncomfortably in his seat. *No. Maybe not. Too young and embarrassingly naïve. Like me really. Back then. No, too close for comfort although how lucky was he? With Mrs Robinson. Lucky bastard.*

The older woman. He'd always fantasised. Of his pale, young, virgin body being seduced by forgiving fingers and demanding lips. Gently and calmly and confidently instructed. All that overflowing heat, controlled and understood and the chance to explore *such* mysteries. Like Mrs S. from two doors up. *Oh God, Mary. Do whatever you like. May I call you Mary, Mrs S.? You won't tell my mother?* But he would have been straining through gritted teeth and she must have known. *I blushed every time I met her, not to mention what was happening in my trousers.* Fear. Embarrassment. Ignorance. What effective contraception they had been. *What a shame. What a waste.* And Mrs S. had never done more than smile knowingly at him.

He glanced mechanically into the rear-view mirror. The motorway was almost empty at this time of night. He looked back again. Nothing much ahead. He yawned. *I would have been a different person you know. Calmer. Confident. Reassured. Instead of being imprisoned in that churning body. Instead of making terrible mistakes. Wouldn't that have been better? For everybody?* His right leg and shoulder were beginning to ache now and he squirmed again in his seat in an attempt to relieve them. *Not far now.*

He smiled to himself in the darkness. He couldn't really complain. Here he was, at his age, driving through the night, dashing to a liaison, his mind and body hungrily sought by a gorgeous woman. She had called him.

'Hallo Alex. How are you? Really looking forward to having you back again. I know it's a lot to ask after a long drive but… can you come tonight? Alex?' Her voice had sounded low and warm but also edged with concern. Had something happened? 'No, I'm fine.' His concern slipped away. 'I'm sorry. Just wanted to be with you. Talk to you. Listen to your stories. You know how I like your stories. Be close… Is that OK? I will understand if…'

He should have switched the television off by now and be contemplating the dark, empty screen, pondering the issues of the day, thinking about tomorrow, what to do. Trying to struggle upright into a sitting position, summoning enough energy to prepare for bed, maybe even considering a hot water bottle. Instead, here he was, gunning his muscle car towards a hot, hungry babe. *Yeah.* He took his left hand from the bony steering wheel and squeezed it between his thighs, feeling beneath the cold denim, hoping for fire and fullness, eyes straight ahead, although nobody could see him. Before, his energised blood, thick with ambition and excitement, would have surged around his body, beyond his control, filling every vein and artery and capillary with hot wonder, making every cell dance, gushing into his loins, making them quiver, engorging, pulling him inside out. But now, there appeared to be little reaction. *Oh, come on,* and he rubbed harder against the material, hoping for some response. There was a faint spark of interest. It was as if his brain and key parts of his body were no longer talking to each other. Not that that was anything new. In the past they had often ignored each other, preferring instead to go their separate ways, sometimes with disastrous consequences. Maybe now, they were sulking. He returned his hand to the steering wheel.

He had been about ten years old when he had had his first ejaculation. Although the event back then had been classified as 'top secret, not to be revealed to anyone under any circumstances', it didn't come as a great surprise, for his increasing manual dexterity and flushed face had led him to suspect some fruitful conclusion for all his efforts. Intuitively, he knew that the impact – if not the outpouring – was of tsunami proportions and that his life was about to change forever. Having arrived, maybe prematurely, at this pivotal moment in his sexual growth, what he didn't know, was, that others had already mapped out his future development. From flaccidity to awareness to virility to ignorance to repression to chronic masturbation to lust and fever to permitted access and more ignorance to mutual disappointment to adultery to abstinence and back to flaccidity. That's how it was destined. That's what was in store for him. And woe betide you back then if you ever dared to question that journey. And then, after almost seven long decades, he had met Samantha, at one of the occasional crossroads along the way, and they had dared to get off.

He had to admit, he was older, much older now. Coming up to seventy. Didn't feel like it though. As long as he kept clear of mirrors and passport booths and didn't bend to stroke pets. Sometimes he forgot his own age. People would smile knowingly. 'Of course you do darling.' But he really did. Had to work it out. This year minus his year of birth – assuming he could remember the present year of course. 'Oh, is that what I am? Knew it was around there somewhere. So how many years left I wonder?' Sometimes he would talk to younger friends or relatives, see them laugh and chatter and wonder if they would be at his funeral. Which ones wouldn't get the time off? Which ones would have the flu? Which ones would just make excuses? He tried to imagine their faces, a lot older. It was difficult and he gave up. Didn't seem macabre though, just inevitable. Weirdly and scarily inevitable.

Life was slipping past now, moving ever faster and faster. It had been like pushing an enormous glass boulder. Uphill to begin with but now, for the first time, it was beginning to slope downwards. Beginning to run away from him.

So, when did it first appear? About the age of ten? Eleven maybe? Something like that. Certainly by my teens.

It was kept in his bedroom to begin with, where he would be alone with it, even when his mother came in to pick up his clothes off the floor. She never saw it of course. Nobody else could see it. *Suppose she had one of her own. Never thought about that before.*

Somehow, it seemed to understand you, your fears and weaknesses. Outside, you might pretend to be somebody else, another version of you, one you preferred but in your inside world, your real world, it seemed to know everything and sat there, vast and dark and immovable, completely unimpressed, filling every corner, sometimes blotting out the very light. To begin with, it was black and rough and you could just about see your reflection in it. There couldn't have been very much else to see. Later it became clearer and smoother, although never totally. You wanted to move it *so* badly, roll it away, roll it on, but you couldn't. Not then. Later, occasionally, it had rolled easily on a level but then, just when you thought you had controlled it, you found yourself toiling uphill, pushing for all you were worth, trying to stop it rolling back on you. Sometimes you thought fuck it, ignore it, but it was always there, waiting, mute and impassive. Now, however, it was beginning to run away like a bowl rumbling towards the one remaining tenpin.

He looked into the rear-view mirror again. Nothing. He glanced at it. A small plastic rainbow hung from it by a silver-coloured chain. Could have come from a boot fair or a charity shop or even a Christmas cracker, but he had no memory of buying it. Perhaps it had come second-hand with the car. He couldn't remember now but he had no thoughts of removing it. It felt strangely comforting, although a bit weird in the darkness. *Can you have rainbows in the dark? Only in your own head I suppose.* Anyway, nothing for a long way back. Ahead, just those lorries in the distance.

He imagined her, now, waiting for him. Maybe she would be lying naked on her stomach, white sheet pulled up, to partly cover those round smooth mounds that now spread below her lean back, like the strangely innocent pictures of the set of 1950s playing cards he had found and showed her. Needed to be stroked gently, with reverence and delight *and* surprise. Surprise at their shape and firmness. That had been unexpected. All those years of standing. Serving customers. Ruined her feet of course. And swimming. Funny how your occupation can eventually determine your body. Like gardeners. Bending, lifting, digging. Always brown, fit and nimble. Be a gardener my son and you will fuck forever… and now she was waiting for him. His chest squeezed and he swallowed some saliva.

She had said it didn't matter. She had said that, the very first time. She had smiled that sweet, sweet smile. It doesn't matter. We're both a little nervous. A little tense. It *will* be alright. I am sure there are other things we can do, but she had sounded uncertain. But there had been. Other things. Far more than he could possibly have imagined. He reached for the denim again and was met with warm indifference. *It doesn't matter. And it's late. Yes, but it doesn't matter. You know that.*

He realised he was driving too fast. His anxiety had spread to his right foot. He slowed down and switched on the radio. It jangled metallically and insolently. *'Hey we're young. We're cool.'* He switched it off. Ahead, a lorry lumbered along the inside lane, its bulk vaguely determined by the glow of four red tail-lights. *Funny how vehicles have tails. Like fish. No not fish. Fish glide and wriggle and dart. These are more like… elephants. Slow, steady and powerful…* His mind drifted and his eyelids became heavy.

'Jesus!'

A lorry pulled out in front of him; red lights shouting and his stomach yelped with alarm. *Off the accelerator. Brakes on hard. Not too hard! Can't overtake. Can't look behind. Steady now. That's close. Too close.* Steadily the lorry pulled slowly ahead.

'Idiot. You bloody old idiot.'

*

He turned very slowly and deliberately into the tree-lined avenue, as if by doing so he could control the feelings now bubbling in his chest. Slow his pulse. Moisten his mouth. Ahead, he could see her car, waiting patiently for the sun to rise again and clear away the acid streetlight. It looked blacker in the false light.

She sits in that. Her body warms that seat. Her long legs move those pedals. Wonder why it isn't in the garage?

He drove quietly into the space behind, switched off the engine and lights and sat for a moment, feeling the motion of the journey plus the encounter with the lorry that had scared him. Made him feel foolish and he snapped at himself, 'Now for God's sake, concentrate. Have you got everything? Key? Got the key? Rhett.' *It was Rhett. Of course it was. It's all in there.* He tapped his head. *Just a bit reluctant to come out.* Slowly he opened the car door, eased his legs out, held onto the door frame and pushed upwards. His knees complained. One vocally. He sighed to himself, pushed the door gently and it clicked shut. He locked it, stood silently and looked up at the bedroom. A soft light flickered through the windows. Around him the street stood stock-still and a cold breeze was the only other visitor. He moved stiffly to open the decorative iron side gate, the hinges yawning and the latch tinkling excitedly, as he dropped it back. *This could be a film. Maybe a spy film.*

Yeah. Gliding like a ghost into a safe house or deftly slipping a lock and silently creeping into danger, senses aching. This is so theatrical. Deliciously so. And exciting. Am I supposed to feel like this? A geriatric James Bond?

He stood in front of the back door illuminated by the outdoor light. She had offered him only *that* key. He had seen it hanging in the kitchen. *Well at least she's taken the tag off.* He had thanked her politely. There had been no need for further words. No querying. He had read the uncertain messages in her eyes, in her body, in the hand that held the key out to him for him to take if he wanted it. *Gently. Gently.*

Behind him the garden, normally so bright and calm, appeared as a strange dream in the harsh electric light. No softness, no tones, no graduation. Every leaf and twig in razor-sharp relief. Dark, impenetrable shadows watched him suspiciously. He slid the key in and tried to turn it. Nothing happened. *Maybe a little harder? No. Try again… Bloody fingers. No not too hard. It'll snap. Shit. Why won't… Try wiggling it. It won't turn. Why won't it turn? It's the wrong key. Ahh, let's have a look. No. It's the right key it just won't… Oh dear. This was not in the bloody script. Now what do I do? Can't phone her. Knock on the door. That'll spoil everything. Shit. I don't believe this… OK. Calm down and try again. Gently. Carefully. Can't let her hear. Move it out slightly. Feel for it. Click. There… Thank God… Some bloody spy.*

The kitchen was very large and modern and lit by a single light. He bent, holding onto the worktop and took off his shoes, immediately feeling the coolness of the slate flagstones. *God, it's about the size of my flat.* There was the smell of fresh vegetables. Onions and in the background, the taste of some potato field. *She's been to the local farm shop. Wonder if earth smells differently in different parts? Must do. A good drop of East*

Anglian loam or the sharp tang of Kentish clay maybe. In the sink, a large, white cup, a plate and some cutlery waited for the morning's hot soapy water. Nearby, on a black marble top stood a card. He knew immediately it was for him. Forty-five years ago, he may not have noticed. Would only have been aware of the throb growing in his loins, dominating everything. Now, he smiled.

Welcome home sweet sexxxxxy man. Sam.

For some reason the words felt strangely uncertain; her small writing moving across the card, neat and controlled but also slanting... *to some conclusion maybe? Looking for something perhaps? And five kisses... all the same height. All the same. Had they started with five?* He couldn't remember. *How many would they end with? Would they still be real kisses then or just symbols? Everyday? Automatic? Would they be almost the end of the alphabet? The end of words? The end of the story? The end?* He pushed the thoughts away and placed his lips on the card.

Next to him was a cupboard full of drinking glasses. He opened it and even in the semi-darkness, they winked and chattered brightly. *Careful, don't drop one.* Then she *would* be alarmed, turn on the lights, call out and the magic would be lost. He stood very still and listened. Nothing. No tick; no tock. Nothing. Only his breathing and the huge unheard sound of his heart thudding and his ears hissing. The fridge suddenly purred and he jumped. *Shit!* Then nothing. He filled the glass carefully with water, switched off the light and waited for his eyes to become accustomed. In the darkness, he looked up towards the ceiling. Up there, just up there she was waiting for him. Up there, pleasures that before he had barely imagined, now waited for them both. He took a nervous sip of water, opened the kitchen door and then stood quite still. In the darkness of the long hallway, light flickered before him, around the bottom of the stairway and he felt a pang of alarm. As he watched, the light settled into a warm, steady glow and his concern turned to curiosity. He moved forward. On the bottom step and every three steps above, a small candle was burning like a runway guiding him home. He smiled broadly, placed his glass onto a small table nearby and on all fours climbed the stairs, blowing out each candle, one at a time, until he reached the landing. There he paused, panting quietly at the exertion. In the darkness, the bedroom door in front of him was ajar and through it played the same trembling light. He stood quite still. There was silence. Not a sound. His senses sharp and quivering; mouth open. He waited, scarcely daring to breathe, then, slowly, pushed the door and stepped inside. The flame of the nearest candle, startled, moved abruptly, and then settled, reassured. Apart from their soft glow, the room was in darkness. Samantha was sitting on the bed, her back against large pillows, bare legs drawn up. She said nothing. Alex realised that his mouth was now quite dry. She was wearing a soft, black top, open to her waist, covered in dark reflective sequins that shimmered in the light. From each ear dangled long silver earrings that she never normally wore. They flashed brightly as she turned her head. Apart from that, she appeared to be naked. She looked towards him, her eyes in shadow, apart from sharp glints as the candlelight caught the movement. With no accompanying sound, Alex felt a sudden stab of irrational fear at this mute creature. Her voice, when it came, was low and remote, as if from a shadow but was loaded with sensuality.

'Hallo…' She paused. 'Good trip?'

Her words, with their strange formality, surprised him, suggesting as they did that nothing else was happening in the room. That the pounding in his head and heart was incidental; that the thick, hot tension building around them was not actually happening. But it was. He nodded, reluctant to trust his voice, and moved slowly towards her. She watched carefully as he gently moved the black material further apart and then stood back to see the gentle light catching the soft contours of her flesh.

'Great.'

She wasn't sure if he meant the trip or the sight of her body. But it didn't matter.

1

In the Beginning

THERE WERE FIVE charity shops along the incline of the high street and approaching from the bottom of the slope, Alex normally visited the first he came to, not out of loyalty to that particular cause, but because he couldn't be bothered to carry heavy donations any further. But he *had* visited every shop at some time. They fascinated him. The windows; dressed like normal retailers but full of other people's plastic fruit and soft toys and cake stands and plates with rabbits painted on and wooden signs telling him where the Heart is. The flotsam of kitsch washed up here. All that brightly designed stuff from the outer periphery of real form and function that people gave to each other for their toilets or kitchen walls and then got bored with. Reminded him of the strange still lives he had tried to paint, years ago and for a brief moment his heart sank.

Back then, in his youth, he had been nervously excited at the thought of entering art college. He had been drawn to the large Victorian building that stood so solidly near the centre of the town, aware of the very tall windows that looked out from the stone structure, of the idealised caryatids and the columned entrance. He had felt reassured by its architectural confidence, reassured that the mysterious activities that took place within must surely have the same gravitas and status. The status that his parents wanted him to have. When eventually he did enter, wearing the suit and tie prescribed by his father and clutching a shiny, brand new portfolio, it felt strangely comforting and yet at the same time the whole place seemed to spin at a provocative and dizzy tilt outside of the normal and everyday. He had gawped at the huge open studios bathed in northern light, reeking of turpentine and the fat richness of oil paint. He had stared at the colourful students, each dressed in their own non-conformist palette, and had felt very ordinary. Some had smiled at him, most ignored him but each he knew was immersed in the strange secret ways of this other culture, secrets that he desperately longed for.

And so, he had started with still lives. Drawing and painting. Drawing, he understood. *That exquisite feeling of pencil tip on paper* and he drew with a fluency and accuracy that attracted a positive response. At that moment he had felt so happy and accepted but then his flush of success had turned cold and he had sat, rigid-backed, looking around, lost and bewildered as other students found alternative and at times audacious meanings to this simple pile of objects before them. They had breathed life into their concepts with paint and brush and finger and rag, concepts that he simply could not understand. The tutorials that followed had left him lost and angry; angry at his own lack of perception and miserably he had applied to change direction and was readily accepted onto an art history course. Despite his disappointment, he was reassured that the world of art – which he had dared to believe really existed – did so, was all around him and took many forms. He had worked hard, published books, risen to a fairly senior level in design education before retiring but always felt a grudging admiration for fine artists, especially his friend Edmund. Now he shook those thoughts away.

Inside the small shops, he had often squeezed past the rows of clothes and piles of shoes and inhaled their human mustiness. Felt their sadness. Once they had been bright and crisp and hopeful. Now they were desperate to keep out of the 'Everything 50p' box. Maybe he'd pick one shop and go in there today. Have a good look around. It felt like a day for an adventure.

He studied himself in the bathroom mirror and ran his hand over his grey close-cropped hair and sighed inwardly. Once it had been long. Shoulder length. Thick and curly. Like his mother's but darker. Usually pulled back into a pony tail, plus the occasional facial stubble. Had represented who he had been. Art student? *Certainly*. Lecturer? *Yes*. Free thinker? *Sometimes*. Revolutionary? *Not really*. Anti-establishment? *Sadly*. He had wanted to keep the pony tail into retirement, maybe shorter, as a badge of honour, one you had to earn, but his hair had disappeared. Slowly. Silently. He hadn't really noticed to what extent until that day in the barber's chair.

'Is that alright sir?'

The mirror had moved slowly over the back of his head and there it was, a bald patch like a fresh wound.

'OK sir?'

But there was nothing to be done, nothing to be said. He had begun to shed the vitality of carefree youth. It had slipped away without him noticing, never to return.

'Yes. That's fine thanks.'

Strange thing was, that his hair now grew in abundance everywhere else. It had slid down from the top of his head and now covered his eyebrows, ears, nose and back. *Even* his back. 'Forget my head. Just trim my eyebrows, burrow into my nose and shave my back please.'

'That'll be seven pounds please. Special rate for senior citizens today.'

Oh God. Is it that obvious? You could have lied. Pretended you couldn't tell. Charged the full amount and hoped my vanity would pay it. Not much to ask.

*

He hadn't shaved today. Hadn't ironed his shirt either which hung limply outside of his jeans. Well, he had nobody to impress and there were far more important things to do. Mind you, perhaps if he undid the shirt, he could show off his Stones T-shirt. Yes, he'd been there. 1976. Les Abattoirs. Heard Jagger sing *Fool to Cry*. Great. Trouble is, it would also show off his paunch. Not so much of one, but it was there alright. The other problem was that he had no idea where that particular T-shirt was. *Not hanging up. Must be in a drawer somewhere. Means it will smell musty. Means washing. No. Not today.* Anyway, he'd taken his medication. Or was that yesterday? No, he took them with that cup of tea. Or was that last night? No, he always took them in the morning... Bloody memory. You spend your life filling your brain. Hour after hour after hour, learning and understanding, feeding its voracious appetite, packing tons and tons of knowledge into the bottomless pit of brain cells and then later, when you want something back... nothing. Maybe his brain was now feeding on all that information piled inside it and would only let you have the scraps it doesn't want, like bacon rind and cherry pips. Maybe it was simply composting. Anyway, no time for that now, he needed to get out into the sunshine. Had already sniffed its warmth through his open window and tasted a sweet tingle on the air like candy floss at a funfair. He pushed his wallet into one pocket and his keys into the other, edged carefully past the piles of books stacked on the floor and closing the door to his small flat with a bang, stepped out into the long corridor that led to the front entrance.

His flat had been rather cool and dark. The sun wouldn't arrive until the afternoon and work its magic. In the corridor, he was struck by the heat coming through the picture windows that looked out onto a large, lawned garden punctuated by flower beds and shrubs. Three large crows were strutting around the grass. *Sarf London crows* with attitude and yet, occasionally, they fluttered nervously at the unexpected movement of a grey squirrel. *Look at him.* The squirrel moved so quickly, so positively, with such focus as though there was no time to waste. *Must be nice to have that attitude. Squirrels don't drift through life. They know what they want. They get on with it.* He tapped on the window. The squirrel stopped, sat up on its haunches and looked directly at him. *Don't look at me like that Mr Clever.* He tapped again. Harder. The squirrel turned and scampered off and the crows lifted their black bodies into the air and flapped lazily away into the trees. *There, all gone.* Except for him. Standing there.

In one corner of the garden stood a pale statuette of a Greek figure, peering uncomfortably through the leaves and branches that threatened to envelop him. He knew it was Dionysus or at least a sanitised version, with his plaster robe draped conveniently across his manhood. He had given lectures on Greek art many times. At college. 'This, is

Dionysus. Also known by his Roman name of Bacchus. Son of Zeus and Semele. God of wine and ritual ecstasy. Shown here as a naked androgynous youth.'

'Sir. Sir.'

'Yes.'

'Why is his willy so small?'

Oh, for God's sake.

'No sir. If he was a god, why didn't he give himself a really big one?'

Oh Dionysus. Protector of those who do not belong to conventional society. Guardian of the chaotic and unexpected. Leader of wild female followers. Please come and rescue me.

Alex looked closer. The original pale, smooth skin of the statue had changed. It had turned darker, smudged with the grime of weather and pollution and ageing, and around his noble head, cocked to one side, the summer growth was slowly covering him. *Discoloured and disappearing.* Alex sighed, turned, walked to the front entrance, opened it, stepped into the car park, walked across the front lawn, through a gap in the hedge and turned left.

The high street was comfortable and slightly old fashioned. At intervals, small silver birch and beech trees grew, their delicacy contrasting with the concrete slabs and stone around them. The street also offered a bakery, a butcher and a greengrocery stall. The stall intrigued Alex. Unlike the smooth segregated sections seen in the local supermarket, here the fruit and veg seemed to have been specially selected, polished, piled and presented. It sat full and luscious, a bright ensemble of colour and form against the green baize, almost defying you to disturb it by buying any. Reminded him of a painting… *Dutch… seventeenth century. Saw it in the Rijksmuseum that time… girl selling something from a large table laden with fruit and veg... Floris... come on you should know this.... Floris van thingy... van Schooten. Yes, Floris van Schooten. That's it. Yeah. Now, apart from old Floris, it might even become a Cezanne or maybe a Matisse.* If he stepped back into the road, held up his hands in front of his eyes to contain just the stall and then squinted... Yes. There. Look. OK, cars might drive slowly around you, drivers too curious to sound their horns.

'See that old guy. What on earth is he doing? Is he alright? Silly old fart. Careful you don't run him over.'

Alex crossed the road and stood in front of the stall containing parts of it within his hands. The stallholder looked at him curiously.

'You alright mate?'

'Oh yes I'm fine, thank you.'

'Got some nice bananas today.'

'Yes, I can see but I was really just imagining your stall as a Matisse.'

'Oh really.'

'Have you never done that?'

'No mate. Just imagined selling this lot and getting off early.'

Alex smiled at him. There was a time when he would probably have been too embarrassed to have done that. No, not embarrassed exactly. More conditioned. Concerned about others and how they saw him. But now, at this age, he had learnt not to worry so much. Not only that, but he realised, it was almost expected. *'Look at that silly old fool.' Isn't that how they see me?* It had been something of a revelation. The realisation that maybe all those white-haired ladies and balding men, shuffling along, already knew this? All this time they'd simply been playing the part. Wallowing in this wonderful freedom and not letting on. Playing the youthful and the confident for the callow beings they are. So, what else did they know? What else went on behind closed curtains? Geriatric threesomes in quiet suburban bungalows? Maybe. But it did mean that the great observer of life had got it wrong or maybe it was different in Will's time. He stood on the pavement and mouthed the lines to himself as best as he could remember.

'The sixth age shifts into the lean and slipper'd pantaloon, with spectacles on nose (*well that's true*) and pouch on side. His youthful hose (*something, something*) too wide for his shrunk shank; and his big manly voice, turning again towards childish treble, pipes and whistles in his sound.'

The stallholder shuffled.

Alex looked at him.

'You have a wonderful time coming to you.'

'Oh good. I'll tell the missus. Now what about these bananas?'

*

At intervals along the high street, the council had placed large baskets of plants above head height. The packed flowers spilled over and trumpeted purple and red in the bright sunshine and waited patiently for the late afternoon to arrive, to turn them up to an even deeper glow. Alex stopped to admire one. *So beautiful.* As he did so, a single bloom fell from the basket and landed before him. It was yellow. *Yellow? Thought they were all red or purple. Didn't see any yellow. That's strange. Hey, maybe it's a sign. My God, it's Dionysus. Must be. From this morning.* He slowly stooped to pick up the flower and placed it in the palm of his hand. It felt soft and limp and vulnerable. *It's an omen.* He looked around, seeking some meaning. There was nothing obvious. He placed the flower carefully into his shirt breast pocket and walked on.

Outside the charity shop, he stopped and peered between three headless dummies wearing women's clothing, placed next to a stand of charity cards. The shop was long and narrow and the door to the rear room was open. Inside, a fluorescent tube threw an uncomfortable light over a number of black plastic bags and a mass of objects piled near the doorway. In front of the room, to one side, a woman was placing clothes onto wire hangers and then hanging them for display. She appeared to be alone and was wearing a yellow tabard. Alex watched her curiously and then something began to tickle in the back of his mind. *Do you know? I think I know her.* He turned away and studied the pavement. *Sure I know her.* Suddenly, in his mind, swam waves of dark, lustrous red against milky flesh dissolving into a painting, a large painting within an over-ornate frame. He glanced back. *No, it can't be. Is it? But her hair's so different. What's happened? It's gone.* He looked again, out of sight behind the shop window dummies. He inhaled sharply. *Yes. Reagan.* He waggled a finger at that thought. *His name was Reagan.* Placed the finger against his lips. *Fancy remembering that. After all this time. Well well.* Looked back. *She must be about my age now. Don't want her to see me… I'm sure it's her. Smaller than I remember. Maybe… maybe just slimmer. Hard to tell beneath that terrible tabard thing. Maybe she's dyed it? Must have… Doesn't want to show the grey. But to lose that glorious copper colour… What a shame… Ain't life cruel. Reagan… She married that business bloke. What an arsehole. Very rich though. Made his money in… oh what was it? Something ridiculous. Like… toilet rolls or plastic ducks. Hardly earth shattering… It was at that private view. Yeah, they were both there. Terrible artist. Don't remember his name. Awful work. Crap. Real crap… She seemed so lost… I went to their dinner party. That's right. Why was that? God it was awful. Think I got drunk. Probably. Usually did.*

God knows what I said. Don't suppose it was very complimentary. Oh no, perhaps I upset her… No, no it would have been him. Pompous prick. And it was such a long time ago… Well, well… Reagan. He spoke the word in his mind again so as not to lose it. *Reagan. Now what was her name? Began with a…? God, she was beautiful. Mmm. Long time ago.* He went to turn away, find a coffee, ruminate on those days but something made him stop and push the door open.

Immediately to his right were several rows of second-hand books. He picked one up at random, looking furtively in her direction and back again. She hadn't looked up when he had entered the shop. *Guess lots of people simply wander in and out, just to see what is in that day. Get out of the rain. Pass the time.* He glanced in her direction, took the book, moved closer and waited quietly to one side of her. *This feels like stalking. Why am I so nervous?*

She placed the last item on the rail and turned. *Those eyes. So pale. So big.*

'Hallo.'

A slight look of alarm crossed her face like the shadow of an unexpected cloud crossing your hot body on a summer beach and she raised one hand to her throat. Her fingernails were the colour of a shiny cherry. *Oh dear, am I smiling too much. Probably look like Mad Jack in* The Shining. *Don't seem to be able to control my features anymore.* He tried to switch his face off. *How's that?*

'You made me jump.' Her voice was soft and cultured.

'Sorry.'

She smiled politely and looked down at the book he was carrying.

'Would you like to buy that?'

Alex continued to gaze at her. *Yes, of course it was her.*

'The book?'

She smiled again. Teeth so white and straight and expensive. She seemed slightly amused now and the wrinkles around her eyes joined in.

'Shall I take it? Check the price?' She tried to take the book from him, gently as if he was a recalcitrant infant. He noticed she was wearing a wedding ring. He swallowed hard.

'You don't remember me, do you?' Waited. Tried again. 'No, well, must be nearly… what, forty years ago now? Huh. Forty years. Mind you I did look very different then. You know. Long hair.' He waggled a finger in a circle next to his head.

Her hand moved nervously to her own hair.

God I wish I'd shaved today. Ironed my shirt. He felt himself begin to panic. Words slipped free from him. 'Dionysus. Yes. Of course. Dionysus. The god. You know. Yes. He sent me. Told me to give you this.'

He fumbled in his shirt pocket, gently retrieved the flower, took her hand and placed it in her palm. It felt soft and warm. She looked up at him. Her eyes had widened in surprise. He let go abruptly, smiled awkwardly, stepped back, raised one hand in a form of wave, turned and moved hastily towards the door. She watched his figure move outside across the shop front, between other pedestrians and not look back.

Alex bounced unsteadily down the high street almost colliding with another shopper.

'Careful Grandad.'

'Sorry. So sorry. Didn't see you.' He waved an apology and as he moved on, suddenly caught sight of himself in a shop window. He stopped in surprise, for there looking back at him was not a gauche lad of seventeen, blood pumping, but an elderly man whom he barely recognised; balding, slightly stooped, wearing glasses, face lined. It wasn't until he returned to his flat that he looked down at the book still in his hand and realised he hadn't paid for it.

*

He couldn't go back the next day. Knew he should, but spent the morning cleaning his flat and washing and ironing every shirt he owned. He had rummaged through a number of drawers and amongst the odd empty glass case, blank thank-you cards, pens, pencils, chalks, rubbers, small scissors, old book markers and piles of white plastic curtain hooks, he found a pair of secateurs which he then used to cut back the fringe of leaves and ivy around the statue.

'That's better. Now I can see you.'

He found himself a plastic garden chair and brushed off the dirt, old webs and dead leaves.

'I think you've got me into a load of trouble. No, OK, I know that. I know *you* didn't tell me to do anything, but you were in my head. You must admit that. Well… anyway. The thing is… now what do I do? Yes, I must take the book back or pay for it. I know that. And soon. You haven't seen all the notices in the shop about people stealing things, have you? Oh, you have. Well, I certainly don't want to be thought of as a thief, now do I? So, right, I have to go back. Pay for the book. Apologise to her? Do I apologise or should I just be mysterious or something? Isn't that what you are supposed to do? And then what? Wish you wouldn't look at me like that. It's alright for you. You're used to the unexpected and chaotic and placing women under ecstatic spells. It's harder for me. Right, so I go back, pay for the book, say nothing about why I ran off? Oh, I don't know… Anyway, why am I so concerned? She's only a woman I once met and do I really want to get involved again? Once was enough and anyway she might not even like me. And not only that, I don't really want the book. It's about spiritual growth. I can just talk to you. Oh yes. One more thing. Do you happen to know what her first name is?'

The sun, having heard it all before, moved slowly across the garden, behind a cloud and left Alex pondering in a cool shadow.

*

Dionysus was wearing a red wig, which together with his pale androgynous appearance, was disconcertingly attractive. His manhood, now revealed from beneath the plaster cloak, hung to just above his knee and the floor of the studio, in which they were all gathered, was deep in yellow flowers. He said nothing, but stood, posing, with a strange, superior smile on his face. Nearby, Alex hovered nervously before a large, blank white canvas and attempted to paint the scene before him. Every brush stroke however, although laden with colour, failed to register a single mark, no matter how hard he tried to apply it. A large clock standing in one corner chimed irregularly, and as it did so, the dimensions of the canvas became smaller and smaller and smaller.

He awoke sluggishly, sweaty and with the tendrils of the dream reluctant to release him. He looked up at the plaster swirls on the ceiling and rubbed his fingers over the dampness of his face and neck. *This is ridiculous. Quite ridiculous. Today, I'll go back to the shop, pay for the book and say hallo. No more than that.*

He showered and prepared to shave, rubbing the steam from the bathroom mirror. His eyes looked the same although they seemed to have shrunk. Maybe it was the eyebrows, still dark but with silver grey now entwined within them, growing bushier and pressing down upon them. If he combed them upwards, he could trim them like you would a hedge although it was difficult to do whilst wearing spectacles. *I need one of those magnifying glasses.* He dabbed his nose with shaving cream. There were two or three small dark hairs growing there. *Would have to be dark wouldn't they? Couldn't be grey and almost invisible.* He shaved them away and studied himself in the mirror again. *They'll be back. Not too many lines around the eyes but two deep ones either side of the nose, pointing downwards. Like a sad clown's face. And that jaw – once it had the clean, sweeping lines of a racing yacht. Now look at it, bumbling around the coast, lumpy with barnacles.* He looked at the back of his left hand, free from holding the razor. It was gnarled and veined and brown-mark blemished. Some days, his fingers ached when the rain fell and cold fogs rolled in.

He turned it over. His palm was covered in lines running in all directions, like cracks in an uncared-for pavement. He turned it back again and flexed his fingers. *My God, look at that. Looks like…* The back of his hand was covered in a myriad of creases. *Looks like old basketwork.* He released the tension, fearful that the skin might tear like old parchment and put the razor down. *And the scars.* The backs of his hands were covered in old scars. He turned them slowly, left to right and back again, counting the small, white marks that sat upon his skin. He couldn't remember how they had happened and briefly imagined the sharp pain of each but had no memory. They were the hands of someone who had pushed out blindly, who had felt uncertainly into an unknown and jagged world. He looked up again at his face, reached and pulled the skin and flesh back to his ears. Ten years dropped away. *There, that's better. I just need to pin it all back. It's like a balloon the day after a party. Taut and smooth and shiny and bouncy when you arrive and then limp and rather sad when you leave. Let's hope you had a great time.* He began to cover his lower face with thick, white shaving foam.

He had laid some clothes onto his crumpled bed. Normally they were piled over the back of a chair, socks lying limply where they had fallen across a pair of old shoes or draped over the large, battered portfolio that was propped up against the wall. He looked at the portfolio. It was secured by a single drawstring – the other had long disappeared and a name written on one side had been crossed through with vigorous black slashes. *Must go through that one day. Sort it out. Not now.* Turning away, he looked down at the socks and realised the colours didn't match. *Do you know, I've never noticed? Been walking around like that for ages. Still, it doesn't matter, does it? I am an artist after all. Well… almost. Expected, isn't it? A bit of eccentricity that's all. It's allowed* and he thought of the greengrocery stall. But still a tremor of uncertainty rippled through him. *Reagan. What's-her-name Reagan. She's very posh and cultured and brimming with etiquette and social graces. Not like you mate.* He felt uncertain. Then annoyed.

'Oh, fuck Mrs thingy Reagan.' *Oh my God. I do hope so.* The intensity of that thought shook him.

He had pondered for quite a while over whether to wear a tie and had finally decided not to. He didn't normally, and it *was* summer and anyway he wasn't quite sure if he actually owned one. If he did, it was probably at the bottom of that long drawer, with his Stones shirt maybe, waiting for winter or a funeral or something, along with that long Merino multi-striped scarf that reminded him of the work of Sean Scully, together with his thermals and that woollen hat, which reminded him of a refugee.

The high street was quite busy. Usually was on a Saturday, but soon enough, Alex found himself outside the same charity shop, once more peering through the rack full of greetings cards. Beyond the splashes of unfocussed colour and words, he could see people moving slowly but he couldn't see her. *Maybe she's in the back room, sorting. Must be really smelly in there.* There was one other woman serving and two or three older ladies browsing through the clothes. *Now what do I do? Must go in. Must pay. Find out.* He took the book, lifted his shirt and stuffed it down his waistband. *Maybe nobody will notice.*

The woman serving was standing behind a small beech-coloured counter, eyes down, checking something in a catalogue. Alex waited for a moment.

'Er… hallo.'

The woman looked up and then smiled, openly. Alex's eye was drawn to a gold-coloured chain that descended towards the fold between impressive breasts. For a second, he imagined drawing them.

'Ah, is Mrs Reagan here?'

The woman didn't answer directly but scanned Alex's face curiously.

'No, she doesn't work Saturdays. But she is going to call in later.' She looked towards one of the two clocks on the wall opposite. Both showed slightly different times. 'After lunch I expect.'

Alex hovered, hoping the woman might tell him more but she just looked at him with an amused smile. The book was pressing into his stomach.

'Lunch. OK. Thank you.'

'Angela.'

'Sorry?'

'My name's Angela.'

'Well thank you Angela. I'll er… I'll call back later.'

Alex hastened towards the exit, stopped and turned. 'What is Mrs Reagan's first name? Been a long…' His voice tailed off.

Angela laughed. 'It's Samantha. Samantha Reagan.' The laughter stopped. 'And, she's a good friend.'

Outside, Alex looked in both directions in the hope he might spot her. In films, the undercover police officer did the same but always seemed to know which way his quarry had gone. Never spent half the film heading uselessly in the wrong direction. *If only it were that simple. Shit. Wonder where she might be?* He turned left and headed for the nearest coffee shop.

Alex entered the dark interior and looked around. *Well, she's not here.* He felt his anticipation deflate. He looked around again. But no. *Maybe she'll come in later. I really do need to sort this book out.*

He hated queuing. Not the need to form an orderly queue, to wait your turn, not even the boredom of it all, but the strange debilitating effect it had on him. How was it that queuing made him feel increasingly powerless and anxious as he inched forward, tray in hand; heading for that gap in the counter; now half on, now fully on, his mind swaying on a tightrope? Sometimes his anxiety forced him to practise his order over and over in his head, each time more uncertain than the last, until when it came to his turn, he blurted out the now jumbled words in a gush of gibberish. Surely the epitome of success was to be whisked to the front, past the sullen queue, by burly silent men in sunglasses and with suspicious bulges.

'Are you being served sir?'

'Pardon? Being served? Oh yes. Err. Small… err cappuccino please. To have in please. Yes. No. Not being served. Well wasn't. Anyway, thank you. Hah.'

With some relief, he found an empty table at the back of the room and tore open the small bags of brown sugar without looking at them… *Damn. Where is she?*

Around him, the walls were covered with images of coffee. Plump beans in rough hessian sacks gathered from exotic places. Photographs of attractive people made even more attractive simply by drinking coffee. Long, manicured fingers, slightly out of focus, caressing white cups with a lover's touch.

The images were in colour and black and white and also sepia. All were mounted and framed, as if he was in a gallery, or a shrine, or a church. *Now there's a thought. Church… Saint Barista. Patron saint of skinny latte or should that be skinny patron saint of… where? Mocha? Is there such a place?* Before him, a speckled pattern floated on top of his cup. *Looks like a bird's egg.* He poured on a small pile of light brown sugar, which hung in the thick cushion of froth and then poured another bagful on top of that. Both reluctantly sank to the depths, leaving a sort of entry wound and giving him a strange satisfaction. He stirred his coffee, sat back and looked around. *Didn't they used to call these places penny universities back in the… what… seventeenth century? About then? Penny for a coffee and the chance for some vigorous debate on the issues of the day. Who dunnit then, set poor old London alight? Was them Dutchmen without doubt. Bigger than their britches. Wonder if that still happens? The debate?* Behind him a young female voice cut through the general hum. She spoke so quickly into a mobile phone that there was hardly a space between each word and sentence. 'Welldone. Goodforyougirl.

Youtakingthefreezerwithyer? Good. Serveshimright. Wanker,' but apart from her, there were no raised voices. No fierce argument. No heated debate. He took a sip of his coffee. Now, it was too sweet.

In the background, Ella Fitzgerald competed with the chatter of voices, the hectic clatter of cups and plates, the constant thud of metal pots and the gurgling hiss and steam of machinery. *God, why is it so noisy in here? They're only making bloody coffee after all. It's positively industrial. Like being in the… Pyjama Game.* He whistled softly and heard the words in his head at the same time. '*Whu wu whu whu whu whu whuu whu. Whu wu whu whu whu whu whuu whu.*' He stopped, sat up, realising how taut his shoulders had become. In front of him, figures were silhouetted against the bright world slanting in through the windows and doors. A snatch of Ella briefly evaded the clamour like the moon slipping past on a wild cloudy night and then disappearing again.

Now knowing Samantha's name made him a little more relaxed, although he wondered what the formidable Angela would tell her. *Oh shit. Forgot to ask when she's next in. Oh, so stupid.* Nearby, two elderly women held hands across the brown tables. They did so in a way that seemed natural and normal. The one nearest to him wore a simple black and grey striped top, blue jeans to just below her knees and coral pink trainers. Her hair, white and grey, was restrained in a small pony tail but it still roamed waywardly over her face and pale glasses. *Where they just good friends or maybe lovers? Hard to tell. Anyway, what the hell did it matter? At their age, they'd earned the right to behave how they wished, without embarrassment, doing no harm to anybody. Not like back then.* He looked around again. *Hey. Look. This place is full of middle-aged women. Perhaps they have secret trysts?*

No… look, seven of them grouped around that table. Agenda today. Husbands. Boyfriends. Children… Same as last week.

''Allo 'ow are you? You OK? What can I get you?'

The staff continued to smile and chatter and clatter around at high speed. Alex watched them for a while. They were part of the act, part of why you come here. *Hey, me Enrico. I have dark consuming eyes and a sweet bum inside these tight black trousers. You just wanna coffee signora?* Alex wondered if this was included in their training. *Today, we are going to look at your role in the customer experience. Divide into two teams. Team A, bang on those saucepans in a jolly way. Team B, run around in circles whilst grinning broadly.*

Through the background noise, Alex heard the empty plastic click of a keyboard. Just to his left, a young woman sat, a look of concentration on her face, one finger of one hand pecking wildly at a laptop. The sound of the keys was strangely audible. Every now and again she paused, took a locket on a chain around her neck and placed it between her lips as if the feeling or taste would inspire or even console her. Alex looked directly at her. She was far too busy to feel his gaze. He took in her low-cut top and polished skin and thought about her breasts. *When you think about it, it's not fair really. She doesn't know much about life, too young. And there ain't no shortcuts. You just have to experience it, don't you? And look at them. Perfect. Perfect ivory globes. Sitting there. Trying to escape. Surfing her top.*

He looked around. The Committee of Seven had reached boyfriends on their agenda. He knew that, by the way they now leaned intently towards each other, each with a curious little smile. *See, they're all covered up. Baggy clothing, jackets, coats, no tight sweaters. Certainly no low-cut tops.* Alex looked at them individually and tried to imagine them topless. The surfing changed to diving. *It really isn't fair.* He picked up his cup and took a sip but by now it was lukewarm. *Young women's breasts should be small and insignificant, maybe droop a bit. Then, as they mature, became more experienced, are nurtured and admired and caressed and loved, they would grow into perfectly shaped firm spheres, like… like… melons. Sounds a bit music hall. Bit seaside postcard. But no, it's right. Fruit and veg grow from small seeds into fully firmed ripe whatever. Don't they? So why do humans do it back to front?* He put his cup down and smiled to himself, his gaze drifting through the chair opposite him. *Maybe I'm becoming a dirty old man. Could be worse. So, what about Samantha Reagan?* He had no idea. He'd seen her at that dinner party of course and was sure she had worn a low-cut dress – everybody did – but he'd been transfixed by her tumbling copper hair and smooth, pale skin. So pale. It was as if somebody had painted her features onto an alabaster doll's head. Pale grey eyes. Red lips. Painted onto translucent whiteness… *wow. Remember, alabaster is deceptively hard, extremely brittle and easily bruised. Oh dear, do I really want to do this?*

A woman stood up to his front and moved away from her table, her back to him. He hadn't noticed her before, being partly obscured by other customers and furniture as well as the dazzling light, but as she stepped backwards from her chair, she revealed a shapely and well-proportioned rear, wrapped in tight jeans atop brown suede ankle boots. He watched, appreciatively. *What is it that makes that combination so attractive? And look at those jeans. Not skin tight, that would be too obvious, but tight enough to accentuate those curves, those delicious proportions. It's almost as though she isn't aware. That what I am enjoying is by accident. Not true of course. She knows exactly what she's doing. That's lovely.*

Wonder how old she is? Could be a young woman of course – certainly has a young shape – or maybe an older woman with the luck or better still the determination to preserve her body. The latter thought excited him; always had done. The older woman. Seducing his young, inexperienced, out of control, exploding body when he should have been doing his homework. *Too late now. Wonder if she'll turn?* She bent to pick up a soft leather bag, stretching the denim tighter. Then he saw them quite clearly. Her forearms and hands. Slim, veined hands and fingers, tipped with dark-red polish, and there, the glint of silver and gold rings. He thought how the rings would have worn and tarnished over the years into a smooth inevitability, their original sparkle and excited chatter now reduced to an accepted calmness. On her thin wrists however dangled two silver bangles. Maybe they were different. Maybe when she slid them on, they began to flash energetically against her mature flesh, singing away like a pop song in a retirement home.

The woman slipped on a short jacket and turned for a moment and faced him. It was Samantha Reagan. *Shit!* Alex gave a small intake of breath and realised he had no idea what to do next, except for the impulse to duck beneath the table. *Don't be so bloody daft.* He watched helplessly. She had taken the ugly tabard off, and now the light pouring in from the street caught the pale glow of her face and red lips. Full red lips. Lempicka lips. Yes, Lempicka lips. Those same soft lips would have left an imprint on her cup. *What am I thinking? What the hell do I do now?* Cappuccino dregs came into his mouth and he swallowed hastily and wiped his face with the back of his hand. Samantha, still standing, looked around. *Is she looking for me? No, she's meeting someone. She must be. A man. Must be a man. Oh, how embarrassing. What*

· 33 ·

am I doing here? No look… she's looking for a table. No, can't be, she's been sat at a table you idiot. Oh God why do I feel so bloody hopeless?

Samantha's gaze moved past him, stopped and then returned. Her eyes locked onto his, gave a flash of recognition and she smiled. *Is she smiling at me or someone else? Someone behind me?* She picked up her bag and walked directly towards him. *What do I do?* In a panic, Alex stood up and waved the book. She stopped suddenly, surprised at this strange apparition. Then recovered.

'Hallo again. May I join you?'

'Oh yes.' Alex swept the empty sugar bags, spilled sugar, a napkin and a spoon across the table towards him. The spoon fell to the floor. He bent awkwardly and tried to pick it up, failed and surfaced, face slightly flushed. *Oh shit, did I shave this morning? I can't remember.* He resisted the temptation to touch his face.

'Thank you.'

She placed the leather bag onto the table and sat opposite him, hands in her lap, legs crossed. She looked up at him, curiously.

'Aren't you going to sit down?'

'Oh yes.' He sat down abruptly. His chair screeched and he looked directly at her hair. *My, it's so different. Had tumbled down her back like a wild copper waterfall – and now? Well, cut shorter but exquisitely. What is that style called? A bob? Certainly shiny, healthy, different. Different red but suits her. This older, wiser version of her. Oh dear she'll see straight through me.*

'Is everything alright?'

'Oh yes. It's just… it's nothing.'

She looked concerned and touched her hair.

'Nothing?'

'It's… just been a long time.'

'Oh that.' She looked away for a second and shuffled in her seat. 'Yes, it has.' She looked back at him and placed the tips of the fingers of her right hand on the table. The other out of sight. 'So, are you still painting? Alec. It is Alec, isn't it?'

Alex sat back. He grinned. 'You almost remembered my name. It's actually Al-ex.' He pronounced it as two syllables, then normally. 'Alex.'

'Oh sorry… Yes, Alex.' She paused. 'I'm Samantha.' He heard the query in her voice.

'Yes, I know.' He wanted to tell her that he had remembered quite easily, even though he couldn't remember what he had had for breakfast but then he thought of Angela in the charity shop. She nodded lightly.

She sat back in her chair and appraised him coolly. 'Yes… I do remember you. And your antics.' She smiled. The fingertips tapped lightly.

'Antics. What antics?' For the first time, he felt relaxed. *Oh, thank you.* Now he could hide, be the clown. 'I don't remember any antics.' She placed both hands on the table top, fingers laced together, and her eyes widened slightly. He could see that her hands were slim, maybe thin and no amount of cosmetics could hide the lines and veins and dark blemishes. Alex suddenly wanted to hold them and reassure her.

'Really? Well I can remember you having… well, some very forthright views at a dinner party.' She raised her slim eyebrows slightly, inviting his memory.

'I was probably pissed.'

She resisted the temptation to laugh aloud. He pulled the book towards him, looked down and ran a finger absently over it. 'Was I rude?' He looked up. 'Not to you.' His voice raised slightly. 'I wouldn't be rude to you.'

She paused, realising his concern, not expecting this vulnerability.

'No, not me… But I can remember you advising my ex-husband to buy some awful paintings for an enormous amount of money.'

'I did…? Oh yes, so I did.' The grin returned. He couldn't really remember too clearly, but liked the idea. He also liked the idea of an ex-husband. 'Oh yes. That's right. Served him right. He only invited me because he thought I could be his pet art dealer. Show me off.'

She looked at him wistfully.

'Yes, I guess you're probably right.'

'So… what happened?'

'To the paintings?'

Alex nodded, but it wasn't just the paintings.

'Oh, he sold them on but at a big loss. He was furious, he…'

'He what?'

'Oh nothing. It *was* a long time ago.'

Alex leant back in his chair and looked at her. Took in the perfect make-up, the exquisite hair, the short, fitted chestnut jacket and the silky top with one button undone at the neck. Her well-groomed, smart sophistication was obvious even to him. Here was a woman used to having money, probably lots of it. Why should she be interested in him? Suddenly he felt nervous and inadequate again.

'So… do you remember where we first met?'

The words slipped out before he could stop them.

She looked up, surprised.

'First met?'

'Um. Yes. Err. Sort of first met.'

'No, I don't really remember. Do you?'

'Think so. It was at that gallery on Dean Street. I was there from the university. It was a vernissage. Ex-student. Successful but hopeless work. No content. You were both there.'

'The gallery was actually on Frobisher Street.'

'Was it? Thought you couldn't remember?'

'I remember that gallery. I never visited very many.'

'I remember you.'

'Do you?' She laughed and looked away.

There was a long pause. Samantha twisted the silver bracelets on her wrist, then suddenly looked up. 'So... what's all this nonsense about Roman gods offering flowers to strange women in charity shops?'

'No, Greek. Dionysus. He's Greek. The Roman equivalent would have been Bacchus and of course you're *not* strange *and* it's not nonsense. In fact, he instructed me.'

'He instructed you?'

'Oh yes.'

'I'm not sure I should ask this but... where did you meet him? It *is* a him?'

'In my garden.'

'Now you're beginning to worry me.'

'Well, technically it's not *my* garden. I do share it.'

'I didn't mean that.'

'Oh, I see. Well, he's only there in statue form although we do talk a lot.'

'You talk a lot.'

'Yes, why not? I bet you talk to the radio and the telly and the dog.'

'Don't have a dog.'

'Cat then.' He paused. 'So, what did you do with it? Did you throw it away?

'The flower?'

Samantha laughed and looked at the slim silver watch on her left wrist.

'Of course not. Look I'm sorry, I really have to go.'

'Oh no, do you? Really? What's the time?'

She turned her wrist towards her, gave another look.

'It's late and I have an appointment. I really only came in to do some shopping.'

'Oh. Well. Um. Will… will you take the book?'

'Book?'

'Yes.' He held it aloft. 'It's from your shop. I forgot to pay for it.' He grinned at her.

She shook her head in mock disbelief. 'Why don't you bring it in yourself? Save me carrying it.'

'OK. Tomorrow?'

'Shop's closed tomorrow.'

'Oh yes. Silly me.'

'Monday then?'

'Yes. If you like. I won't be there but…'

'When are you there then?'

'Tuesdays and Thursdays.'

'OK. Tuesday then.'

She stood, picked up her bag, and looked directly at him.

'Thank you for the flower. Good to see you again.'

Alex stood abruptly. The chair screeched again. She waited. *Do I shake her hand? Maybe kiss her on the cheek?* He did neither.

'You too. Bye Samantha.'

'Bye.'

Samantha made her way towards the entrance, through the bustling interior, around customers, and for some reason, felt slightly annoyed. She squeezed around a table and as she did so, swung her hips, provocatively and deliberately, side to side.

Oh my God, why did I do that? How embarrassing. She felt an urge to turn, look back, see if he had noticed, was grinning or even worse looked shocked, but she daren't – that would just make things worse. She felt the heat rise in her face and she headed purposefully for the coolness and sanctuary of the street. Outside, out of sight, she stopped for a moment, to gather herself. That movement of her body had been so spontaneous and so surprising, like bumping into an old friend you hadn't seen or even thought of in decades but had never truly forgotten. But at her age? She began to walk, more slowly than usual, ignoring the pace of the busy high street, looking at other women passing her. The young, crisp, brisk and confident, paraded before her. She admired their fashions, had imagined herself wearing them but felt afraid of clothes that were too young for her. She was also aware that they simply ignored her eyes completely and she felt not for the first time invisible. Ahead, a woman was pushing a pram up the slight incline. Inside the pram, a young baby sat. The weather was warm and so the heavy clothes of winter and autumn had been universally discarded and Samantha could see the young mother's full figure straining in a tight skirt and how her heels and the need to bend slightly forward to push against the slope emphasised the rhythmic sway of her body. The mother suddenly found a space, stopped and half turned. Their eyes met and a smile spread from one to the other.

'Little girl?'

'Yes. My second.'

'Oh really. I have two. Two girls. Grown up now of course but no grandchildren… sadly.'

The mother smiled. Samantha rubbed her fingers lightly over the baby's cheek.

'So pretty.'

'Thank you. I want another. I would like three. Maybe a boy this time.'

'I wish you luck.'

The mother smiled again and nodded. A man brushed past them, his eyes resting appreciatively on the mother. On her body. They both noticed.

'An admirer.' It was Samantha who spoke.

'That?' The mother laughed, then spoke softly, like a conspirator. 'Some mums give up and I don't do it to have admirers. I just want to be me. The me I want to be. Want to feel… you know? And forever. Actually, sometimes it scares them, the fellers. Sometimes they like it. Mostly I don't care.'

'I wish…' Samantha stopped. 'I wish you good luck again.'

'Thank you.'

'Bye.'

'Bye.'

So, when did she stop being a woman? A real woman? When did she give up? After the divorce maybe? She stood more upright and lengthened her stride up the high street, all thoughts of the encounter with Alex pushed away.

*

He felt crestfallen. Not only had he behaved like a clown, but she had left so hastily that by the time he had finally picked up the spoon from the floor, she had disappeared. Not even a cheery 'see you again' wave as she left.

Why did he do that? Play the buffoon. Why couldn't he just be himself? Except he didn't really know who he was anymore or how he was expected to be. This elderly man. He sank his forehead onto his folded arms, stared at the table top and inhaled the dankness of carelessly wiped plastic. He looked up and around. Nobody seemed to have noticed. Nobody seemed to care. He was invisible now and he slumped back into his chair. What had happened to him? He had felt like a naïve little boy again. Shy, hapless, tongue-tied, hiding his ineptitude behind silly behaviour. He bounced his fist angrily onto the plastic. His coffee cup rattled.

'Shit. Shit. Shit.'

You would have thought that by now, he would feel comfortable enough to have a reasonable conversation with an attractive woman, if no longer able to sweep her into his wicked grasp. He had in the past – swept them up. Oh yes. They had been enticed by the long curly locks that flopped enticingly over his eyes and which drew female fingers to tidy them away. Fascinated by his audacity and disregard for convention and of course, that easy association and knowledge that the artist had of the naked female form. This plus an appetite for booze, drugs, sex and rock and roll proved irresistible to many, and many had drunk from that multi-coloured well.

They *had* been kind. Drinks, speeches, farewell gifts. Then they had shoved him out into retirement, waved, closed the doors, found a replacement and forgotten him. He was no longer dashing, he knew that – with his balding head, lines and wrinkles, a spine that was slowly collapsing, an unreliable bladder and a cock that seemed now to have developed a mind of its own. No longer riding with the renegade gang who had fought the dark forces of conformity, who had stiffened his spine, bolstered his behaviour, fed his resolve and given him strength. Now he had been forced to hand in his coat of many colours and in return found himself almost alone in a grey, foreign world.

'Oh, come on. Don't be so bloody pathetic.'

*

Meanwhile, Samantha glanced anxiously at her watch.

'Damn.'

She had to call back briefly at the charity shop with some shopping for Angela and now also felt the need to talk to her. But Angela would be leaving soon. If only she hadn't stayed to talk. She quickened her pace.

'Sorry Angie.'

'That's alright love. No worries. Got caught up shopping?'

'No. Very strange. Met someone I haven't seen in forty years. Rather unsettling.'

'Not the guy who was in here? Looking for you? Tall. Bit posh. Bit of a looker.'

Angela was a large lady who wore bright red lips and dark outlined eyes and for some reason a small seahorse tattoo on a wide ocean of pink upper arm. When asked, she simply laughed and talked about the dangers of getting pissed. Around her neck she wore a gold chain from which dangled the letter 'A'. At times it almost disappeared between her considerable breasts. 'Stands for available. A for available,' she would explain and then laugh very loudly. But with her, Samantha always felt comfortable.

'Was he? In here? Sounds like Alex.'

'Alex eh? So where does Alex fit in?'

'Oh, he was an artist. From a long time ago. Might still be. They don't really retire do they?'

'An artist. Really? You'll have to watch him then. Have you stripped off and posing before you can say Harry Picasso.'

Samantha smiled. 'Don't think so.'

'So, do you fancy him then, this Alex?'

'Oh no. It's all a bit confusing. Bit of a shock really. He's changed so much. You know, physically. Bit like going back to a school reunion and not recognising people you once knew. *And* something awful happened.' She looked around.

'Awful. Go on then. Tell.'

'Well, it's a bit embarrassing really.'

'Go on.' Angela stopped hanging clothes. 'Go on. Spill.'

'Well,' she whispered, 'as I left, I actually wiggled my bottom at him.'

'Aah… Wiggled yer bum? Good for you girl. Wiggle mine all the time. Doesn't do me much good though.'

'No, I didn't mean to. Not sure why I did. So embarrassing. What must he have thought?'

'Who cares. You fancy him. That's why.'

'I don't know. Think it might be that the attention made me feel like a woman again. Been a long time. Or maybe the woman I once was?'

'And still are darling.' Angela did not tell her that Alex couldn't remember her name.

'Really? It's all a bit confusing.'

'So, will you see him again?'

'Don't think so. Don't think I want all that relationship bother again. Not now.'

'Oh, I do. Love it.'

It wasn't until that evening that Samantha remembered that Alex was bringing the book in on the following Tuesday.

2

_____

Samantha and the Wolf

S AMANTHA SAT BACK in her cream-coloured armchair and slowly stroked the broad armrests. The leather felt cool and smooth under her fingertips. She closed her eyes and raised her fingers until they barely brushed the surface. Barely touching. Caressing really. Alex would be here soon.

In front of her stretched a bright wall of windows framed at either side by black curtains touched with gold. She liked gold. Preferred silver though. Didn't really know why. Cooler? Quieter maybe? Beyond them, through and above the trees in the garden, white clouds moved, slowly but relentlessly, left to right, changing and forming. There's a face. Now here's a country. There… a huge castle. There a ragged wisp torn away. *Keep up. Don't get lost. Don't get left behind… No chance. This can't be stopped. This rolls on and on, forever. Is that why it's so compelling? Bit scary. Will I be up there? Will I pass by? Will anybody notice?* She stirred from her thoughts and looked around the spacious living room. Opposite the settee hung a large semi-abstract painting and beyond, in one corner, against the curtains stood a cluster of white glass globes, each drooping downwards on a white metal stem like some strange electric bloom. At their feet, on the thick white carpet, stood pots in earthy browns and greens from which protruded a variety of yellow, green and cream silk flowers, punctuated with slender stems of russet brown grasses. To her left, a frame in rosewood showed an old-style monochrome photograph of her grandparents, head and shoulders only, heads resting together in an unashamed gesture of affection, cheeks slightly pink from the colourist's brush, he in a stiff collar and tie. She knew that below, out of sight, somewhere down the wall, they would be holding hands. The items hanging on the warm white walls looked down upon the everyday, ticking away below, wondering if anything there would one day be special enough or maybe safe enough to join them. But nothing had for a long time.

Nearby, newspapers and magazines had been scattered across the long settee, and ragged empty envelopes, receipts and leaflets dropped onto the black marble coffee table and left where they fell. She would tidy up of course but before that she felt the need to study them for a while. Study their patterns and shapes and colours. Like Alex might have done. Alex the artist. The mind of an artist. So fascinating. And difficult.

She looked again at the objects on the table. Just ordinary objects. Just dropped at random. Do artists do that? Work randomly? Employ mistakes? She vaguely remembered a programme. Television. The artist was dripping paint from a stick. She hadn't really understood and now she tried equally hard to see the table top in a different way, but she really couldn't. They just seemed to be what they were. Ordinary. Maybe untidy and disordered. Was that it? Is that what they represented? Maybe. No, must be more than that. Suddenly she felt herself becoming excited by a glimmer of understanding. Possible understanding. Untidy? Disordered?

No, they're the wrong words. Unconventional maybe? No, not even that. She had looked again and moved one or two of the items around, trying to improve… improve what? She wasn't sure, except the composition, if that's what it had been, now seemed worse. Less satisfactory. Why was that? What had she done? Before, the composition had been… what…? Natural? Intuitive? Spontaneous? Bit like Alex really and now she had ruined it. She had interfered and changed it and now she didn't know how to get it back to where it was and the thought worried and confused her. She sat back.

He *was* fun, certainly different, there was no denying that and she thought of the yellow flower and smiled. She seemed to smile when she thought of him and she seemed to have thought of him a lot since the coffee shop. Well, of course, she did remember him from the past. Very clearly. Maybe too clearly for he had been magnificent and wild back then and she had been what…? Attractive? Maybe. Physically attractive yes but also rather lost. Lost and uncertain. Uncertain about so many things. She was surprised that he even remembered her. Now she felt the need to reach out, to touch her table, the table that could be her and then to touch the papers that could be him. The table felt cool. The papers felt warm. She suddenly felt annoyed, although why, she wasn't sure, and she stood, collected them roughly in a bundle, looked around, and hid them behind a cushion. There. Gone.

A triangular corner peeked out. *No.* She gathered them up again, crossed the room, opened a drawer, thrust them in and closed it. She felt her cheeks beginning to heat. Now the table was clear and safe. Perhaps she preferred that? She looked around. *Come on. You're supposed to be tidying.* A lone plastic bottle of mineral water stood on a rich Persian rug. *How incongruous.* Nearby CDs had slipped from their stand.

She removed the bottle, replaced the discs, and turned towards the long settee. It had several cushions stacked at angles along its top. Each one was different in colour and pattern and she had enjoyed searching and shopping for them. Blues, reds, yellows, purples, greens, some striped, some plain, looking like a row of multi-coloured jars in an old sweet shop. She plumped and rearranged them, wondering if Alex would notice her design achievement and then looked around. The room was tidy. Immaculate. Organised. Like a show room. She had tidied everything away and in doing so had removed all traces of *her*. All intimate traces at least. Left the room clean, but also nervous and vulnerable. Vulnerable enough for someone else to strew themselves around it. Isn't that what happens when you tidy away to invite someone to visit? To stay maybe? Isn't that why you sit waiting nervously, because your space is about to be violated? She had an overwhelming feeling of confusion and uncertainty.

She had showered and put on new underwear, a little more daring than normal. The shop assistant had commented on it and smiled at her. 'It's lovely.' Probably thought it was a present for her daughter or even granddaughter. But she *did* enjoy wearing it. Made her feel special and attractive. Although a long look in a full-length mirror made her doubt herself. She was no magazine beauty. Not anymore. *But they are heavily airbrushed, aren't they?* She had looked again. It would take an awful lot of airbrushing to smooth out all the wrinkles and creases. But she felt like her room now, clean, tidy but still vulnerable. Maybe he would take advantage of that, read the signs, make advances. A hot flush began to spread across her chest. Did she really want that? Maybe she did but at the cost of him spewing and smearing and littering his traces around her room, her home, her domain, like a wolf marking his territory?

Alex had returned to the shop on the Tuesday and finally paid for the book, even though he didn't really want it. He had worn a slim dark-blue tie, the knot of which had refused to sit neatly within the spread of his white collar and he constantly felt for it. Samantha had considered not going in that day, but that seemed rather childish and part of her recognised that then she might not see him again. And yet she had been strangely disappointed, maybe expecting something more flamboyant; he had smiled shyly and lingered for a while but at the same time had seemed anxious to leave. *Why was that? Maybe he felt shy in front of Angela, who had grinned at him constantly. Maybe it was too formal for him? A sort of commitment?* That thought had flickered across her mind and was reluctant to leave.

'I'll just put that in a bag for you.'

'No, it's OK thanks.'

'Won't take a moment, I'll just fetch one,' and she had returned with the book in a paper bag and smiled at him. She wasn't quite sure what her smile meant.

'Thank you. See you,' and he had left.

Angela had eyed every movement and after he had waved to them from the doorway, could hardly contain herself. 'Oh, he's so sweet. So cute. Makes you want to pick him up and give him a *big* cuddle and he fancies you Samantha. Oh yes. No doubt about it. You're in there girl. And he did say he would see you. Don't look like that. He did. So… are you going to see him again? Are you Samantha?'

*

When Alex returned home, he had made for the small garden and sat down. Dionysus stared implacably back at him.

'Yes, I know, but I've only just got back. Thought I'd explain what happened. Well, I returned the book, even paid for it. *How to Achieve Spiritual Growth.* That's what it's about. Don't know how that's going to help although she was I think keen that I read it. Maybe she thinks I need it. What do you think? Do I need to find my higher self? If I'm honest, I'm having enough trouble with this lower one. But she did put it in a nice bag. Do you want to have a look?'

He slid the book from the bag and placed it on his lap.

'There. Yes. You know, I thought that something special would happen. Thought you might weave some magic for me. Not too much to ask. All I've got now is a book I don't really want. How did that happen? What on earth do I do now? I can't go back again. Can I?'

He idly opened the book and saw it immediately. A yellow Post-it note stuck to the inside cover.

'Please phone. Samantha Reagan' and a series of eleven numbers.

3

My God, It's a Twombly

'Hallo.'

'Hallo Samantha. It's me.'

'Alex. Alex James. Is that you?'

'Yes. Hallo. You asked me to phone.'

'Oh yes… look… um… I have this painting.'

'Painting?'

'Yes. Henry and I bought it in New York. Well Henry did really. Must have been in the early seventies. Gosh doesn't time fly?'

'Henry?'

'Oh. Yes. Henry. My ex-husband.'

'Oh. OK. So, who's it by?'

'The painting? Well I don't really know. Can't remember and it doesn't appear to be signed. I know there's something on the back, but I can't move it. I'm pretty sure it was an American artist. Just wondered if you would have a look. No rush of course… maybe when you are not so busy. When you are in the area… if you want to.'

'I'd be delighted.'

'Oh good. So… er I'm not at the shop tomorrow. Will tomorrow be OK? Is that too soon?'

'No, no. That's fine.'

'Can you come for lunch? About one? Is that OK? Do you like fish? Least I can do for your professional advice. Shall I give you the address?'

'Er… yes please. Can I park?'

'Yes. Park outside. Residents' parking.'

'OK. See you tomorrow then. At one. Bye.'

'Bye Alex.'

Click.

*

Alex arrived at her front door exactly at one o'clock, having parked his car and waited around the corner for ten minutes. He had spent the morning preparing himself and poring through a catalogue for the older man, searching for some sartorial assistance and had finally decided to be casual, wearing his shirt outside of his trousers as usual and agonising about how many shirt buttons to leave undone. He had abandoned his black, blue and acid green trainers with the right large toe beginning to push through the soft material in favour of a pair of brown brogues, in which he felt quite strange and unsteady. He had also made an attempt to clean the interior of the car, removing crumpled newspapers, parking tickets and sweet wrappers from the floor and traces of chocolate from the front passenger seat. Unusually, he stood in front of his only mirror to check that everything was satisfactory. His pulse thumped.

What on earth are you doing Alexander? You look like a schoolboy on a first date. Got your clean hanky? Cleaned your teeth? Been to the toilet? Let's hope she hasn't prepared spaghetti. It'll be everywhere. No, she said fish. Why am I doing this? Oh yes. The painting.

The painting intrigued him, and he felt quite flattered that she should want his advice. *Yes, that's all it was. As she had said, my professional advice in return for a lunch. That's all it was. So why did she leave the note inside the book for me to find? Bit clandestine, wasn't it? Maybe she didn't want Angela in the shop to know. Yes, that would be it. You know how much they gossip.* He picked up the bunch of flowers and put them down again. Should he? Seemed a bit extravagant for a business lunch. Had he taken the price off? Sort of thing he'd forget. Oh yes that's right, the assistant in the shop had done that already. He picked them up again. Oh well, why not? Just a friendly gesture.

'Hallo Alex. You found it alright? Oh, what lovely flowers. And yellow.' She smiled at him. A conspiratorial smile. 'Thank you. How sweet. Come on in. Forgive the apron, I've just been preparing lunch. Do you like pasta? Are you a vegetarian? Sorry I should have asked you that before. You can have a salad instead if you wish.'

Alex stepped onto Italian ceramic tiles covering a large entrance way. In front of him were glazed double doors leading into the living room, which appeared to be covered in a thick, white carpet. To his right came the smell of cooking.

'No, not a vegetarian. Pasta is fine thank you *[what happened to the fish?]* As long as I can have a bib.'

'A bib?'

'Just joking. What a lovely house you have.'

'Yes. Henry was very generous. Although I do rattle around in it on my own.'

'Oh.' Alex paused. 'Smells delicious. You must have gone to a lot of trouble.'

'Spaghetti alla puttanesca. No, I love to cook. Henry employed a cook in our house – chef he liked to call her. We got on very well. I learned a lot from Maria. So, cooking is

fun; cooking for others at least. Not so much fun for one…
anyway, oh dear I'm talking too much. Shall we have lunch
first, it's just about ready? I've laid a table in the dining room.
Through there Alex. Take a seat, I'll be with you soon.'

Samantha turned into the kitchen and leaned against the
black marble worktop. *For goodness' sake Samantha, slow down.*
You've almost just invited him to live with you. What's wrong with
you? She stood upright, took a deep breath and called out.

'Alex will you open the wine? Sorry I forgot. Supposed to
breathe isn't it?'

They sat in the dining room with sunshine slanting in
through large picture windows.

'This is delicious Samantha. It really is.'

'Do call me Sam. Everybody does. Except my mother of
course and Angela.'

'OK. Sam it is.' He looked around. 'Nice to have a dining
room.'

'Don't you have one then?'

'No. Just a room. Multi-purpose.'

'Multi-purpose?'

'Yes. Somewhere where you can have a meal, watch telly,
mend your bike.'

'You have a bike?'

He grinned. 'What I really meant was, it's nice to have a
room where everybody can get together to share a meal.'

'Instead of balancing it on a tray.'

'Exactly. And I love this.' He stroked the surface of what
was a large, worn table. 'Wonderful. Goes so well in this
room. Nice contrast. Is it oak?'

'I selected it myself. I'm so glad you like it. Yes, oak.' She
beamed at him.

'So, where's the painting?'

'It's in the living room. Too big for here. Perhaps we can take our coffee in there later and you can have a look. Tell me what you think?'

'Looking forward to it… And what happened to *your* portrait?'

'My portrait? Oh, you remember it?'

'Yes, of course. It was exhibited at the gallery remember, where—'

'Oh yes. I'd forgotten that. Henry's idea. Guess he's still got it.'

'Didn't destroy it then? Slash it or something?'

'Oh no, he wouldn't do that. He paid good money for it… Did you like it?'

'Oh yes… but it was something of a beautiful monster.'

'Monster?'

'Yeah, it was like a bank statement or the crown jewels or a bloody great Rolls Royce parked outside your front door.'

'What do you mean?'

'Well, I got the distinct impression that it was just something else he owned. He was just showing the world – look what I've got.'

'You don't hold back do you?'

Alex waved his knife rather dangerously in the air. 'Sorry, but…' He shrugged.

They ate in silence for a while.

'He wanted me to pose nude for it.' Samantha flushed slightly.

'He did?'

'Yes, but I refused. I think I would have been too embarrassed. You know standing there. Like that. And yes, maybe you're right, he would have shown it to all his associates.'

Alex paused to mop his mouth with a linen serviette. 'I'm sure you would have looked superb.'

'Maybe. Anyway, he got very angry. Called me a prude... More wine Alex?'

'I shouldn't but thank you.'

'It was well painted though, wasn't it?'

'Superbly well. Based on *The Bridesmaid*, by John Everett Millais, 1851.'

'Really? You are clever knowing all these things... I do remember the artist showing me some pictures from an art book before he started.'

Alex nodded. 'Who chose the frame?'

'Henry did. Why?'

'Thought so. Dripping with gold and ostentation. Pretty awful, *and* the wrong period.'

'It was?'

'It certainly was. French Rococo. Eighteenth century.'

'Is that wrong?'

Alex nodded again.

'I thought it was a little ornate. I remember Edmund laughed when he saw it.'

'Edmund?'

'Yes, the artist. His name was Edmund. Can't remember his surname except it was double-barrelled. He was fun. Dark curly hair and a little beard and moustache. Frilly cuffs. Looked like a cavalier.'

Alex grunted. 'A cavalier. He'd like that.'

'Do you know him then?'

'Yeah. He was a visiting lecturer where I worked and we went to college together, many years ago. Told me he was painting you. Told me about Henry as well. That it took ages to complete.'

'Oh dear. Henry would not stop asking questions. Giving suggestions. In the end, Edmund became a little frustrated I think.'

Alex carefully dabbed his mouth. 'Did you know that he added a comment in the painting? A little symbolic message.'

'No. He never told me that. Oh dear, now you've got me worried.'

'Don't worry, most people wouldn't notice it. It was quite common to do, back then. Made it truer to the subject really.'

'So, what was it? I hardly dare ask.'

'Well, in the original, the bridesmaid is holding a ring and superstition tells us that if she could pass a piece of wedding cake through the ring nine times, then she would see a vision of her lover.'

'But I wasn't holding a ring.'

'No, I know, but also, in front of the original model was a salt cellar which was, of course, a phallic symbol.'

'It was?'

'Well it *was* a wedding.'

'So…' she paused for another sip of wine, 'did I get one of those?' Her eyes shone.

'One of what?'

'You know, a phallic symbol.'

'No, afraid not.'

'Oh, what a shame.' She looked up at Alex and pushed her glass away, just a few inches, towards him. He paused. Smiling but uncertain.

'No, well, Edmund replaced it with that dark-blue Victorian dropper bottle. I remember him showing it to me.'

'Oh yes, I remember too; it was such a lovely deep colour.'

'Yes, it was. And the ivy? Remember the ivy?'

'Yes, I do. Wasn't sure about the ivy but Edmund said it was alright. Said it represented eternity or something. Henry liked that.'

'Well in fact the bottle wasn't just there for the colour. Symbolically, it represents containment. And the ivy, as a female symbol, means a force in need of protection. So…'

'So, Edmund thought I was trapped and in danger?'

'Guess so.'

'And I thought it was so well hidden.' She slowly pushed her half-eaten plate away, face sad.

'Oh, I'm sorry. Please. I didn't mean to…'

She pursed her lips. Said nothing.

'No, I'm sorry. Really sorry. I just thought you would want to know the whole story.'

'Not very sensitive are you?'

'No. No I'm not. Sorry. I know that. That's what…'

There was a long pause. Alex sat nervously, not knowing what to do or say.

'He wasn't all bad you know… Henry. Things are never just black and white. Surely as an artist looking at the world, you can see that?'

'I can see so much in a painting. Subtle meanings, delicate inferences, technical brilliance but—'

'Not in people.'

'No.' Alex felt the wine and the situation beginning to redden his face. Still felt the need to justify himself. 'I suppose it's just that Henry and I are at opposite ends of the spectrum… you must admit he was a bit of a philistine.'

Samantha looked fiercely at him. '*He* would call *you* a well-meaning but non-productive loony left winger. Without people like Henry you wouldn't be able to *sell* your paintings. *Live* your lifestyle. *Teach* from your ivory tower. Henry employed hundreds of people, gave them a wage, paid taxes and supported the economy.' She wanted to add, 'So what was your contribution?' but suddenly felt weary of it.

Alex sat back, stung, half considered the accusation of being 'loony', dismissed that, turned to 'non-productive' and 'ivory tower', was considering a suitable retort but knew he was already drifting out of his depth. Suddenly, he wished he was back at his flat, shoes off, feet up and alone. He grinned at her instead, like a naughty puppy. Maybe, if he rolled over, she might tickle his tummy. She did not grin back.

'Now you're sticking up for him Sam.'

'Samantha. No. Just pointing out *his* contribution.'

They both sat in silence, looking away from each other, embarrassed and rather annoyed at their outbursts. Samantha pulled her glass back towards her as if defending it and rolled its stem between her fingers. She looked sideways at him. Alex looked like a lost little boy, eyes downcast and for a second, she wondered if she could be bothered with all this again. Just give him his coat, close the front door behind him, kick of her shoes and… resume her empty life? She sighed.

'He *was* good to me to begin with. Swept me off my feet. Lavished me with gifts. Weekends at the Waldorf. Paris. Rome. Rooms full of flowers and he just made things happen. He was like a bow wave slicing through the world. I had never met anybody like him before. I felt like a princess; a real princess. He would get angry if people weren't attentive enough to me. He once tried to get a waiter fired because he forgot to bring me something… a fresh napkin or… I don't know. Poor man.'

'So how did you meet?' Alex spoke tentatively. Hoping he was forgiven.

'I came down from university in 1962.'

'With a good degree?'

'I managed a two one in statistics. Suppose you did better?'

Alex shook his head. 'No. Go on. Please.'

'Well… we met at a club in London. Can't remember the name now. Anyway, there he was, this breath of fresh air, this tall, handsome, moustachioed man, who told me how beautiful I was – but in a totally natural and believable way. As if it was a known matter-of-fact. Beyond flattery. Beyond compliment and I believed him. He really understood women – which was rather unusual back then. Maybe that's what came of living in a two-up two-down terraced house with two sisters. In fact, he knew so, so much but with no real formal education. I had spent all those years studying hard and yet he made me realise how little I knew about life and how it ticks. He called me his lovely innocent. "Brain crammed full of bloody numbers which won't add up." That's what he used to say. "Can't let you out on the streets on your own." At first, I thought he was joking… later… Well anyway it didn't matter; after all those stuffy academics and gauche undergraduates, I was spellbound. It was like landing on another version of my own planet; but just around the corner and full of colour and surprises.'

'Sounds too good to be true.'

'Oh, he had his faults alright, but he was totally fascinating which made you forget them. Had this hunger for knowledge which would shame most students and was fearless when it came to discovering new things, even at his own expense. Once, he took me to a restaurant and ordered a bottle of Martini from the wine list. He just didn't know.'

'So, what did you do?'

'Drank the whole bottle. He knew from the waiter's reaction that he had got it wrong but he just grinned, poured out a glass and toasted the whole restaurant. Wonderful.'

Alex knew that interest was slipping from his face and he was having trouble stopping it. *Bloody Henry.*

'Sorry Alex. I'm talking too much. I'm sure you don't want to hear all this.'

'No, go on. Please.'

'OK. Well, it wasn't all wonderful of course. And probably only was, because I was so naïve. In fact, a lot was very dark indeed.'

'Really?'

She looked uncertainly at Alex. He nodded encouragingly.

'Well, Henry came from Hoxton, in the East End of London. One day he came home and found his father molesting one of his sisters. Henry ended up pushing a wardrobe on top of him. So, he was thrown out, onto the streets. At fifteen. Walking the streets.'

'What on earth did he do?'

'Not sure. Drifted. Got into trouble. I do know he did nine months in Wandsworth. He refused to tell the police the names of his accomplices. Misguided loyalty the judge said and added more time to the sentence.'

'So, what had he done?'

'I don't know. He never said but I suspect it was for some violent crime. Assault maybe.'

'I thought he was a businessman?'

'Oh, he was. A real natural. At some point, he acquired a breakdown truck. I don't know how. I learnt not to ask. He used to listen in to the police radio and turn up at accidents and breakdowns with a big roll of notes before the official lorry arrived.'

'Notes?'

'Pound notes. Back-handers for the police. And from there grew a large multi-million haulage and car sales company.'

Alex smiled and took another sip of his drink.

'So why did you leave? Sorry, it's none of my business.'

'No, it's good to talk.' She looked at him, this still-handsome man, his face full of interest and compassion. She had never told the full story before and now she was about to do so to an almost complete stranger. Why was that? She looked into her wine, like a crystal ball, occasionally glancing up at him.

'Well, there was a darkness to him. A black, empty space, deep inside him, that I knew I could never fill and which at times spilt over. And he was so unpredictable and at times so controlling. Used to finish my sentences for me and yes, sometimes literally wouldn't let me out onto the streets. I never worked. Not really. Only in his office and later, in the show rooms. And only because I insisted. One day he threw a glass paperweight at me. Really threw it. Went straight through the window of the hotel we were staying in and into the street. Amazing it didn't kill somebody.'

'Could have killed you?'

'Yes, I know. I was so frightened I just left.'

'So that was that?'

'Yes. The girls had already gone. He never really wanted children. Frightened him and they wouldn't put up with it like me. Maybe it was partly my fault. Maybe I couldn't give him what he really wanted... I often think about him. Wonder what he's doing? He did give me such a lot.'

'Did he? Doesn't sound much like it.'

'Oh yes, he did. He gave me security. That's what he gave me. Security, two beautiful daughters and a glimpse into another world. A real world. A world I didn't even know existed. I don't suppose it was the same for you?'

'Well sort of, although there was never a Henrietta.' He laughed uncertainly. 'My parents were middle-class. Not that I knew what that meant back then. Dad was a financier.' He stopped and smiled. 'No, he wasn't. He was a dark-grey accountant in a dark-brown office, engaged – to my mind at least – in dark-beige calculations.'

'That's very poetic.'

'No. Just how I saw it. In fact, he was apparently very good at it, certainly successful enough to allow my mother to indulge in her great passion, which she did with an enthusiasm unfortunately not matched with any significant ability.'

'Which was?'

'Oh, she painted. Copies of watery Highland landscapes and that's maybe where I got it from. The art thing.' He paused, looking beyond her into the past, then laughed. 'Do you have a second first name?'

'No. Just Samantha.'

'Well, I have several.'

'Really?'

'Yes. Afraid so. An A, an R and an N. All chosen by my mother. She might have been a romantic Scot, all whisky-coloured hair and dewy eyes, but in matters domestic she certainly prevailed. Hence the R… Raeburn.' He winced and looked at her, hoping for some positive reaction.

'That's a nice name.'

'Maybe. Let's forget about the N for now. I try to. Anyway, my father's profession suited him and I suppose, protected him with its balance sheet mentality. If you asked him for an opinion, what you usually got was a very, very long silence. You could almost hear all the cogs whirring and the columns being filled and calculated, by which time you would have lost any interest in the outcome. Maybe he was simply relieved not to be involved in the daunting decision of my many Christian names which seemed to have been obligatory back then but which of course I have never used. They simply sit there lonely and unloved. Maybe post-war, they simply wanted to feel bountiful and hopeful for the future?' He stopped. 'I'm talking too much.' *See. That's what happens when you live alone. Only talk to statues. She'll think you're a bit pathetic.*

'No. Please do carry on. It's so interesting. You know, sharing the same times.'

'OK. Well, anyway, they survived the war, looked at the grey fifties and wanted better for me. That meant the eleven plus. Passing the dreaded eleven plus. That was so important to them, I could see that, so I worked very hard – I've always worked hard to make up for the lack of any real talent – I passed and was segregated. Leaders to the right. Workers to the left. That's how it worked then didn't it? But they were proud. So proud. Huh. Bet you passed?'

'I did and it was the same for me. I can remember my mum taking me to buy the grammar school uniform. Then I had to wear it everywhere, even when she went shopping.'

'Yes. Me too.' He smiled at the memory. 'School cap, blazer, grey short trousers, school tie and socks and a huge satchel full of pencils and a ruler and a beautiful Conway Stewart pen. Mottled green and black it was. Lovely. And a compass and a protractor. Whatever that was. And a hymn book. Yeah, all bright and shiny. Had new boy stamped *all* over it. First day, the school bully threw my cap over a wall into somebody's garden. My very first experience of the exercise of power and the public-school system.'

'You went to a public school?'

'No. Just had pretensions of being so. You know, black gowns, canings, bullying, rugger, cold showers, raising your cap to the masters and no money.'

'Well at least you didn't have to wear thick brown lisle stockings and grey knickers *which*, I must add, they used to check on every now and then.'

'Check on? Who did?'

'Mrs Merryworth. She was the RE teacher. Religious Extremist. Used to pull up the horrible grey flannel skirt we had to wear, to check on our knickers. Imagine doing that now. She'd end up in court.'

'Obviously thought that grey would ward off the devil. Was she a lesbian?'

'No idea. We didn't know that such people existed.'

'No. Didn't know much did we?'

'The girls used to try to be attractive. We had this navy-blue pudding basin hat with the school badge on that we had to wear. We used to crease the crown and pull it to the back of our heads to show off our fringes and roll up our skirts when no teacher was looking, but I think the idea was to make us as unattractive as possible.'

'Yeah didn't want any lust. It was the same for us of course, although we didn't wear grey knickers. Mind you, come to think of it we probably did. Don't remember clothes being washed that much or even bodies. No washing machines of course. Just coppers of boiling water and a mangle. No wonder they only did the washing once a week.' They both stopped for a moment, lost in their memories, glad to be friendly again.

'Do you have any sisters Alex?'

'No, unfortunately not. Wish I had. Only child. Girls were a complete mystery to me, and very scary. Best avoided.'

'Scary?'

'Yeah. Witches. They seemed to know everything. Seemed to know what I was thinking before I did. I felt completely inadequate. Still do really. Sometimes.'

'Really?'

'Oh yeah. Every now and again I get that feeling of being hopeless and helpless. That empty feeling in the pit of my stomach. Not able to talk properly. Not that I had much to say to them back then… Girls knew nothing about football.'

'You must have had a girlfriend.'

'No, not really. Too difficult.'

'Difficult?'

'Yeah. If you went out with a girl for more than a month, they wanted to take you home to meet their parents and started looking in jeweller's windows. It was hopeless. You couldn't have a girl who was simply a friend. So, I didn't bother.'

'So, what did you do?'

'Masses of homework and masturbated for England.'

'Oh Alex!'

'You could stand my pyjama trousers up on their own.' He grinned at her. Inanely.

'Oh no!'

'Everybody did it if they're honest. Just as well really, otherwise we would probably all have exploded. And school didn't help. There was no sex education unless you happened to do A-level Biology and the reproductive cycle of the rabbit. But it wasn't rabbits that had the problem.'

'Poor Alex.' She laughed aloud.

'Don't laugh, it was awful.' He grinned back at her. He felt excited at his own words, daring even but also rather silly at the same time, aware that the alcohol was loosening his mind and words and control. *I need to stop before…* He reached for his glass and took another mouthful. 'Must have been the same for you Sam?' His voice felt very loud. She noticed the diminutive.

'Worse in some ways. I had a big brother who obviously knew about your pyjama trousers and all those others across the land and frightened off most boys. He was very protective. And if any boy was brave enough to ask me out, then you immediately became a couple and no other boy would approach you. You're right, you couldn't just have friends. And to make it worse you then had to break it off with the first boy. It was all very silly.'

'You know, society was determined to segregate the sexes as much as possible and then marry them off. Bastards. There was no real alternative. Not in my little one-horse town at least. I mean where else would you buy something so big without trying it out first or at least having an instruction manual. It's a wonder the bloody species survived. You know, I was so ignorant. Everything I knew came from rumour or dirty jokes or lavatory walls. Mind you, wonderful form of contraception – ignorance. I had no idea what to do with it and was terrified at the same time. So, thank God for pyjama trousers.'

They both remained silent for a while.

'More wine Alex? We might as well finish off the bottle.'

'Thanks.'

'Did you never get married?'

'Nope. I was lucky.'

'That's a bit cynical.'

'Well, imagine meeting somebody intimately for the first time on your wedding night. Somebody you have just vowed to be with forever. And then finding out you're not compatible. What a bloody daft idea.'

'So, nobody special then?'

'Nope.'

'Must have been somebody.'

'Not really.'

'Not really?'

The wine drifted around his mind like a delicious warm fog, seeping into the locks of secret vaults long since shut tight, teasing them. Grey eyes watched him softly, curiously.

'Well… I was in a relationship when I was at college. Long, long ago.' He waved one hand vaguely.

'Oh… And?'

'Nothing. Came to nothing.'

'Sorry. I didn't mean to pry.'

There was a pause whilst Alex drank some more wine; relieving his dry mouth. 'No, that was a different world I suppose; art college; back then; when I think about it. A world where people actually queried the rule of Church and State and what your parents had done. It was more liberal; different possibilities. Bit of a shock at first if I'm honest. And not very serious really. Bit of a game. A dangerous game.' He paused, uncertain. 'I guess, I've just drifted around since then. Not really had time. Never found anybody who would seriously put up with me.' He looked up and laughed.

'And children. Did you not want children Alex?'

'No. Not really. What about you?'

'What, children?'

Alex nodded.

'Just the two girls. Debbie and Lisa.'

'Oh yes, you said… I would have liked a daughter. Someone to spoil. Dress up. Must be nice for you to have had two other females around. You know, shopping and girly things.'

'I rarely see them these days. They both live abroad. One in New York and one in Florence.'

'New York and Florence! Wow how perfect. The Guggenheim and the Uffizi. Absolute bliss!'

'Oh Alex. There's more to life than art galleries, surely.'

'Is there. Well, I've never really found it. They're my best friends. Always glad to see me. Always offering themselves. Wanting nothing in return. Always full of surprises and new thoughts and understandings. Never shouting at me but simply talking; whispering even. No, that's not quite true. Sometimes they do shout. Sometimes they rage, but always for my own good. They never tell me what to do, what to wear, what time to go to bed. They don't try to control me. They are only ever concerned about me, never themselves. Unselfish. And I don't even have to remember to buy them anniversary cards.'

'Wow Alex. That's quite a speech.'

'Yeah. Sorry. Must be the wine. I know people think I'm a bit weird but everything I need is there.'

'Everything? Are you sure?'

'Well almost. Yes, I need food and drink and shelter and medicine and er… sex sometimes.'

'Sex? Thought you had your pyjama trousers.'

'I will ignore that. You know, some of the most erotic images can be found in my galleries. Wall to wall painted Viagra. Painted by artists who understood, relished, enjoyed, worshipped, celebrated the female form. Better than any porn. So yes, I am human, despite what some might think.'

'But you must miss human contact. You know, physical contact, don't you? I know I do, sometimes.'

'Sometimes, but unfortunately human contact comes with humans and I don't really miss humans.'

'Oh Alex. That's a bit sad, isn't it?'

'Maybe, but they have a habit of trying to control you or change you. You must know that.'

There was a long pause. Sam thought about her marble table.

'Sorry Sam. Too much booze.'

'Hardly booze. It's a 2005 Bordeaux.'

'Is it! Well it's delicious anyway and I think I've probably drunk most of it. Sorry about that. Didn't mean to get all personal.'

'No. Not at all. You know I'm very happy to talk to you like this. Never really had the chance before. Never found anybody I could talk to so openly. So honestly. You are rather different, aren't you?'

Alex laughed. 'Yes, so I've been told.'

'But that's good, isn't it? Maybe you know the answer? Or is it too late?'

'Too late?'

'Well it's obviously not too late for you but I'm not very attractive now. Not at this age, not for a woman, and you have to attract someone don't you.'

'Of course you're attractive.'

'But I'm nearly seventy.'

'So what?'

'Oh Alex, you are such an… an innocent at times.'

'If that means I see things for what they really are, then I'm happy to be an innocent.'

'But my body—'

'There's nothing wrong with your body.'

'Not covered with clothes and make-up maybe. Oh dear. Can't believe I'm saying all this. Yes, you're right, must be the wine.'

'Do you know the work of Dorothea Lange, American photographer? No? Doesn't matter. Took photographs of destitute workers in the Dust Bowl in places like Oklahoma in the 1930s. Farmland turned to desert. Terrible privation. There's one photo called "Migrant Mother". It's actually about a woman called Florence… Florence Owens Turner. Just imagine; starving; with seven children; sold your tent and the tyres of your truck for food. Living in a lean-to. Eating little birds caught by the children. This woman literally only has the dress she stands up in, she is painfully thin, no make-up, probably not even a brush for her hair and yet there is a strength in her face, a haunting strength. OK, yes, there is also sadness and maybe resignation but her inner soul shines through. You cannot stop looking at her… I often wonder what happened to her and the children.'

A long, thoughtful silence thickened the air around them; pulling at them; filling their skin and pores and nostrils; quickening their pulses; shining their eyes.

'Would you like some brandy or something? Then we can look at the painting?'

Alex moved rather unsteadily into the main lounge, glass still in his hand. He fumbled for his spectacles and gradually put them on whilst walking towards the painting, which covered most of the far wall. He moved slowly from one end to the other in silence, occasionally stopping to peer closer.

'My God.'

'Is something the matter? Alex?'

'My God. It's a Twombly. Got to be. Just got to be.'

'Is that good?'

'Cy Twombly? It's very very good and very very valuable. I never imagined for a single moment… Wow!'

Samantha stood close to him, feeling his infectious

excitement, like the little boy who had just collected the final cigarette card to complete his collection. She felt the urge to place her hand on his arm.

'Look at that. So beautifully done. God, you are *so* lucky. This is a major piece of work.'

Alex paced up and down in front of the painting, sometimes peering closely, sometimes standing back, his face beaming. The glass of brandy in his hand bobbed around, forgotten for the moment and Samantha removed it to safety. He hardly noticed.

'When did you get it?'

'Must have been around 1972, in New York. I don't have a receipt, but I have found this card at the bottom of a drawer.'

'Well '72 fits. Can I have a look?' Alex read aloud. '"Leo Castelli Gallery, West Broadway, Soho, New York". Wow!' He turned and grinned at her. 'Wow.'

Samantha laughed. 'I get the impression that you like it Alex.'

'Oh yes. It's wonderful. Major American post-war artist. Completely out of step with all the other post-war movements. Complete rebel.'

'Bit like you then?'

He grinned back.

'So, what is it painted with Alex, or should that be drawn? Looks like chalk. You know, the sort of chalk you used to use on a school blackboard.'

'Probably is. His work is often very calligraphic.'

'Yes, I remember the dealer saying that. Like handwriting.'

'That's it. So, do you like it Sam?'

'I do. Keep seeing different things in it although Henry liked it more. It was Henry's choice really.'

'Really?'

She nodded.

'Guess I misjudged him.' He looked slightly sheepish.

'Yes, he used to sit for ages in front of it. Used to say that the blue-black background disappeared into the past and the chalk marks were words or feelings trying to escape or even speak. I think it reminded him of his own background or maybe at times his state of mind. It sort of haunted him and also helped him, I think.'

'So why did he let you have it?'

'Maybe it was too painful for him to keep? Too many memories?'

'Well, apart from its considerable value – if you ever fell on hard times – maybe he wanted to remind you. Have a bit of him looking down at you every day. Keep you feeling guilty or maybe sorry for him.'

Samantha stood quite still and stared at the painting for a long time in silence.

'Perhaps I should cover it up?' She turned to him, a look of anguish on her face.

'No, you mustn't do that. Just make it *your* painting. Make it belong to *you*.'

'I don't know how to.'

'I'll help you Sam. I'll help you.' And he felt the urge to put his arm around her.

*

The painting moved slowly up the wall and spilt over onto the white ceiling above, spreading pools of blue-blackness until every inch of white was flooded and filled. Below, Samantha lay naked. Staring upwards, she could see what looked like bruised storm clouds brooding above her and she tensed for the crash of thunder. It never came. Instead, hundreds of thin white stripes came floating up to the surface that looked down upon her, covering and building like a torment of scars until there was room for no more and then, slowly at first, they began to drop and float down upon her. Below she braced herself, but each landed lightly, on her face and mouth, her thighs, her breasts until she was completely covered and slowly buried. She struggled to breathe, flung them away in panic, but many more took their place.

'Alex!'

She awoke with a start and looked uneasily at the ceiling. Even in the early light she could see that it looked the same as every other morning. *Oh, thank goodness.* She lay back and closed her eyes and then opened them quickly. Had she called out or was that call also in her dream, safe in her mind? Had Alex heard her? Oh no. She hoped not, he might come into her room, concerned about her and see her in her nightdress. See her bare arms and throat and the shape of her body beneath the thin material. At least she still had her make-up on, not being brave enough to remove it. Just in case. She quickly tried to control her hair with both hands and at the same time listened intently. Nothing. Not a thing. She lay back and pulled the duvet up to her neck. *Of course he won't just barge in. Of course not. He'll knock and call out 'Sam, are you alright Sam? Sam?' and I'll say… what will I say? I could say 'Come in Alex. I've had a bad dream. Come in, get into my bed and hold me. I need to be held… Oh dear.'*

She quietly climbed out of her bed and padded to where a full-length mirror stood. Normally, she used it to check everything before she went out. Hair OK. Yup. Make-up OK. Yup. Scarf to hide that scrawny neck OK. Yup. Arms covered OK. Yup. This was the same mirror she had stood before and decided to lose her hair. Her long, tumbling auburn hair, her young hair, her hair beginning to lose its rich colour, her past hair. She had felt the shock as her locks were trimmed away, as her youth disappeared and had spent a lot of money on the new style, the new colour. It was also the mirror where she had first felt the lines around her mouth, where the lipstick's easy glide had been interrupted by them. Now she stood and looked at herself. Or, of course, he just might not say anything. But he did mention her body. Although he was probably just being nice. She sighed and pushed her breasts up and together. *There, that looks better. If only they would stay like that. Such as they are.* Outside her room, she heard a toilet flush.

Alex had stayed the night. 'No, I'll be OK.'

'But you've had a lot to drink Alex.'

'I'll get a taxi.'

'But there's plenty of room. You're most welcome to stay.'

'I don't have a toothbrush or anything.'

'I've got a spare and an electric razor.'

'Electric razor?'

'Just in case anybody stays.'

'So, do lots of men stay then?'

'No Alex. They don't. Just the family. And you now. OK?'

She'd been a little surprised and curious at his initial reluctance. Why was that? Male chauvinism? Embarrassment at his inability to drive home? No. Alex was the least chauvinistic man she had ever known. Maybe he didn't like her? Didn't fancy her? Maybe he did? Maybe he couldn't…? She moved to her en-suite bathroom and stood beneath the hot water that hissed down and covered her body.

*

They sat opposite each other at the breakfast table. Alex, face in hands, elbows resting on the table, looking mournfully at her. Inside, as well as feeling unwell, he felt uncertain and a little foolish about his alcohol-fuelled words from the previous night. It was true that his world had been dark at times, like a grimy unwashed window pane through which things had often appeared dismal and vague, when all he had wanted was to escape inside one of those paintings he admired, sheltering in the purple shadows of a red-hot Fauvist sky or feeling the swell and taste of salt air in a Turner seascape. You would have thought that his upbringing would have produced a healthy balance between the implacable rock of his father and the hot wind of his mother, but it hadn't. He could never remember his parents telling him that they loved him. His father tended to swallow such difficult words, which then stuck like brickbats in his throat. His mother sort of made up for it by gushing a great deal but often to the background of his father's mental or sometimes actual tut tuts. However, it didn't seem to make much difference, because deep down, somewhere, he knew that they did, although he could never articulate exactly what it was they did, except that generally it felt like a good thing. And so, he had simply carried on in the same way. Reluctant and nonchalant and assuming with varying degrees of disaster, when it came to relationships.

'What would you like for breakfast?'

'Coffee. Just coffee.'

'Only coffee?'

'Feeling a wee bit fragile.'

'Oh dear.' She stood and moved away. 'Poor Alex. Would you like some painkillers?'

He looked sideways at her. Looking for sarcasm or even humour. She simply opened one of the bright white cupboard doors. He looked back at the worktop, resisting the temptation to rest his head on the cool marble.

'Yes… Well… I'm sorry about that. Hope I didn't misbehave. Say something stupid. I'm quite good at that. Very good in fact.' She thought about his pyjama trousers as he rubbed his face vigorously in circles around his eyes. 'Not used to alcohol anymore. Never liked it much if I'm honest. What it does… *You* don't drink much do you?' He smiled weakly but it sounded a little bit like an accusation.

'Just the occasional glass of wine with a meal that's all and you were the perfect gentleman.'

'Oh dear. You mean boring.'

'You are hardly boring Alex. Enthusiastic, but that's OK, isn't it?'

'Oh that. Yes. Well. Do you think I could have that coffee now… before I die?'

'Of course. Mug OK?'

'Bucketful would be better.'

Alex watched as she moved around the kitchen, her back to him, took in her trim figure, sat back and looked around. The kitchen was large and modern and minimal, straight out of a glossy catalogue, crisp lines, inset ceiling lights twinkling on stainless steel and white units above black marble standing on a black slate floor. *Modernism within the Victorian setting. Study in black, white and grey. Good subject for a lecture or some dissertation.* He wondered if the same neat orderliness followed her into the bedroom. Did she iron the sheets and have a demarcation line down the middle of the bed? He thought about his own kitchen. *Oh dear. You wait till you see mine. Kitchen chaos.* He swallowed uncomfortably as fumes of undigested brandy escaped into the Mouth Desert. His head pulsated. *God, why do I do this? Feels like acid compost down there. Perhaps I was showing off again. Haven't done that since… can't remember when. Just when I thought I'd grown up a bit. Got away from that particular devil.* The smell of fresh coffee galloped to the rescue.

'Would you like to stay for lunch Alex?'

He looked up, still grasping the mug between both hands, resisting the urge to sip frantically. Her eyes seemed to be waiting, anxiously. He glanced briefly at the neckline of her dark-green blouse. *Has she undone another button? Shit, can't remember. Wish this fog would clear.* Her flesh glowed, a small creamy-white triangle within the darker material, the tiniest impression of the beginning of a line that indicated the division of her breasts. Wonder if she knew. He put the mug down.

'Sorry?'

'Lunch?'

'Err no. No thanks. I've got a lot to do.'

'What have you got to do Alex?'

'Oh, you know. The usual stuff. Washing, ironing, shopping, housework, saving the world.'

'Can't you save the world later?' She picked up his spoon from the worktop and held it. 'After lunch?'

'Well, I *was* going to prepare something for *you*.'

'For me?' She smiled, put the spoon down and sat opposite him again, crossing her legs and pulling her skirt towards her knee. 'How lovely.' She paused, gleaming, waiting for him.

'Yes, I thought I'd go through my art books and pick out some examples for you, also see if there are any good exhibitions on in London, at the Tate maybe.' He resisted the urge to belch.

She continued to smile directly at him, just looking, saying nothing.

'Yes, you remember our conversation yesterday? About your painting? I said I would help you. You remember?'

'That would be lovely Alex. Thank you *so* much. I do appreciate that,' and she placed a hand on his arm.

Alex gathered his coat, checked his car and door keys and they both walked to the front door. He turned rather nervously to face her.

'Thanks so much for the lunch and breakfast. Sorry about…'

'My pleasure Alex… thank you for telling me about the Twombly and you *will* contact me about the paintings? The gallery?'

'Of course.'

'Make it soon.'

He nodded and bent to kiss her lightly on her cheek, a friendly, neighbourly, nothing kiss, but she moved her head at the same time and clumsily his lips caught the very edge of her mouth. They both felt the shock.

A moment passed between them. Not an ordinary, everyday, tick tock moment that would soon flitter away and add to the giant heap of forgotten moments. This one stopped and dallied. Half a second passed. Neither said anything.

Alex turned away and waved a cheery hand, his back to her.

'Bye Sam.'

'Bye Alex.'

He looked towards her as he drove quickly away. Saw her wave.

4

Journey to Georgia

ALEX SAT IN the waiting room. Beneath him, the hardness of the long wooden bench pushed uncomfortably into his bones and at his feet stretched a large expanse of wooden floor, herringboned in pattern and badly scuffed. He crossed his arms, looked down and studied the shapes for a while, hoping for stimulation, but soon, even with his eyes wide open, the floor swam away and he looked instead into his troubled thoughts.

What am I doing? Not sure. Anxious? Am I really? Yes. A bit. Why's that? Not sure. Is it the waiting? Maybe bored? You're always bored. No, I'm not. Well maybe. Sometimes. But anxious and… and trapped. Trapped? Trapped? Yes. Really? Well uncertain then… Come on. Enough. Let's pretend. Let's go somewhere else. Hard. That hard feeling. Bare room like a… police cell. A suspect. Yes. Down Mexico way. South American state. Unshaven. Hair wet. Tangled. Sweat running down my back. Flies buzzing. Smell of…

He stopped. Sat up. The herringbone swam back into focus. He took a deep breath. *Actually smells faintly of disinfectant and… paint and… damp people.*

He sighed quietly to himself. *Anxious?* The watch on his

left wrist called out to him again. 'Come on then, look at me. You know you want to. Need to.' It had been doing that all morning. *Oh, ignore it. Come on be strong… Maybe the bus had broken down. She would have left her car at home. No, she would let me know. It's OK. We'll just catch the next train. No rush. Got ALLLL day.* He placed his shoes exactly together and compared them. Left and right. Right and left. Both knots in his laces slanted to his left. *Wonder why that is?* He looked up again. *Shall I wait outside? No, it's cold and wet out there. Be something to do. No, stay here. At least it's dry in here and almost warm although I do feel as if I'm on display. Why do we have to face each other like this? Humans weren't built to face each other. Not really. Much better in rows. On buses, in queues. Or side by side… like… in bed.* His stomach rustled. *Think I'll clean my glasses.*

Opposite him, on the wall, brightly coloured illustrated faces, impossibly attractive, beamed encouragingly out of a poster. 'Great Day Out'. 'Visit Historic London'. *Imagine that. Just a short train ride to the capital. Forget all your cares and woes. Off we go, singing low… and you'll lose twenty years and gain perfect teeth.* Below the poster, one traveller was reading a free paper picked up from the bench. It had been crisp and eager but now it was limp and discarded after several readers had sucked out its contents. Alex watched him. *Look at him. You can tell there's nothing of interest by the way he flicks the pages over – almost angrily. Now he's folded it because it's empty and put it down. He'll look around next and then at his watch… There, told you so. Strange, restless creature, homo sapiens. Always needing to do something. Write a sonnet; explore a jungle; start a war.* He sighed. *What are the others doing?* The other three travellers sat silently, their empty 'waiting for trains/ buses/anything faces' switched on. One, an older woman, sat upright, her bag on her lap, knees clasped together, staring straight ahead. The other two, a younger couple, sat close to each other, the woman with her legs crossed, each occasionally whispering. *I wonder why people always whisper in waiting rooms? Sort of makes sense in a doctor's or dentist's surgery; just fear, anxiety; but waiting for a train? Perhaps they sense something? Some impending disaster?* He looked out of the window and then down at his shoes again. *Oh shit. Odd socks. How did I manage that?* He looked up to see if anybody had noticed and then tucked his feet away beneath him.

What's the time? He looked at his watch again. It looked back. *You're alright. Ticking away. Regular work. Nice and warm on my wrist. Travelling free.* He looked up. *She should be here by now.*

Outside, the pavements had been wet and shiny and large raindrops had plopped into puddles but now the rain seemed to have stopped. Seemed a bit brighter. In the waiting room, folded umbrellas leaned next to their owners, each brolly leaving a small puddle of water like a naughty puppy dog. Alex looked absently down at the floor again, out of the nearest window and then ran his fingers over the seat. His fingertips caught the names and letters scratched there. Moments of love? Passion? Hope? Despair? Existence? Maybe he should carve their names? Alex. Sam. Alex and Sam. Alex AND Sam. Oh such an enormous word for just three letters. He looked down; saw the names slowly disappearing beneath layer upon layer of grey paint. One moment, proud and recognised; then gone forever. He shuffled uncomfortably, stretched his long legs and reluctantly looked again at his watch. Ten minutes yet. He yawned and rubbed his aching knees.

Look, so much space. So much space at what is just a suburban railway station. For so few people. How many? Let's think. Four in here. The man selling tickets and handing out timetables, that's five. Then there's the little Asian girl selling mints and magazines. Six. Me, that's seven and outside, acres of platforms that stretch away left and right and that huge gap between where the track is and then this stadium of a waiting room. Hey, that's what this is, isn't it? Two long platforms of wooden benches facing each other and that big gap in between; that's for the tracks. Used the same plan twice or maybe it's just a railway station planner's mentality. Imagine what his front room must look like. He looked at his watch again. Nine and a half minutes yet. He looked up just as Samantha walked past the window, glanced in and opened the door.

'Hallo. Been waiting long?'

'No. Only just arrived.'

Alex stood, placed his hand on her upper arm and kissed her lightly on her turned cheek. The other three automatically looked up at her arrival and then turned away, save for the older woman, who watched the show of affection with a tiny smile. Alex's touch felt strange against the fabric of her coat. Not warm; the material was too cool and smooth and damp for that, but it was as if he could sense her beneath. *Come on Alex. It's only a greeting. Never used to be. I know, but times change, times change.* A fresh fragrance, strangely androgynous, drifted into his nostrils and toyed with his brain. *Smells like sweet lemon and hot toast.*

'You seem to have shrunk a bit.'

'Oh thanks Alex.' Samantha glanced nervously at the other four. 'Just wearing sensible shoes if we're going to trudge around galleries.'

'Not trudge Sam. Skip excitedly.'

'Think my skipping days are over.'

'But you do want to go?' Around him four sets of ears pricked up at the possibility of an impending drama.

'Of course I do.'

Please don't say silly.

'Come on, let's wait outside.'

The four slumped back and resumed their waiting faces.

*

The carriage was almost empty, maybe five or six other passengers.

'Do you want to sit on the inside, Alex?'

They sat next to each other, arms brushing.

'Is it always this empty? Can't remember the last time I travelled by train. It's really quite exciting, isn't it? Hope the weather doesn't spoil it. Suppose you do this quite a lot? Travel to London?'

He smiled at her, at her enthusiasm and wanted to hold her hand.

The train sped past trees and fields, soggy allotments, back gardens and glistening parks, stopping from time to time at almost empty pale-yellow brick stations. Samantha watched Alex curiously as he looked out of the window, occasionally turning his head to keep sight of something.

'What can you see, Alex?'

'Oh sorry. Didn't mean to neglect you.'

'No, it's OK. It really is. You seem to see so much. Wish I could see through your eyes. Is that what you're going to show me?'

'You make it seem like some special talent.'

'Oh, but it is.'

'Not really. Just learning to see and not just look… and being curious.'

'Hope I can do that.'

'You will Sam. You will.'

Samantha looked out at the passing scene, hoping to see something new and different, but it flashed past, tree after tree, field after field, like a demented speeded-up film making any recognition difficult and soon she gave up. *Alex will show me* and she felt a twinge of excitement.

The train began to slow and then finally stopped. They sat wondering for a while.

'That's strange, the main lights have gone out.' She spoke quietly.

'And there's no power. Listen.'

They looked at each other curiously and then sat in complete silence except for the occasional muffled words from further down the carriage.

'I do hope we haven't broken down.'

They both looked out of the train window.

'Hope not, 'cos we won't be walking. Middle of nowhere.'

Suddenly, the train purred into life and slowly moved forward, stopped at a station and switched off again into silence.

'Conductor to see driver.'

The announcement sounded abrupt.

'Now what?' Alex stretched his legs and closed his eyes, in anticipation of a long wait.

The conductor appeared at the far end of the carriage, his body bending towards an unseen passenger. His words sounded fuzzy and indistinct at first, before suddenly and viciously punching them in their chests.

'A woman has jumped… from a bridge… train in front!'

Samantha gasped. Moving one hand to her mouth she grasped Alex's hand with the other.

'Oh no.'

The conductor walked towards them. His brow shiny.

'Did you hear that?' His voice was quiet but firm.

'How awful.' Samantha's voice trembled slightly.

The conductor nodded and moved on.

'Oh Alex. Poor soul.' She turned towards him, eyes moist and wide in her pale face. Her hand soft and warm and alive. 'Why would she do that?' She looked into Alex's face for answers, but he had none. She turned away and stared ahead of her in the hope of seeking some understanding. Seconds ticked past in absolute silence. The sky, grey with grief, closed in and shrouded them. Outside, the world, unaware, buzzed and ticked and pulsed as usual but inside they all sat quite still, in silence, their thoughts bruised and dislocated.

The heavy stillness was broken by a man's voice somewhere behind them, speaking quietly into a mobile phone. 'Yes, accident on the line… my meeting at twelve… several hours… could you? Yes… thank you… bye.' Samantha moved her hand and placed it around Alex's arm.

'Why would she do that Alex? She must have been so desperate.'

'Don't know. Maybe a terminal illness or a broken marriage or depression… I really don't know.'

'Imagine her getting up this morning. Putting on her make-up… bet she did that. Imagine how she felt, knowing… while we were so happy about meeting… being together. Oh dear. So sad.'

'Hope she was successful… you know. Imagine if…'

'Oh Alex. Don't…' and she closed her eyes and shuddered.

They sat for a long while. Alex looked outside. It had started to rain again and drops ran haltingly down the window. On the platform, puddles trembled and branches sighed and shook. Leaves tumbled down helplessly and were blown away. Quietly the conductor had appeared at their shoulders.

'This could take a couple of hours I'm afraid but we're arranging for buses to take you on.'

Samantha turned and looked up at him.

'What about the driver? Is he OK? Will they take him off?'

'Oh yes. They'll do that…' He sighed. 'Not nice. Not nice,' and moved on.

They both sat in silence for a long time, immersed in their own thoughts. Ahead of them one or two passengers had stood to stretch their legs. Alex recognised them from the waiting room, now shyly talking, sharing the trauma, trying to shake it off like gazelles narrowly missed by a hunting lion.

'Makes you think, Sam. How fragile life can be and how brutal at times. How lucky we are.'

Samantha turned, looked at him and squeezed his arm. 'We're moving.'

The lights came on and the train throbbed back into life. Alex counted the next two bridges and knew they must have passed the spot where a life had just ended. The train moved slowly, almost gently, almost with reverence.

'Alex. Look. Look at the sky.' The rain had stopped and the grey clouds covering them had parted allowing a soft lemon light to peer through. 'She's there.'

He felt the emotions bubble up into his chest and threaten to spill over.

'I really do hope so.'

They sat in silence for the rest of the journey, watching more passengers joining them, until the train was quite full. They watched them chatting, reading, sending messages, full of their own thoughts, unaware of the trauma they had just shared. At their destination Alex helped Samantha down from the train. As they walked towards the barrier, he felt her hand slip into his.

'Think we need a coffee or something Sam.'

She nodded.

They sat within the station concourse, aware of the hustle and bustle but also detached from it, as if they had a secret that separated them from the wide-eyed travellers around them, anxiously seeking train times and platform numbers and taxis and Tube trains.

'How you feeling Sam? Are you alright?'

'Yes, thank you. Bit shaken, that's all.'

'Strange, isn't it?'

'What's that?' She slowly stirred her latte.

'Well, we weren't even in that train, the one ahead and yet we still became so involved.'

'We *could* have been on that other train. Quite easily.'

'Yes. Of course. But it was more than that. It was that oppressive silence, wasn't it? Just crushed you. We just sat there and felt all of that. Maybe it was because we were on a train. Same as the one in front and couldn't go anywhere, do anything. Was that it? The other passengers that got on later would have known or guessed. An incident on the line or fatality on the line – isn't that what they announce and yet it didn't seem to affect them so much. I really wanted to say something, something comforting.'

'Did you?' She stopped stirring.

'Yes. Comfort myself if I'm honest but all those thoughts pressed themselves into me. Squashed any words.'

'I understand. I felt the same. I'm so glad I was with someone… with you.'

They looked at each other.

'So, what do we do now? Do we go on or just call it a day?'

Alex sat upright and tapped the table with both hands.

'Oh, we have to go on. Life *must* go on. Mustn't waste a moment. Are you ready?'

She looked directly at him and smiled.

'Almost.'

They crossed the busy mainline station, hand in hand, Alex leading the way, threading between the criss-cross streams of intent travellers, then descending into the dim scurry of the Underground and through the District and Circle Line barrier. Alex found a space and ushered Samantha onto the escalator in front of him. He placed one hand on her shoulder.

'We'll go to Blackfriars first. Have a look at the new station. OK?'

Samantha felt his hot breath on her cheek and ear and nodded.

They descended from the clatter of the train into the space and freshness of a new Tube station and rode upwards into a large hall. Alex turned slowly on his heels, face alight.

'What a great space.' He spoke to nobody in particular.

In front of them another escalator rode endlessly upwards towards the railway station.

'Come on, let's have a look.'

At the top, they stood taking in the parade of shiny grey shapes above their heads and the wide expanse of pale marble platform. Ahead the barriers winked red and green but were open.

'Well, we've got to cross the river to get to the Tate. Wonder if we can cross here, along the platform? What do you think Sam?'

'Well, look, right at the end there. There's a woman pushing a pram. Doesn't *look* as if she's waiting for a train.'

They watched as the woman suddenly turned right and disappeared.

'Come on Sam. Let's go.'

They strolled onto the platform, stopping to admire the view of London through the panoramic windows that opened up the whole side of the station.

'Imagine building a railway station on a bridge over the Thames. That's clever. That's exciting.' Alex stopped to smile at Samantha.

'I didn't know you were interested in architecture, Alex.'

'Oh yes! It's all linked. "Architecture is inhabited sculpture".' Alex spoke the words slowly and rather grandly and swept his arm to embrace the station.

'Oh, that's clever. Did you just make that up?'

'No such luck. Constantin Brâncuși. He was a sculptor.'

'Brâncuși. I don't think I've ever heard of him.' She stopped and looked a little lost.

'Oh come on Sam. Doesn't matter,' and he put his arm around her shoulders. 'Come on. So many beautiful things to see,' and he walked her along the platform. Samantha placed her arm around his waist.

They turned down the new, wide staircase and suddenly came face to face with a monumental patchwork of strong bright colours – gold, red, white, and blue.

'Wow, look at that.'

Samantha read the huge words outlined in a gold colour. 'London Chatham and Dover Railway. Eighteen sixty-four. Invicta.' She turned towards Alex. 'So, this must be the old railway. Some sort of badge or shield; coat of arms and I know about Invicta,' she pointed to the white horse prancing on the red background of the top shield. 'It represents Kent. I had an aunt who lived in Tunbridge Wells.'

They stood for a while.

'So, what does it feel like Sam?'

'Feel like?' She looked at him in surprise.

His voice had softened. 'Yes, feel like.'

She stood for a moment, uncertain what to say.

'Look back there Sam. Back along the new bridge.' From where they stood, they could easily see the outline of the railway bridge stretching across the river. 'Tell me what you see.'

'Well…' She paused. 'Well, all those panels that form the roof look like wings. Don't they? Jutting out. Like an airport.'

She looked quickly at him. He nodded encouragingly. She continued, 'I think it's rather beautiful. In a quiet sort of way. Like… like a host of insects with metal wings have landed but all very disciplined. All in the right place. Very symmetrical. Is that right?'

He smiled at her. 'And what about this?' He pointed towards the brightly coloured shield.

'Oh that. Well, that's big and bold and… proud? Shouts confidence. Victorian confidence.'

'Certainly does.'

'And of course, very different materials. That must make a huge difference. What is this Alex? Iron? I suppose the materials you use have characteristics of their own. Personalities I suppose.' She turned to face him. 'So how did I do?'

'Top of the class Sam. Top of the class.'

They walked beside the grey river, with Samantha now looking around, knowing she had to be curious, noting the water buses and sidestepping the slow perambulation of tourists and impatient darts of the occasional jogger. The rain had stopped and the sun had appeared, weakly apologising. There was an air of briskness and excitement.

'Listen.' Samantha stopped. 'Can you hear it?'

'What?'

'Music. That's a saxophone. Isn't it? Where's it coming from? It's over there.'

She left him, walked to the river wall and looked over. He was aware of her jeans stretching tighter behind her as she did so. She turned and waved excitedly. 'Look Alex.'

They leaned together, shoulders touching, and he felt a surge of energy run down his arm. Below them, on the stony shoreline, stood a young man playing a tenor saxophone. He was quite slight with wispy ginger hair that trembled in the breeze and from above, his instrument glowed honey gold, even in the tepid sunlight. Before him stretched a rectangle of blue material, in the middle of which stood a cheap red plastic bucket centred on a large painted bullseye. Around, he had weighted down sheets of white paper, with his story scrawled in large red letters on them.

MY NAME IS TED.
I'M A MUSIC STUDENT IN LONDON
WITHOUT A STUDENT LOAN.
IT'S HARD.
EVERY 10P YOU GIVE ME
GIVES ME TEN MINUTES
OF PRACTISE
INSTEAD OF TEN MINUTES
OF PAYMENT.

Around him were dotted a number of coins and a single, crumpled banknote. From below came the sound of a quiet blues number. It faltered from time to time.

'Oh Alex, we must give him something. Poor young man. He's trying so hard and it's not easy when you're first starting out is it and we have so much, don't we?'

'Do we?'

She turned and looked steadily at him for a moment. Then she smiled and rubbed his arm.

'Of course we do.'

She turned away and scrabbled in her bag, pulling out a leather purse and clicking it open.

'Here, see if you can get these in the bin. Bet you do.'

Alex missed by a few inches. The young man looked up at them and nodded, still playing.

They passed the row of delicate silver birch planted outside, entered the cavernous Tate Modern beneath its towering brick chimney and walked amidst the chatter of voices and languages.

'Alex, it's enormous.'

'Come and look at this,' and he led her towards a railing. Below them stretched a vast concrete space that sloped down into a grey dimness. Light poured in from tall, slender windows above another entrance and small children, many dressed in bright pinks and reds, rolled joyously down the slope to the feet of their waiting parents.

'What a magical place. The girls would have loved this.'

Alex felt a cold shiver touch him, then fly away. 'Shall we go and have a look at Miss O'Keefe?'

Samantha gulped in one last sweeping look. 'OK. Can we come back later?' Her eyes shone.

'Of course.'

They walked up to the second floor and entered the world of Georgia O'Keefe. Samantha was immediately struck by the change in atmosphere, from the outside bustle to a feeling of quiet reverence, concentration and space. Lots of space. It reminded her of stepping into the church that sat on her clamouring high street but without its echoing contemplation and quiet shadows. This world was light and bright and people moved almost dreamily through it and in virtual silence, stopping only to contemplate the jewels spaced on the white walls. She wondered if it was always like this or whether this was simply the impact of the paintings of one woman. How powerful that would be. She held tightly onto Alex's hand, not feeling confident enough to venture too far on her own and entered O'Keefe's world of colour and flowers and the landscape of New Mexico. Although Alex had outlined the history of the artist, she was still completely unprepared for what she was now facing. If the other visitors felt the same, they did not seem to show it, moving slowly and confidently, sometimes with a little inward smile. She had expected some sort of debate but apart from the occasional whisper, there was no discussion. Was it that they had all come to worship at the altar of O'Keefe or was it that like her, they had no idea how to respond and so simply kept quiet?

'Sorry,' she mouthed silently, realising she had moved in front of another visitor, blocking his view. The man, quite elderly, smiled slightly, gave a small nod and turned away, then looked back briefly, his small white pony tail bobbing as he did so. *Oh dear, there is obviously some sort of etiquette here.* She wanted to ask Alex, but he was too engrossed. She watched him; the silent concentration on his face, the way he turned his head slightly from side to side as if somehow that helped him to understand; how he bent forward to see a detail and then stepped a few paces back; the tiny nods of appreciation and then occasionally, he would turn to her with a little gesture of his right hand and with raised eyebrows, like a chef indicating a perfect dish.

'So, what do you think Sam?' He couldn't keep the excitement from his voice. 'Don't you think the colours are wonderful?'

Her stomach tingled. *That's just what I was thinking. How amazing. Got that right.* 'Yes, and what's more that young girl over there,' – she indicated with a little movement of her finger – 'she's actually wearing the same sort of colours. Don't you think?'

Alex turned slowly and then turned back. 'So she is. Well spotted.' She glowed for a moment and then felt a pang of uncertainty bordering on panic.

'Do I look OK?'

He looked surprised.

'Yes, of course you do. You always do. Why?'

'Well, these people seem so different somehow,' she whispered. 'They dress so… individually. A sort of individual style. Artistic I suppose. Not always smartly but quite often expensively. That young girl for example,' and she nodded in her direction again, eyes not leaving Alex. 'I feel like the country cousin in the big city for the day, with Selfridges and Jigsaw written all over me.'

They stood together, whispering earnestly, like two pebbles catching the splashes of a stream, as those around them flowed confidently onwards.

'Oh Sam, you look wonderful. You always do. And…' he leant a little closer, 'I've noticed a number of men looking at you. You know…'

'Huh, don't think so.'

'Oh yes.'

'Well who then?' and she looked shyly around.

'Well him for a start.'

'Who?'

'Him. The old guy in black with the arty fading-rock-star pony tail.'

'Oh no. I just got in his way. He was just being nice.'

'Samantha; I know that look. I know what that look means.'

She smiled impishly at him. 'Why Alexander. I do believe you're jealous.'

'Huh. Come on. We're supposed to be soaking up Georgia O'Keefe not chatting up strange men.'

She snorted aloud, causing a few nearby to look casually in her direction. They grinned at each other like naughty children.

'Do you want to sit down? Space there.'

She nodded, surprised at how much her legs ached and how much was spinning through her head. They sat with some relief in the only two spaces left on a simple wooden bench in the centre of the room and she tried to gather her thoughts. She had dutifully read the titles to each painting hoping for some enlightenment and also the information presented on large white boards at the entrance to each section. Sometimes the language was difficult and dense but she understood enough to be intrigued about this other world that Alex inhabited and about the artist herself. She continued to observe the others around her, viewing the exhibition. *Wonder if some of these people also dress for each exhibition. You know, this is my Picasso dress. This is my… oh dear can't think of another artist's name… anyway my famous artist's hat. My O'Keefe colours.* She wanted to tell Alex of her discovery but decided not to, just in case she was hopelessly wrong.

'So, what do you think?'

'Well if I'm honest I'm a bit confused,' she whispered back.

'That's good.'

'It is?'

'Oh yes. Shows you're involved.'

'I might be involved but I still don't understand.' If she was honest, she also felt rather overwhelmed and inadequate and increasingly exhausted. And at this age. Suddenly, she was in the back row of the dreaded fourth-form Latin lesson with Amanda, her friend Amanda. Amanda. The gerund from Amare, Worthy To Be Loved. That's about all she could remember. They had clung together, both with that sinking feeling of being lost amongst the conjunctions and complications. But Amanda had died young. In childbirth. Obviously not worthy. That's love for you. She shivered. Alex was saying something.

'Sorry Alex. Miles away.'

'I was saying that I deliberately didn't give you my opinion, because I was interested in what you might think.'

'Really?'

'Yup.'

'Trouble is, I don't really know how to respond. Do I respond emotionally? These huge paintings of flowers are a complete surprise, they are very beautiful, but do they represent more? Am I supposed to intellectualise them? I mean are they not flowers after all and why are they so big? Are they also about me? You know I think they might be. Just when you think you've got it all sussed, something comes along and spins you off somewhere else? And she was also a woman of course. Is she, Georgia O'Keefe, telling me there is more to myself, Samantha Reagan? Much more to come? Oh dear.' She let out a large sigh and turned towards him. 'You know, I want to read all about her.' Suddenly she was fourteen again and full of awe and need.

'Wow Sam. Wish you'd been one of my students. Although "sussed" is a bit vernacular for a posh bird like you.' He was grinning and holding her hand tightly.

'Oh, stop it Alex. It's just a lot to take in… Do you understand it all?'

'No.' He shook his head and laughed lightly.

Oh, thank goodness. That's the right answer. Honest, straightforward Alex.

'But I love being here, trying to understand, trying to fit it to my own life. It's a privilege.'

Sam looked around the room. 'So, it's up to me to try to understand but maybe more importantly to take something from it. To make me consider, reassess? And just when I thought I had got my life… sussed. Phew… what a day.'

'Hope it's not been too much Sam. Didn't mean to wear you out.'

'No, it's been fascinating, but I must admit my feet are aching and I could do with a drink.'

'Come on. There's one more thing we *have* to see. Ready?'

He took her hand and gently pulled her to her feet. 'Just one more room. Promise.'

They turned into the final room and before them, a small group stood in front of a large painting, the top of which could be seen above their heads. The group stood in complete silence, not moving, almost transfixed and for a second, their attitude chilled Samantha and she froze at the thought of another disaster. *Don't be silly. How could that be, in here?* In front of them a couple moved away, almost reluctantly, allowing Alex and Sam to take their position.

Before them, hung a painting of a flower, petals white and cream, leaves surrounding it, in darker greens. Samantha felt herself drawn immediately towards it, more than any of the other paintings, recognising a simplicity and honesty but also a worrying fragility. She bent forward to read its title. *Jimson Weed / White Flower No.1. 1932.* She stood up, surprised. *It's a weed. A common weed. Oh my goodness.* Then, as she watched, the petals appeared to shiver, just for a moment, as if caught by some light New Mexican breeze. She held her breath, doubting her senses and then suddenly felt a deep hurt for this simple flower, afraid that it might be dashed and blown away and she thought of the woman trembling on the railway bridge. In that moment, she recognised once more the brevity and fragility of life. She turned towards Alex, beside her. His face was pale, and a tear had rolled down one cheek.

'Alex.' She looked around, anxious that others might have noticed, then stood before him.

'Alex. Are you alright?'

Gruffly, he wiped the tear away with a sleeve. Then again, almost savagely.

He suddenly put his arms around her. She felt the strength of his body vibrate through her in a wonderful shock, then confusion, then embarrassment. She stood quite still, her hands on his waist. He let go, almost as if he was unaware of what he had done and wiped his eyes again. 'Come on. Let's rest our legs and have that drink.'

They left the building; out of its bright intensity and into the cool night air and found a seat in the nearby Founders Arms, surrounded by the loud chatter of the evening. The bridge that they had crossed now glowed with smudges of blue light across its span and in the near distance London was speckled with dashes of bright white, yellow, blue, green and dark red. Samantha sat and looked, occasionally sipping from her glass of dry white wine but her mind was on Alex and 'Jimson Weed'. They sat very quietly, the reflected light dipping and rolling on the high tide.

'Ready?' Alex finished the last drop of his orange juice and rattled the ice cube loudly around the glass. He seemed to have completely forgotten about his emotional reaction to the painting, although he tried not to look her directly in the eye.

Samantha nodded.

*

The train was still quite full of commuters, even though the evening was sliding past. Samantha slipped her feet from her shoes, feeling a welcome coolness and looked out of the train window at the dark world rushing away. They both sat without speaking, each immersed in the day's thoughts.

'Next stop.'

'Can I give you a lift Alex?'

They stood next to Samantha's car in the station car park.

'No thanks. I'll walk. Need to stretch my legs.'

'Are you sure?'

'Yes. It's only five minutes from here. That's why I left the car.'

They paused for a moment.

'Thank you for a lovely day.'

'Thank *you* Sam. Certainly eventful. And as you can see, art can sometimes make its mark.'

Samantha had waited for Alex to talk about his reactions to the exhibition and to that painting in particular, but she had been met with silence. Certainly she was bursting with thoughts and observations of her own, but knew to say nothing. It was as if he had needed the time that followed to recover and quietly collect himself but now his eventual response felt inadequate and incomplete. However, she smiled and touched his arm.

'See you again? Soon?'

'Oh yes. Of course. I'll phone you tomorrow Sam.'

'OK.'

He stood uncertain in the orange streetlight. Samantha placed her hand on his upper arm. He didn't move. She leant and kissed him. Her lips felt soft and warm.

'Goodnight Sam.'

He turned and walked away, one hand waving without him looking back.

'Goodnight Alex.'

She stood and watched him, until he had disappeared into the night.

5

———

Secrets and Understanding

A LEX HAD GOT up late, and now looked rather forlornly
through one of the large outside windows, into the
garden where Dionysus stood. The bright summer colours
had gradually dripped into the autumn pool and become
muddied and dull, and the grass, left long, had lost its spiky
plumpness and was now flattened into light and dark
whorls, flecked with wet silver. A lone pigeon fluttered fatly
into the open bird house, looking for soggy breadcrumbs
and now stared out, head bobbing, into the heavy drizzle.
Nothing else moved, except for the occasional tremor of
leaves and slim branches and the electric dancing of tiny
drops on the wet pathways. There was an uneasy calm, as
if the garden was waiting anxiously for something. The
end of the cycle. Spring, summer, now autumn, winter to
come.

He had felt reluctant to consider it, even in his mind. This
was so silly. It was nothing monumental. Nothing serious or
out of the normal. Not on its own at least. He looked up to
where the sky had been, closed his eyes and spoke the words
out loud.

'We kissed.'

He opened them and looked towards where Dionysus stood, still partly hidden by wet leaves. *I know. Just a kiss. Nothing much in your book. Hardly an orgy. What? Well… soft, warm, full… delicious really. It had been one hell of a day. Firstly, that poor woman on the railway and then… I don't want to go into that, and she kissed me I think. Yes, I probably did respond but she'll think… What? Oh, I don't know. It was only a kiss and it has been a long time. A very long time… Maybe I've just forgotten and people kiss all the time now. Never did in my youth; so now it's confusing, not sure where you are… Yes, I know, on the mouth. No, I don't know what happens next. She's a friend and God knows, I don't have many of those and she's fun and interesting but… well, if I'm honest, it worries me… I don't know why. Not really.*

He returned to his tiny flat, plumped up the cushions on his battered green armchair, sat down and stared for a long time at the daylight drifting dimly through the slats of the venetian blinds. Nearby on his phone, a green light winked incessantly at him. He knew who the message was from. Knew that he had promised to phone and hadn't. Knew that part of him wanted to ignore it and part wanted to snatch it up eagerly. He stood stiffly, moved to the winking phone and hovered uncertainly over it as if it was some malevolent one-eyed monster. *Shit. One moment I'm free, carefree even. Safe. On my own. Can't be touched. Not answering to anybody. Do what I like, when I like. Shave when I like. Change my socks when I like. Fart when I…* He sighed deeply. *Shit, shit, shit*

He picked up the phone.

Her voice, even recorded, sounded unusually low and quiet, tired maybe.

'Hallo Alex…' *Not 'Hi Alex.' Why so formal?* 'Are you OK? Anyway, thank you for a lovely day. Quite memorable really.'

Why memorable? 'I really enjoyed it. Learnt such a lot. Would you like to come for lunch on Saturday? Usual time.' *Usual?* 'Around one? Got lots of things to talk about now.' *Things? What things?* 'Get back to me. Bye.'

He played the recording again and then phoned her.

*

Alex brushed the curled leaves from the bonnet of the old Volvo and peeled off those stuck like transfers to the bodywork and windscreen. Normally, he wouldn't have been so meticulous but today, he felt the need to delay his departure. He sat for a while in the driver's seat, smelling the musty interior, tapping the steering wheel lightly. Around him, trees had almost shed their summer finery, just a few limp leaves left, empty-yellow and scabby, leaving bare branches pointing defiantly skywards. *Wonder why they don't relax now? Hang down during the long winter? Have a rest? I would.* He sprayed the windscreen and watched the wipers sweep the wash away. Swish swish, swish swish, before the blades finally staggered over a dry area. He switched them off. In front of him, a single, silver drop of liquid made its way cautiously downwards, leaving an uneven wet trail, stopping from time to time, uncertain whether to continue, before rushing the final distance and disappearing. He watched, reminded of a stricken aircraft falling from the sky. *Oh dear, the omens don't seem so good today mate.* He fired the engine and moved slowly away, reaching for the radio as he did so. The genius of Borodin poured out, telling him rather passionately, that he could be in paradise, but that help was at hand. He switched it off.

He parked outside Samantha's house, aware of the long, white Mercedes stretched out in her neighbour's drive and then stood for a while, taking in the classic Victorian lines, neat front garden and black iron railings with their decorative finials, standing confidently against the red brick. Eventually, he opened the front gate, walked slowly along the geometric tiled pathway and knocked loudly on the front door with his knuckles. His stomach gurgled. Through the stained glass, he saw a vague figure appear and then the door opened.

'Alex.'

For a second, he was silenced by Samantha's appearance. The jeans and blouse had gone and in their place was a russet-coloured jersey wool dress, high at the neck with three-quarter-length sleeves and dark shoe boots. A single silver bangle hung from one wrist. There was no silver watch this time.

'Hi Sam. Hallo. You look very nice.'

'Why thank you.' She beamed, pleased at her decision. 'Makes a change from jeans and a jumper. Didn't get too wet?' *No flowers this time.*

'No. Stopped raining now.'

He stepped inside, wiping his feet, deliberately, lengthily.

'Come on into the kitchen, I've just put some coffee on.'

She walked ahead, the wool following her shape as she moved. Alex watched, and realised that he had never seen her legs before. He felt his inner strength begin to crumble.

'I've just made us a simple chilli con carne.' She pronounced the words with a slight accent. 'One of Maria's favourites. You remember me talking about Maria? Is that OK?'

'Oh yes. I'm sure it'll be delicious.'

She half-turned. 'I'm beginning to know what you like.' The smile had gone.

'And, I have some Negra Modelo to go with it or an Argentinian Malbec if you prefer.'

They had reached the kitchen. Samantha turned and faced him.

'What would you like Alex? What do you want?'

Oh my God, I wish I knew.

'Well… I usually have fish and chips and half a lemonade if I'm honest. I've not heard of Negra thingy.' He laughed nervously. Samantha looked at him blankly.

Oh shit. Do something.

'Sorry. I'm just not used to such fine things.' He placed one hand on her upper arm, just under her shoulder, trying to reassure, an unspoken apology maybe… *such slim shoulders, like a child, a child woman, under this soft material…* He smiled weakly. She felt his touch, imagined it hot on her, knew that she had wanted him, way back then; when her breast was firm and proud, her flesh young and silky. Back then. Now. Here he was. At arm's length. Bittersweet. She looked up into his wavering smile. Searched his face silently.

'Just a peasant really,' he continued.

'Hardly. I think you are the lord of all you survey.' She turned away. 'Coffee?' Her back to him.

Alex balanced uneasily on one of the chrome stools. 'Lord of all I survey? Lord Alex eh. Lord Alex of where? Where do you think?' He stretched out one hand theatrically.

'Where?' She turned, leaned against the marble worktop, like a boxer in a corner and looked directly at him. Her words arrived; coolly charged, deliberate.

'Oh, I think, lord of the vast plains of his… *reluctant* soul.'

He heard the emphasis and in the clean, clinical space between them, the atmosphere, which had been rather cool, suddenly changed like an unexpected squall turning a calm sea into cold trembling waves, and with no warning.

'Reluctant?'

The word sat there, looking backwards and forwards between the two of them. Alex felt its intent instantly. Hard and dark and heavy with edges sharp and probing. He had been expecting it, always expecting it, always ready. A protective armour just below the surface with watchtowers, ever alert, conditioned and ready to retaliate. Now, deep inside, he felt cold and sick but outwardly he was tense and prepared, had been prepared ever since then. Never again.

The kitchen was still full of tepid light slipping in through the windows and the ceiling lights sparkled but as they faced each other, the air between them growled and their surroundings lost focus and began to slip away.

'Reluctant. What do you mean?'

Maybe the word had been carelessly chosen, tossed in without any great thought. Maybe she would laugh, that deep, warm laugh and cleverly remove it, with wit. Maybe he would grin foolishly, allowing her to win, so he could back away out of this shadow into the warmth again but with a tiny barb caught in the back of his mind, where it would itch and occasionally catch sharply and remind him, along with all the others attached there.

She didn't remove it.

'I like you so much Alex, but you really won't allow anybody in, will you?'

He had tried to prepare himself in that short time, his brain running at a million miles per hour, overheating with the smell of burnt reason. He tried to remain cool and calm, choosing words carefully, words that might explain without telling, keep him safe, defuse, resume, but he failed. Instead he drew a dagger.

'Exactly what business is it of yours?'

His words, cold and unexpected, flew at her with a cruel force, scattering hers like ten pins, removing colour from her face. For a millisecond, he felt victorious, powerful even, as she faltered.

Samantha recoiled and felt the hardness of the worktop edge press into her back. Somewhere inside her, a snarl echoed. She knew it from Henry. She shivered.

'None, it's none.'

Their words had swollen and filled the room, sucking out the air, threatening them both with suffocation. Outside a bird sang. A simple song, nothing glorious but it was more than they had. At that moment, much more.

Alex slipped from the stool. Her words had slapped him hard, leaving their mark on his flushed cheeks, but he also knew they were justified. His made him feel hot and heavy with shame, for he knew their motive. Survival and revenge. He looked at Samantha. Her face was deathly white, her eyes huge and dark. He knew at that moment, he must turn away his icy history and pride or lose her. He also now knew he could not bear to lose her.

'Sam.'

He moved uncertainly towards her, clumsily, hands extended. She watched this strange slow mime until he stood against her, felt his hands encircle her waist, felt the fabric of his shirt against her cheek, the smell of him and inside his trembling resistance. She did not hold him.

'Sorry. I'm so, so sorry. I can explain. Please.'

*

They sat, once again, opposite each other, across the large oak table. Alex placed his hands on the rough timber, could see the table's age and history and through his fingertips, imagine the depth of ingrained experience that lay there. Many had sat where he now sat and where Samantha sat. Lives had come and gone as theirs would, with the same passions and feelings, mistakes, lost and magic moments. A patina of people. Under the table, he stroked the smooth reddish-brown timber with his foot, hoping for an answer but there was none, except for a feeling of deep regret and humility.

She had said nothing but gently removed herself from his hold and moved to the dining room, where he heard her placing plates and cutlery. She had laid the table long before but now needed to do something. Anything. Anything that felt like normality. And not to allow him to see the tears filling her eyes. Her mind whirled and she realised that she was uncertain who the tears were for.

'This is really delicious Sam.'

'Glad you like it.'

'And the beer. Goes so well. Really does.'

'Good.'

Their words, heavy with courtesy, staggered around each other, hardly settling in the still-heavy atmosphere. The sounds of cutlery on plates seemed greatly magnified, even aggressive, and both tried to avoid such clashes, eating carefully; daintily. The food, delicious as it was, sat heavily in Alex's gut, as his body and mind still trembled from the spectre that normally only visited him in the privacy of the night shadows. He knew very well the demons that whispered into his ear and roamed through his mind. When he conformed, they became his companions, part of the gang, falsely reassuring. He also knew that he had allowed them to grow fat and black, engorged on his self-doubts and weakness. Now it was almost out. He glanced across at Samantha. She avoided his eyes.

He looked into his glass. *When I finish this, I'll tell her. I will.* He picked up his glass and gently swilled the brown liquid around, looking down into it, put it to his lips in the pretence of drinking, put it down again and stared at his plate.

Samantha looked at him as he stared downwards. He wasn't Henry. Henry had been dark and controlling but at the same time self-assured. Henry would always survive. She wasn't sure that Alex would. *But he's right. What business is it of mine? I don't have to be involved. I can simply walk away. I don't have to take on other people's problems. I can always be on my own.*

'Sam.' He spoke her name softly, eyes closed.

'Yes.'

'Sam… I had a son.'

'Had a son?'

'No.'

'No?'

'I didn't really have him.'

'Sorry. I don't understand.'

'He was a twin.'

'A twin?'

'Yes. He had a sister. A baby sister. Yes… and they took them away.'

'Took them away? Who took them away?'

'The people at the hospital… the authorities… oh I don't really know.'

'Why did they do that for goodness' sake?'

'Because we weren't married… so I never saw them. They gave them to someone else.'

'Oh Alex, that's terrible. But didn't the mother…?'

'She had no say in it. They simply took them.'

She placed one hand at her throat. 'Oh, how awful.'

'It was at university… art college. She was an alcoholic… I didn't know. Didn't understand… we all drank a lot… and the drugs. She carried my son and my daughter… our children, our twins. God, it was terrible.'

She said nothing. Afraid to speak.

'Sorry.' He smiled weakly and rubbed his face with both hands. 'Sorry.'

'You've nothing to be sorry for, you poor man.'

He held up one hand. It trembled slightly. 'I've never told anybody before, not even my parents. They would have been appalled.' He looked away, shook his head. 'Absolutely appalled. And ashamed. The stigma. I couldn't… and they would have intervened. Well my father, certainly. Made us marry. But she wouldn't. Things were so, so different back then. Now… well.'

'We all make mistakes.' Samantha flinched at her trite words but had no others. Now her anger had gone and she simply wanted to hold him, comfort him, pleased he had told her, just her, felt her emotions bubbling up into her mouth and eyes again.

'We thought we were so clever, so rebellious, so loud with our disdain for society, for convention. Thought we could change it, thought that it didn't apply to us.' He laughed. 'But we were pretty stupid and worse than that, so naïve. Thought we were in love, but it was just lust and excitement. So shallow. We knew nothing. Absolutely nothing. Especially about sex. How could we know? Rumour? Lavatory walls? Nothing from our parents or teachers.' His voice grew louder, stronger. 'They kept that very quiet. Didn't they? They did Sam.' He looked at her imploringly. She nodded gently.

'Your son. What was he called?'

'I don't know.'

'You don't know?'

'Not really. We were going to call him Jak. His mother registered him – we weren't married of course – she may have named him something else. I don't know. And the girl. My daughter. God… how that word hurts.'

'Sorry. I don't understand. Weren't you there?'

'No… Oh God this is so difficult.'

'It's OK. You don't have to tell me.'

'I want to. I have to.'

She waited silently, hardly able to breathe. 'And what happened to the mother?'

'Rachel? I don't know. She refused to see me… she needed help and the hospital wouldn't let me in, so….'

Samantha looked at him uncertain of what to say or do.

'I know. I did try. I went to the hospital hoping to see Jak and Georgia, but they were whisked away almost immediately. It was hopeless.'

'Georgia?'

'Yes. That was the name we chose, or at least Rachel chose. After her favourite artist.'

'So, your daughter was named Georgia. After Georgia O'Keefe?'

'I expect so. I don't really know.'

'Oh Alex. I'm so sorry. I don't know what to say.'

'Rachel went back to her parents and the bottle I guess. I just wanted to run away. It would never have worked… Never. Georgia would be forty-seven now although I always see her as being about ten years old. Isn't that strange?' Tears ran slowly down Alex's face. He made no attempt to stop them or dry them.

'Georgia.' Samantha spoke the name softly as if by doing so she had finally introduced her to the world. 'Pretty name.'

'Yes.' Alex's face lit up. 'I think so. And Jak. Think he might be a musician or maybe an actor with that name. Jak James. Sounds good. Except it probably won't be James.' He gave a pale smile, picked up his glass to wet his dry mouth and wiped his face roughly with his hands, as if that's what he deserved. Samantha wanted to stand and hold him to her, tell him it was alright, but at the same time felt the wooden barrier between them. Perhaps he had chosen that, that separation, that distance. He *had* kissed her back, with warmth and softness, at the end of that emotional day, the day of the train and she had felt it, but that was almost a week ago and now he seemed to be still keeping them apart while he released his story or was that just coincidence? But he *had* told her. After all those years of holding back the pain, he had told her; trusted her with this dark secret. Is that why he behaved like a clown at times? Hiding behind the funny costume and thick grease paint. Is that what had happened in front of 'Jimson Weed'?

'So, what happened then?' She urged him gently, carefully on.

'Oh, I finished college. Funny, I worked really hard as if that could somehow make up for things, looked for a job…' His voice tailed off.

'And you never got married?'

'Heavens no. Not after that. Frightened me. Really frightened me. Just drifted. Person to person. Buried myself in my work I suppose. Did well in that respect but, well, probably too late now. Too old. Too stuck in my ways.' He looked up at her.

She wanted to challenge that, ask if she was also part of that drifting, just casual flotsam or even jetsam but knew he was too raw.

'I'm so glad you told me.' She smiled at him. 'Are you alright?'

'Yes,' he laughed. 'Think so.' He inhaled a large breath and patted his chest.

'Nothing seems to have fallen off.'

She looked at this man. Clever, funny, sensitive and now, courageous and vulnerable.

'I suppose it was meeting you again. Someone from my past. Brought it all back and you can't keep carrying it around forever. I know that.' He spoke as if he had just engineered the whole scene but wasn't sure that he had. He didn't really know why that had just happened. He felt slightly sick but hugely relieved and rather light-headed and the demons seemed to have scattered for now at least. Maybe they would rally later in the early hours but for now, he felt able to chase them away. With Sam's help. Yes, with Sam.

'Hope you know you can trust me Alex.'

'Oh yes. Of course. Wouldn't have told you otherwise. Really wouldn't.'

He grinned weakly at her. The little boy grin.

'Come on. Leave the plates. Let's go and sit in the lounge.'

They stood. Alex walked slowly around the large table and followed Samantha. He didn't take her hand. He really wasn't sure why.

*

They sat close to each other on the long settee. Samantha grasped his arm tightly, protectively. She had always felt guilty about Henry. Didn't really know why but felt that somewhere, somehow, she had been partly responsible. She couldn't really articulate those feelings but nonetheless, the guilt had never left her. Just like Alex. Maybe, as he had said, it had been simply a lack of experience and knowledge. They had all been so ill-prepared for marriage. Embarrassingly so. Dangerously so. Now, things were so different. And he *was* badly damaged. Even without knowing the full story, that was so obvious. Was that too big a risk to take? There was always going to be a risk. Could she turn him away now? Could she really live happily on her own? Not be lonely. If they were honest, really honest with each other, couldn't they make this work?

Alex felt uncomfortable and weirdly different, being away from the emotional glow of the dining room; away from the heady emotions that had poured out of him. Now he felt unsettled and with a strange sense of loss. Was that all there was to it? Was that all he ever had to do? Just tell someone? Years and years; layer upon layer of strangling torment tossed into the air in a moment. Walking into the lounge was like turning another page over. He heard it rustle, but wasn't sure what was on it. All he knew was that his dark secret had suddenly vanished in seconds; possibly ending the empty nights of anguish and chattering voices, but also leaving him exposed, removing the excuse to feel sorry for himself. Now he knew he could never turn back. Never.

'Are you OK Alex?'

'Yes. I'm fine.' He heard the quaver in his voice and quickly turned to face her. To confirm. 'Yes, I'm OK; thank you.'

She had been shocked at how aggressive he had been, at the very sudden change of character but then equally shocked at his story. Did things like that really happen then? Not so long ago. She knew that there would be a lot more of the story yet untold, but she also realised how he had carried that pain for most of his life. Why he hid behind the clown's mask.

For now, he would have to be treated very gently. The merest spark might consume him; her heart swelled with compassion and at that moment she knew she couldn't let him go. She turned to him.

'I wanted to thank *you*.'

'You did?'

'Yes. That day. That very long day we went to the Tate. It was like entering a new world. A fascinating new world. Anyway, when I came back here, I sat for a long time and looked at my painting.' She indicated the Twombly stretched on the wall in front of them. Alex leant back into the softness of the leather. He felt more at home now.

'Oh Alex, I've been *dying* to tell you this.' She sat upright and grasped his hand with both of hers. 'It was different. I saw it quite differently. Not immediately I don't think. But I sat here. Kicked my shoes off – my feet were killing me – and just soaked it up, like we did with Georgia O'Keefe. It suddenly made sense and so strongly. It was weird. Suddenly it became friendly. Paintings can be friendly, can't they?'

'Oh yes. They can be anything. Many things. Often all at the same time. So, what did you see?'

'You won't laugh?'

'Of course not. Go on, tell me.' His voice had become very quiet.

'Well…' He watched her face. It had lit up, like a young girl discovering something new and extraordinary. Her first shooting star; sound of a nightingale; first kiss. 'Well, suddenly it wasn't about the past at all. I think I carried that in my head because it came from the past. Does that make sense?'

'Perfectly.'

'I realised it's about the future, my future. It's not telling the future, like a crystal ball. But it's saying what the future can hold, could hold. The main colour is dark but that's not necessarily a bad thing, a negative thing, *because* it's blue. You know, the colour of space, the sea, full of mystery and the unknown, waiting to be explored and understood… oh and our planet of course.' She put her hand to her mouth. 'I've only just realised that… Doesn't mean it's always going to be easy. Look,' and she stood up and pointed to parts of the painting. 'See, here and here. These darker patches. Sort of hovering behind… how does he do that?' She continued before Alex could answer. 'They could be problems, issues to overcome but nothing evil, impossible, the whole image is too positive. And here, these lighter marks. Chalk maybe? I know I mustn't really identify them as real objects and I try not to, except they feel like… and that's the important word isn't it Alex? They *feel* like writing or words or some sort of message or communication… calligraphic you said… yes, messages.' She stopped for a moment, both hands held as if in prayer, as a thought suddenly struck her. 'They could be from the past, couldn't they?' She turned and looked at Alex. 'Couldn't they? Or the present? Or tomorrow or every day? Telling me there is a future. A future as important as the past. Maybe more important. It's up to us, isn't it? If we're brave enough to take it, make it our own.' She stopped, stood in front of the painting, eyes gleaming, hands on hips, a figure in russet, auburn haired, glowing against the endless blue behind her. She turned towards Alex, now perched on the edge of the settee, watching her, fascinated.

'You're brave Alex. You were brave today, in front of me.'

'Hardly.'

'Oh Alex, you were. You men think it's braver to hide something away than to expose your feelings.'

'Our generation I suppose… and the one before. The one we learnt from.'

'OK. I expect you're right, but can you be brave about the future, make it your own… on your own… or… maybe with me?'

There was a long pause. Samantha kicked off her shoes as if being barefoot somehow brought them closer together and sat next to him, facing him, grasping his hands again.

'It frightens me too you know. After Henry. The thought that all that unhappiness could be repeated and just when you think you've got over it. Well almost. You never quite get over it, do you?'

Alex slowly shook his head.

'No. But we're older now. Wiser. Probably stronger. Know what we want.'

She looked around the room, almost desperately. 'I have all this. All this. I can buy what I like, go where I like, do what I like. No more nine to five. No more lives dependant on others' concept of time. Have breakfast at noon—'

'Cornflakes for dinner?'

She paused. 'Do you really?'

He grinned.

'Of course you do, and why not? Oh Alex, I have all this and yet my life is empty. Angela and the girls in the shop. The cleaner. The gardener. The occasional coffee. Cake on a birthday. Bit of gossip.'

'What about your daughters?'

'See them once a year. If I'm lucky. They have their own lives and no grandchildren. Maybe because of me. Not very good role models, were we?'

'I'm sure they made up their own minds on that. Much more worldly-wise than we were.' There was a long reflective pause. It was Alex who broke the silence.

'I was an only child, so I was used to being on my own. Guess that's why I ended up with a creative career. Spent my childhood alone with really just my imagination. We became good friends.'

'I don't want to stop that or control that in any way. Nobody has the right to do that. That's where it all goes wrong you know, when people forget that they each have their own life to lead.'

'And that one day it will come to an end.'

'Of course.'

They both sat in silence again.

'Alex, I want you to be who you really want to be, and I think if we're honest with each other, say exactly what we want and what we don't want… Oh dear I can't believe I'm saying all this.' Her voice trembled slightly. 'Seems so brazen. Do you think I'm a brazen hussy?' Her skirt had ridden up slightly but she made no effort to rearrange it.

'No of course not but… well I'm a bit confused. I hadn't really thought this far ahead. I'm still recovering from the kitchen.' He looked away. Embarrassed.

'I'm sorry. I just feel gripped with the possibilities. For the first time in my life I can see clearly. It's so obvious. We can do whatever we like. We can make up our own rules now. We're not beholden to anybody. We don't even have to love each other. We can be who we like… friends, companions, flat mates—'

'Lovers?'

Samantha quietly pulled her skirt down again.

'Don't think you would want to see my poor old body now. Pity you didn't seduce me in that gallery all those years ago. Had a bit more meat on me then. I looked pretty good, if I say so myself.'

'Seduce you? You mean you would have let me?'

'Maybe. Well, you were very handsome in a wild, exotic sort of way, with your long hair and strange clothes and hot eyes. I used to imagine all that passion… you know.'

Alex slumped back onto the settee, raised his arms and then dropped them, heavily. 'Oh shit.' His emotions had been battered throughout the day and felt in retreat. This was the final straw. He struggled upwards, face puzzled.

'So, what exactly are you saying? Is this some sort of contract?'

'That sounds a bit business-like, but in a way, I suppose it is. I've been thinking about this for some time and I really would like you to do the same… if you want to of course? Hope you do. Look, I do like you. Very much in fact and we seem to get on although of course you never know until you live together and of course that's the whole point, we don't have to or at least not all the time.'

'Now I am confused.'

'Well, that would be up to us. If I'm honest I wouldn't want to live with *you* all the time – not after Henry – and neither would you with me I suspect. Would you?'

'I certainly like my own space.' He looked at the immaculate order around him. 'My own messy space if I'm honest. I do *try* to be tidy and I am in my own way. Just… not your way. I do know where everything is, trouble is, it's usually underneath something else. Anyway, I've got more important things to do with my arty world.'

'Oh dear. You make me feel like I'm wasting my life.'

'No, I love coming here. Seeing you. I feel different.'

'Different?'

'Yes. It's like Christmas at home when I was a child. It was the only time I was allowed into the front room. It was the only time it was ever used. My father would light a fire and I would sit there on my own, feeling the chill, smelling the coal smoke, enjoying the solitude and order. Think I was a rather weird child.'

'I don't think you're weird. I think you're rather unique.'

'We're all unique Sam, if we know how.'

Samantha took his hand and rubbed it. 'So, you were about to tell me about the important things you have to do.'

'Oh, maybe not so important.'

'Of course they are. Important to you. Please tell me.'

'OK. Well, there are my books of course. Love books, except now there are so many, I don't know what to do with them all. And drawing. I've always loved drawing. Should do that again really. Got loads of old sketchbooks and bits and pieces. And my independence I suppose and freedom.'

'Freedom?'

'Yes. Freedom of choice. You know, I can sit on my own all day. Do what I like. Make my own decisions without them being tampered with. Modified. You know? Don't have to speak to anybody. Can sit there with my own thoughts… back in my parents' front room I suppose. It's not that I don't like people, I do, but at times I prefer my own company, my own solitude, pull up the drawbridge and people who are close to you always seem to want to change you, mould you to their needs. Yes. You're right, you forget you have your own life. Does that sound odd? Selfish?'

'Not at all.'

'We've made our contribution to society, well you certainly have – educated, married, children, career, taxes – exactly as society demanded.'

There was a pause. Samantha realised his reluctance at getting too close to her and could now understand his embarrassment at never inviting her to his flat, but at the same time felt encouraged by his words.

'So how many books do you have?'

'Oh hundreds. Maybe thousands.'

'Where do you keep them all?'

'I've got an old bookcase and the rest are piled on the floor, under my bed and in the bath.'

'The bath!'

'Yes, but only the appropriate ones. *Moby Dick*, *Twenty Thousand Leagues*, *Treasure Island*…'

She laughed; a deep, warm laugh. 'Oh Alex, you are funny.' She took his hands. 'Look, why don't you store your books here? We could easily turn one of the spare rooms into a library or better still use the annexe. Yes, you could use the annexe. It's empty. In fact, you could turn it into a library *and* a studio. You could work there in peace and comfort. Wouldn't you like that? I'll get you a key and you can come and go as you wish. In fact, you could stay there. It's got heating and lighting. Quite comfortable really. Wouldn't that be great? Alex?'

'What about my flat?'

'You can still keep that. Move between the two when you want to.'

'Sounds a bit one-sided.'

'Oh no. I need my space as well, if only to do girly things. Don't want you around then, now do I? But also, it has been so exciting getting ready to meet you. You know, the preparation, that feeling of anticipation, not taking each other for granted. Learning from you. I thought all of that had ended. But it hasn't, has it?'

'No, it hasn't… so what about love?'

'Love?'

'Yes. Isn't that supposed to be part of the equation?'

'Not necessarily. You know I loved Henry or at least I thought I did. But when that died it hurt like hell and confused me. The "all consuming, til the end of time" emotion turned out to be so fragile and fickle; switched from red hot to icy cold in a breath. As soon as you utter those three little words then you seem to lose part of yourself. Having said that, I would kill for my children, but that seems to be different.'

'Don't think I ever knew what it was – yes, apart from my children and of course I never even saw them – but the feeling was still so powerful. Shook me. Still does when I see a little girl or a little boy with their dad.'

'Oh Alex. Wish I could help you.'

He smiled.

'Come on brave man. You look so tired.'

'Yes. It's been a long day. Well, feels like it and there's such a lot to think about now. Big changes. Unexpected changes. I just need to get my head around it. Mull it over.'

'Have a word with Dionysus.'

'Probably.'

'He could come here as well of course. Find him a nice sunny spot in the garden… or in the annexe. Maybe get him a lady statue for company.'

'One wouldn't be enough. He would want a garden full.'

'Now there's your first drawing.'

*

They said goodbye at the front door. Alex held Samantha, smelled the perfume in her hair and this time kissed her on her cheek. Somehow that seemed appropriate, anything else would seem to confirm the arrangements they had been discussing, and he wasn't ready, knew he mustn't say anything, not yet, even though he was bursting inside.

'Bye Sam. See you soon. And thank you.' He felt emotion beginning to bubble up inside him again.

'Bye Alex. Hope so.'

This time she stood in the doorway, with her arms wrapped around her against the chill air and returned Alex's wave as he drove away, watching until he had turned the corner. She shivered, closed the door and returned to the kitchen. On the large oak table were the remains of their meal. She stood and looked for a while. Those were the clean, bright plates she had proudly carried in, to be enjoyed. All now stained and cold and empty. She moved to the sink, turned on the tap and placed the plates and cutlery in the hot soapy water. Something ticked nervously in her throat. She picked up the plates and slowly washed them clean; washed away every trace, made them new.

*

'Where am I?'

Alex drifted out of sleep into panic, which quickly softened into confusion and then the relief of realisation. *My own flat.* Around him the thickness of the night had retreated from the single moonlit window into the dark corners of the small room and the air trembled with a brittle chill. He felt warm under the duvet but moving his hands and feet sideways convinced him that he was surrounded by Greenland.

'God. It's fucking freezing.'

He turned and lay on his back, staring at the semi-dark ceiling, and thought about light switches. At night, half asleep, when he had to get up – and that seemed to be happening more frequently – he groped his way to the bathroom, instinctively finding the light switch to guide him. Then at Samantha's, he had to learn a new set of switches so returning to *his* flat should simply return him to familiar territory. Shouldn't it? So why did he flail around, blindly sweeping dark walls for switches that seemed to have been moved in his absence? He stroked his nose with the back of his hand. It felt cold. *Wonder if I can see my breath?* He hurred into the cold air but saw nothing. *Maybe if I put my glasses on?* He reached a warm arm out and found his spectacles, put them on and the room swam into focus. Somehow, he now felt slightly warmer.

Damn storage heaters. Take ages to warm up when you first turn them on, are blistering hot in the morning and then cool in the afternoon when the sun goes down. Perhaps it's knackered. Bit like me. Need a warm body in here with me. A warm, soft body. Samantha's warm soft body… That would be nice. He reached down and stroked between his thighs, felt a sleepy tingle. *Wonder what she wears in bed? A nightdress? Pyjamas? Maybe nothing? That would be nice too. Something natural and almost primeval about that. What should I wear?* He sat up and looked down at his thick, striped pyjamas. *Oh no. Can't wear these. Old men's pyjamas. What do men wear today? What's trendy? No idea.* He turned and looked at the pillow next to him. He had inherited the double bed and had bought a new double mattress and bedclothes. Had told the young male assistant that he might get lucky. The young man had smiled. A professional smile that also silently doubted that. Now, Alex tried to imagine Samantha's head on the pillow, but the image swam away. He looked at the ceiling again. *Wonder what she would smell like?* He knew she spent a lot of time preparing for bed. He had heard the shower running when he stayed with her and then the long pause before the light clicked out. *Maybe she wears a special fragrance. Specially designed to inflame my desires. Trouble is, I'll have to do the same and not just crash down with my socks still on. And what if I snore, or talk or dream violently or worse? And what about legs? The protocol of legs? Whose go where? God, it's so complicated. Do I really want all that?*

His next thought struck him and he slumped back. *What makes you think she wants to anyway? Not exactly seducing you; dragging you kicking and screaming. Maybe she doesn't want a physical relationship, just to be friends. But she did kiss me and that felt more than a friend. Didn't it? Think so. Maybe she's worried… like me.* He stopped stroking, lifted the duvet and looked down. His pyjamas lay soft and flat. *What happens if I can't? Can you sleep with somebody without…? Is that possible? S'pose anything's possible. Not as if we're going to have loads of kids anymore. No worries about pregnancy or condoms or caps or menstruation or mood swings or any of that nonsense. Just do it. All day and all night. Wow!* Under the duvet there was a slightly increased stirring.

More light filtered into the room. He swept the duvet aside, felt the cool air suck away his body heat; stood and stumbled forward stiffly, using the wall for support.

He had gone home to his small flat, sat in his battered armchair and looked around. Normally it felt comfortable, homely, a bit bohemian maybe. He had enjoyed being here, playing the eccentric role. He had felt safe. Now he looked at it with different eyes. It was still exactly as he had left it, but now he could see that it was also tiny, scruffy and frustrating to keep things in order, even to find them at times, let alone keep clean. And he had just been offered a library and a studio. Why wasn't he jumping up and down on the bed and whooping? *Is this all about my pride? Being taken in as the poor relation? Can't make it on my own. Being reliant on someone else – a woman – to achieve my dreams. Oh God. I don't believe I just thought that. How sexist. How chauvinistic is that? Oh, come on.*

If the roles were reversed wouldn't you do the same? Of course. Probably. I think so. Yes of course I would. But that's different. Why is it? Because then I'm… you're what? I'm in control. Then it feels good. It feels right. I'm giving, not taking. Oh great.

He got up and paced from room to room. *What do you think, lounge? Well, be better for me of course. Give me more room. Get rid of some of this junk. What about you, kitchen? Well, be a lot tidier and cleaner. Have you any idea how many peas have rolled under the microwave? Bet she wouldn't allow that. And you can always come back of course. Yes, there's always that. And you, bedroom. What do you think? Well, don't think I could cope with two of you. These springs have seen better days. Be rather noisy.*

Alex sat on the edge of his bed, Samantha's words echoing in his mind. *Pity you didn't seduce me in that gallery all those years ago.* He clasped his hands together between his legs and slowly shook his head. *Imagine that. What a waste. What a waste. Imagine her, then. Lying on a huge soft white bed, her hair spread across the pillows like a rolling field of barley at sunset and that full body; milk-white; pale and delicate; needing only the gentlest touches so as not to blemish it. Full red lips, pale eyes, pink tipped breasts and russet vee, the only spots of colour in that soft, wan landscape… Oh my goodness. Where did all of that come from? I know.*

He spoke aloud. 'She excels all women in the magic of her locks, and when she winds them round a young man's neck, she will not ever set him free again.' *That was Lady Lilith of course. Dante Gabriel Rossetti, 1828 to 1882. He certainly knew how to shock the Victorians. Will she ensnare me? Do I care? And then there's Swinburne of course.* 'For this serene and sublime sorceress, there is no life but of the body.' *So, was she a sorceress? Samantha? Maybe. She was certainly very beautiful back then. No doubt about that. And quietly sensual. Is she still, despite the passing of all those years? Even if the body fades, does that sensuality still remain, tucked away now, but still burning brightly? Oh shit. Could I keep up with her?*

Alex stood, walked into the lounge and picked up the phone. Samantha sounded quiet, a little uncertain until she heard his voice. 'Hi Sam. It's me. Alex. Sorry did I wake you? Yes, fine thanks. Are you free tomorrow morning? OK. About ten? OK. Yes, I'll come to you. OK. See you then. Bye. Bye.'

6

Journeys

'So, this is the bedroom, quite small. If we move the bed out this could be your library. Maybe a desk and chair? What do you think? I've put the heating on and opened the windows for now, just to air it a bit and this, in here, is the lounge. Quite big don't you think? Could be your studio. The carpet's old so doesn't matter if you make a mess. Isn't that what artist's do? And then there's a small kitchen and bathroom with a shower. Isn't it exciting?'

Alex had spoken to Dionysus, apologised for not consulting with him, explained that this was a decision he had to make on his own and promised to visit him again soon. The statue remained mute and Alex wondered if he was a little upset. *That's the problem with women; you have to leave your friends behind.*

He had folded the rear seats down in the Volvo and piled as many books in as possible along with a portfolio, sketchbooks and the few drawing materials he had. His flat looked strangely empty and a little bemused.

Meanwhile the bed in the annexe had been dismantled and now stood against one wall and in its place, they had heaved a leather armchair from the house. Samantha had arranged for a local carpenter to put up long rows of shelves, on which stood a single book as Alex pondered how to arrange the remainder. The few original contents of the now new studio had been cleared to the garage and Alex's portfolio and sketchbooks stood rather forlorn and lost in the space. He knelt and undid the single tie on the portfolio, opened it and laid it flat. Inside was a thick pile of drawings and a few works in colour, in different sizes and textures of paper. He leaned back on his heels and stared at them; his life, his being for all those years. Better than any photographic album, he knew that, for they were part of him, back then, produced by eye and hand and lodged forever in his brain. He knelt forward to inhale them, hoping for the smells of the studio – paint, turpentine, charcoal – but they had long drifted away leaving just a faint smell of ageing.

It was strange that his past had been tied up, tucked away for so long and now he was opening it again. He started to spread them out, handling each piece with care, until he was surrounded by an audience of images like a king surrounded by his courtiers, each waiting silently for the royal decree. Except, he felt far from majestic. *My God. How did I manage all this? The quality. The skill. This was a different me. So confident, so strong, so aware.* Suddenly he felt a wave of panic wash through him. *I can't do this anymore.* He held his hands in front of him. They trembled slightly. He could see a swollen network of light blue veins and straight connecting bones running just below the thin, wrinkled skin, dappled with brown spots like algae. Deep inside his thumbs was a dull ache. *How could they possibly…?*

'Oh Alex.'

He hadn't heard Samantha knock lightly on the studio door. He turned and saw the look of surprise on her face. Had he done something wrong, made a mess? He felt cold anger rise inside him. *What the hell, I've only just got here?*

'They are so beautiful.' She looked at him. His anger crept away with its tail between its legs. 'Did you do all of these?'

'Yeah, I did. Long time ago though.' His knees had started to ache. He held out his hand to her. 'Can you help me up? Poor old bugger.'

He stood surrounded by his work. Absently rubbing his fingers. She stood, eyes flicking from one drawing to the next, surprise being replaced by a wide smile.

'I had no idea; no idea.' She spoke softly. Almost to herself. She turned, eyes sparkling. 'You must put them up on the wall, so we can see them properly. Can we do that?' She turned to him, needing his agreement. He nodded. 'Have you got some tape? No? I'll get some, no, it's OK. You wait here.' A reassuring hand on his arm, anxious to be involved, to make this work.

Gradually the walls were covered, with Samantha holding each piece carefully along its edges for Alex to position, looking silently from the wall to him and back again, noticing his command, noting the importance. 'Up a bit. Left a bit. Stop. That's it.' Occasionally he would pause, look intently, give a small secret grunt and then move on. Eventually, both long walls were covered, with a few pieces positioned at the end, either side of a window. Samantha moved slowly from one to the other, only stopping to smile at Alex. He watched her. The same intensity, the same concentration, the same thoughtfulness she had given to Georgia O'Keefe.

'I love the… er… nudes?' Her voice had queried the correctness of the final word but had also faltered slightly and she wasn't sure why. Wondered if that was in fact the first time she had ever used that word in her life. How odd. She looked back at him, raising her eyebrows slightly, keeping her face neutral. He nodded confirmation. Yes, nudes. She turned back.

'How you capture their shape, their fullness, their er… delicacy in just a few marks. Gosh, you need lots of words, don't you?' She looked closer. 'Is that pencil?' He nodded again. 'All those different lines with a pencil? Just one pencil or lots of different ones?'

'Just one.'

She shook her head in disbelief.

'And are they all models or…?'

'Mainly models.'

'Must be hard work, standing like that for a long time, without moving.'

'Certainly is.'

'So, have you done it then. Posed nude?'

'I've posed, but not nude.'

'And this girl, this portrait. There are a lot of her. Was she a model?'

'No.'

'No?'

'No… Georgia and Jak's mother.'

'Oh.'

Samantha turned and studied the drawings of her in detail, moving slowly from one to the other.

'She's very pretty.' She spoke without removing her gaze. 'And very intense. She's staring out at you.' She moved further along the line. 'Oh, and this one is in colour… She has red hair.' She turned and looked at Alex.

'Yes. She was a redhead.'

Samantha said nothing. Alex wondered if he should offer some explanation, some comment but felt overwhelmed by the complexities of that thought.

Alex pushed the crisp leather chair into the centre of the new studio. The exertion made him pant slightly and he took several deep breaths. *Will be strange sitting in a different chair; Samantha's chair.* He sat down uncertainly, leaned back and sank further than anticipated, lost control, struggled upwards and perched on the harder front edge. An unexpected feeling of annoyance and frustration spiked at him and he thought of his own dirty-green armchair, waiting patiently, alone in his flat, like a faithful old heavily-jowled hound. He was so familiar with it, knew its quirks, how to avoid that hard lump in its back, knew that its seat moved imperceptibly downwards towards the floor like a leather glacier and of that sharp metal pin that protruded from beneath one armrest, which he could rub deliciously with his fingertips. He dreaded to imagine what lived between the sides and the seat. *Years of crumbs, a shrivelled pea or two, the odd biro and spare change in several currencies?* It had always been there, travelled with him, shared a lot. It was a chair you put on like an old overcoat. *Perhaps he should have given it a pet name, or several maybe, according to its personality that day. Like the Seven Dwarfs. Lumpy? Grumpy? Dumpy? Baldy? Tatty? Baddy? Sadly? Yes, at the moment. Sadly.*

Samantha's chair was quite different. Soft, young, excitable, waiting for the next walk in the park. Welcoming? Yes, or was that devouring? *And now I'll have to learn it all over again. Oh, come on. It's only a bloody chair. You are pathetic at times.* He sat back again, carefully, stroked the cool, smooth sides, drummed his fingers impatiently and looked around. The room was more at ease now, with his work taped in neat rows to its walls. So many memories here. His gaze stopped in front of a nude drawing done in pencil. *That model... what was her name?* He cupped both hands over his nose, thumbs under his chin and looked into the distance. *She was excellent. Used to diet in order to keep her figure, could hold a pose for ages... what was it? An...? Angela? No. An...? Anita? No. Yes, Anita.* He clasped both hands together and shook them in a triumph of memory. *Used to change in my office. Oh yes… the day I locked the office, went home, with her clothes inside. Oh dear. She wasn't happy.* He smiled to himself. *They were an interesting lot; models. There was that male model who looked like a tramp; loads of straggly white hair; came in with his dog and played Chopin on that piano in the staff room. And Stella of course.* He grinned to himself. *Stella the stripper from Soho. Used to walk around the college stark naked. Sometimes, in front of visitors. Oh dear. Caused some raised eyebrows and then, there was that woman with the heavy make-up that stopped at her neckline. Undressed, it looked like a sunset over a polar icescape.*

He followed the lines and marks that described the landscape of Anita's body. Stronger incised lines to show the angular tip of an elbow, the hardness of a hip. Soft sweeping lines, smudged with a judicious finger, to follow the smooth roundness of a buttock, the firmness of a thigh, the delicacy of a breast. Simple lines and tones that conjoined to present the solidity of the body and its essence and character. *But can I still do it? Come on. What would they say to young students, just starting out? Don't worry. You just need to begin at the beginning. Collect some interesting bits and pieces, natural forms, bring them into the studio, study them, then it would start to feel right. Build up more materials, different media, an old drawing board. Wonder if they still use them? Hope so… then perhaps it will soon come back. It will come back. Maybe the line, the marks I make will be different, not so confident but maybe I'll see things differently now, after all this time. Yes, that might be interesting.*

Not the first artist to approach old age. Hey, artist. Called myself an artist.

He smiled to himself. He had never told anyone, but he had imagined Samantha as his secret model back then, when she was still with Henry. She could have been his own Lady Lilith; his own Lizzie Sidall. His own young Pre-Raphaelite beauty. But that had meant a painting and he had felt inadequate, especially by comparison with Edmund and that time had now long slipped away, as it had before with Rachel. *Now we're so much older and that youth and vitality will never return. Does that matter? Am I still obsessed with the past? The past staring at me from this wall? The past that was so narrow, so constructed by others? And does Sam sense that? That comment about redheads? Am I really that shallow? This has to be a new opportunity. A different one. A chance to be myself. Certainly the last one, that's for sure.*

*

He had asked her to wear a blouse, which she had fastened almost to her neck. He had undone the next button. The certainty of his fingers had slightly alarmed her but also sent a little thrill.

'I need to see your neck.'

'Don't put in all the wrinkles, will you?'

He sat and looked at her for a long time before disappearing behind a mask of concentration, his eyes scouring her face dispassionately, only concerned with its structure and form; a strange seriousness that she had never experienced before, and which made her feel uncertain and caused her to smile nervously.

'Don't smile.'

The words appeared quietly but firmly, his eyes never meeting hers. The smile slipped away.

Sometimes he sat back, holding the drawing board at arm's length, turning his head to one side, assessing his progress, before continuing in complete silence, save for the tiny scratching of pencil on paper. Occasionally he would stop to sharpen his pencil in an old silver-coloured pencil sharpener, his eyes never leaving the drawing, except for a final inspection of the new point; graphite and curled wood shavings falling unconcernedly to the floor. He continued for some time, with Samantha trying not to move in the armchair, then stopped, took a long look at his work and then looked at her, connecting for the first time.

'That'll do.' He looked again, made a final tiny mark. 'Not bad.'

'Can I see?'

He motioned with one hand and sat back, waiting for her reaction. She gasped. It was her. Without doubt it was her, but it was not someone she had ever seen before. It was not the portrait of an old woman that she had expected but of a woman who had matured with experience and understanding. There was a strength that she never knew was there and yet a softness at the same time. A few marks, carefully selected, indicated the passing of time but in a way that was sensitive, almost celebratory and without flattering. It was as if he had captured her likeness both outside and within, and in just a few lines on paper. She noticed also that he had drawn her shoulders uncovered and a few tentative lines indicated the beginnings of her breasts. Her eyes gleamed.

'Oh Alex. It's wonderful. Just wonderful. Can I keep it?'

'OK. Need to fix it first though.'

The air reeked with pear drops as the fixative spray covered the delicate lines.

'There you are. Just let it dry for a while.'

He sat back and grinned, stood, stretched, held his back and looked around.

'Whoops, made a bit of a mess.'

'Oh, don't worry about that.' She looked up at him. 'Thank you so much.'

'That's OK. Hope we can do a lot more. Try different things.'

She smiled at him. Wondered what that might entail.

*

Samantha couldn't bear to leave her portrait in the studio; it was as if part of her would then be detached and so she brought it through into the lounge and looked at it constantly. Alex ignored it.

Later, as he dozed in front of the television, she picked it up and stealthily made her way to the kitchen, away from him. There was something more about the drawing; not it's uncanny likeness but the look in the eyes, the shape of her lips, the softness of her features, an expression coming from within her. *Is that possible? Am I imagining it? That look?* There was a sensuality about her face, the face she knew so well, saw every day in her mirror, pondered over, reflected on, covered in make-up. But this was a look she had never noticed, except maybe on the silver screen, had only felt, imagined. This was a face of quiet sensuality – almost passion – not quite – not yet. How did he know that? How *could* he know that? How could he even imagine that, her most private feelings? How could he transfer them, unseen and unknown, from within her into his own mind and then down through his hands onto paper. Images she had never seen herself. And were they there earlier? When she had first gasped at the image he had made for her? Had she simply not noticed in the euphoria of the moment? The thought excited and troubled her in equal measure. She slipped back into the lounge.

In sleep, Alex looked so relaxed, so quiet, almost childlike. She smiled down at him, wanted to kiss him on his sleeping forehead but daren't. Not now. She headed quietly back to the kitchen, put on her coat, picked up the portrait and opened the back door. Outside it was dark and she shivered in the light wind, as she crossed the short distance to the annexe and took out her key as the exterior light came on.

This was the first time she had been inside on her own, since Alex had arrived, and she realised how much things had changed. New smells, new look, new purpose, if a little untidy. Perhaps she should tidy it up? No, this was Alex's now and she knew she mustn't interfere. She knew she couldn't offer it to him and then tell him what to do with it.

Most of his drawings had been replaced in his portfolio, with only the nudes remaining on the walls alongside his new drawings, taken from strange, often contorted items found in the local woods or on the beach and which were now dotted around the room. She had been fascinated by the process, watching him select and discard items, seeing their potential, becoming excited, pulling out strange objects at junk shops – 'Wow look at that. Isn't that amazing?' – before transforming them into powerful or delicate or lonely or forceful images, or whatever he saw or felt.

But now the drawings she wanted were in his portfolio, leaning against the wall. She untied the single tie and carefully laid the portfolio flat onto the floor. Her hands trembled slightly and for some reason she daren't breathe too loudly. Suddenly, there was a tap on the window and she looked around with a start, mouth dry, heart pounding. The branch, moving in the night breeze, waited and then tapped again. *What on earth am I doing? What happens if he wakes up? Finds me here? Like a thief in the night. Oh, come on. It's your house. You're just looking at his work again. Didn't want to disturb him. That's all. It's OK.*

She searched through the pile in front of her until she found what she was looking for. The drawing of the Girl with the Red Hair. She knelt and placed her own portrait next to it, although she wasn't quite sure what she was looking for. Did she really think that she was prettier than someone forty years or so her junior? Not really. Or was it a nagging concern that she was this woman's replacement, a sort of clone, an attempt to re-ignite a love lost so terribly all that time ago? Or maybe he just liked redheads. Men did that of course. She knew that. Had a thing for leggy blondes or busty brunettes. Sad really. OK, women did the same she supposed, the tall dark, handsome syndrome – if it really existed – but of course she knew that they were much more attracted by traits such as kindness or gentleness or by being attentive or not being afraid to show their feelings, and she thought of Alex across the oak table. That hadn't changed, had it? Although today, young women seemed far more positive, sometimes more aggressive than her generation had ever been. Maybe now they *were* more concerned with physical attributes, really did want to know size from the outset.

She looked from one drawing to the next. They were obviously both by the same hand and although the young girl was drawn in a stronger, more assertive way, hers was a softer, more delicate approach and had been able to show her so much. A thought suddenly struck her. Was that about her or about him? Was the sensuality straining in her face really about him, what he wanted to see, what he imagined he might see? He had spoken once about being lovers. At the time, she wasn't sure he had meant it, he certainly hadn't pressed the point and she had been equally elusive, concerned about the physical state of her body with its wrinkles, sagging flesh and blemished skin. How could she let him see that?

Maybe he had the same concerns about himself? She knew little about his body, except for his face and hands of course and that little white strip of flesh that occasionally appeared between sock and turn-up. He was certainly quite slim, his small paunch hidden by the shirt that always hung outside of his trousers and he seemed to be quite fit, although he did rub his knees when cold wet weather blew outside. She knew his hands were strong despite the long, tapering fingers that gave the impression of delicacy and the clean, manicured nails that seemed at odds with his laissez-faire appearance. She wondered if the rest of his body was as strong and sinewy. His hands were obviously important to him, whether creating beautiful images or exploring objects. She had certainly watched him stroking many items as if their feel revealed their beauty or history in some strange tactile language or complemented what his eyes were telling him and she knew she wanted him to stroke her in the same way, a way beyond mere touching. But she shook the thought away as she had as a teenage girl dreaming for the unachievable mouth of the young local vicar.

She replaced the young girl's drawing in the portfolio, retied it and propped it back against the wall. She needed to get back. She stood up and came face to face with one of the nude drawings. It was Anita stretched out on a single bed, head lifted slightly against two pillows, face looking out at the viewer. She tried to imagine Alex drawing her. She had tried to watch his face while he completed her portrait. Then, it appeared to be dispassionate, caught in a fierce concentration but was that the same when drawing Anita, a naked woman? Did he feel her body through the point of his pencil, did he feel aroused at its sweeping movement along her thigh, trying to recreate the smoothness that he was so aware of, or did the few marks that raised her nipple out of the nothingness of the paper harden in his mind, ready for his lips? Did his pencil, long and hard and penetrating, really represent much more to him?

She turned, about to go, when another thought stopped her. What about Anita, lying there, naked? How did she feel being scrutinised, minutely studied, of having her body recreated through the intimacy of the eye and hand of another? Of a man? Was that remoteness even more erotic when restricted to her mind? Did the calm, quiet, ordinariness of the situation hide an inner turmoil? Was there the most enormous longing? Did she feel as if her body had been taken by him, slowly, inch by sensually drawn inch? Did their eyes meet afterwards? Suddenly Samantha felt a heat cover her face and chest and she knew she badly wanted to change places with Anita.

She turned off the light, stepped outside, locked the door and stood for a moment, welcoming the cold breeze. When she returned, Alex was watching the television, odd-stockinged feet crossed on the low table. He put them down as she entered the room. She expected him to ask where she had been but to her relief, he smiled but said nothing. She sat down and turned towards him. His dark eyes seemed to have retreated further into their sockets. Was that the drama of earlier? Was she driving him away? She knew that she desperately didn't want that. Above his eyes, the young eyebrows she would have known had grown into a thicket of interwoven silver and dark, curling away from each other. Here and there an occasional hair escaped sideways, downwards or upwards and she wanted to comb and trim them. Was that just being helpful or was it her wanting to change him?

Alex could feel her watching him, feel her questions bubbling away silently.

'Shall I switch it off?' He didn't look at her.

They sat in silence for a moment.

'Alex.'

'Yes.'

'Do you mind me asking you a question?'

'No.'

'About your drawings. Just curious really.'

He turned to face her.

'Yes, I just wondered what it was like when you were drawing?'

'What it was like?'

'Yes. Drawing a woman, like that?'

'Like that?' He smiled, a small teasing smile.

'You know, a woman with no clothes on.'

'You mean naked?' The smile broadened.

'Yes.' Now she felt slightly ill at ease. Maybe this wasn't such a good idea.

'Good word, naked. Quite different from nude don't you think? Nude always feels like a rather giggly, behind-the-bike-shed sort of word. *And* rhymes with rude of course. Whereas naked, well… comes from Old German, Norse I believe. In-your-face sort of word. Very explicit… charged. Don't you think?'

'I'm sure you're right.'

'Interestingly, it was never used. Naked. Maybe for that reason, to take any heat out of the situation. Nude *was* used but usually the word "life". They were "life models". That was suitably ambiguous, although if you think about it…'

'So, was there any heat?'

He looked at her, his smile now more curious, bushy eyebrows raised slightly.

'Ah, I see. Well,' he turned, pursed his lips slightly and looked thoughtfully away. 'Seriously? I suppose there could be. Maybe before and after.'

'Before and after?'

'Well, before, the model would wear a robe and only remove it as she began the pose. At that moment, you could appreciate her body, but very soon you're thinking about the pose you want to set and then, when you start drawing, it all changes; you become totally involved. It's very high concentration you know; you hardly notice there's a naked woman in front of you.'

'Yes, I saw that; the concentration when you were drawing *my* portrait.' She paused. 'And after?'

'After? Well… always seemed a bit odd to see a fully clothed man chatting casually to a naked woman, between poses… before she put her robe back on.'

'Back on?'

'Oh yes. She would always be covered when she wasn't working.'

'So, you didn't fancy her then, with her model body?'

'Who, Anita?'

Samantha nodded.

'Probably. She *was* rather gorgeous.'

'So, were they all?'

'What, gorgeous? Heavens no. They came in all shapes and sizes; colours, class, creeds… and ages. Did I tell you about Elizabeth? Elizabeth Writton? No? I'd forgotten about her. Well she was remarkable. Nobody knew how old she was and she wouldn't say. Reckon she was in her eighties. Tiny, thin and very lined. Many of the drawings of her were very tender, fragile but she didn't like those. Wanted her inner light to shine through. Used to get quite annoyed with the students. "I'm in there somewhere," she used to say. "Just got to look harder." Then one day she never turned up. Think she must have died.' He turned towards her. 'Anyway, why all the questions? You thinking of being my next model or something?'

'Heaven forbid. No, I was just curious that's all.' She drew in a breath. 'Um. Fancy a cup of tea? Some supper?' She stood up. 'Are you staying tonight? Your room's ready and it's a foul evening.'

'Thank you. That will be lovely.'

He watched as she left the lounge. Did her hips swing just a little more than usual?

*

That night, Samantha prepared for bed in her room. She slipped on a new silk nightdress that came down to just above her knees and looked at herself in the long mirror. In the subdued light, she thought she looked good, somehow better than usual, her body shimmering faintly through the sheer material. She had left her portrait in the lounge. It had felt a bit weird to take it to bed with her. But in her mind, she still carried it, hoping to see that same look recreated but somehow it didn't seem to transfer to the face she now saw in the mirror.

But he saw it. Didn't he? It is there. She looked for a long time and then slipped the nightdress from her shoulders, felt it float to her feet and she stood there, naked. *Yes. He's right. Naked is the right word for how I feel right now. Yes. That same restless visceral desire. That hot itch.* She watched as she ran her hands slowly over her stomach, then up over her breasts, knowing already that her nipples had hardened. *I wonder if he'll ever know what that feels like?* Those overt messages directed into his fingertips and palms. Her hands dropped to her thighs and then moved gently to her centre and rested there. *And what about his… thing?* Even as a private thought, here in the sanctity of her bedroom, she felt uneasy with the language. *Why on earth was that?* At university, she had gathered eagerly with the other girls around Monique. Monique, the mature exchange student with those huge, dark, knowing eyes.

'So, what's he like in bed?' They had whispered and giggled at the thought of Monique with *him* – powerful, unattainable, intellectually razor-sharp and… married.

'Not bad. A little small for me. You know?' And she had wiggled her little finger at them.

'And his foreskin, it is not to my liking. I prefer a cut cock… don't you?' They had giggled loudly to hide their ignorance and surprise.

Samantha had slipped away and sat alone with a cup of coffee, pretending to sip it but really immersed in what she had heard. So, was it as simple as that? A simple anatomical fit. A fits B rather snugly. That had never really occurred to her, she had never considered that she had any choice in the matter. After Henry, once the few men in her life had unzipped or unbuttoned, what sprung forth was rather like the outcome of a hectic game of pass the parcel. An increasingly frantic uncovering until that final surprise. And it was always a surprise and sometimes a disappointment over which she had no control. Or did she? *Is that what happens today? Boy meets girl; they start courting. Courting? That sounds so old fashioned. Do they still do that, or do they simply go to bed and conduct a road test? Present their qualifications. That way if they decide to live together, there would be no need to play pass the parcel. Is that better? Or does that trivialise the whole thing? And what about Alex? What do I do about that now?*

Another thought arrived and struck her with such clarity. She remembered long ago, slipping silently out of her bed and standing stock still, dry mouthed, listening for the slightest sound from her parents in the next room. But they slumbered quietly, turned away from each other like old book ends containing dusty unfulfilled dreams. Then, as now, she had slipped her nightdress from her shoulders, her then flawless shoulders and it had fallen to her feet leaving her young body naked in the moonlight. Thirteen. Just thirteen. She had touched her tiny breasts with a sense of wonder and pride, had stroked a single finger into the damp heat between her slim thighs and trembled. In the strange, cold light, her body had pulsed hotly, filling the room with a strange presence. In the middle of her uncertainty, her immaturity, she knew she had this and it was powerful, too powerful to ignore. She danced slowly, the only sound being that of her tongue on her dry lips and the awful tom tom of her heart. Her dance then had been slow and sinuous and primitive; without art or conceit. The dance of a virgin pulling away the barriers to womanhood in the silent stare of the mute moon. Samantha shivered, maybe with nostalgia, maybe with desire, turned and moved to the bed, plumped up two pillows and lay looking out to the mirror, in exactly the same position as Anita had done, all that time ago, that thirteen-year-old burning away again inside her.

7

———

Steam

Alex looked up. The sky was empty, expressionless, cadaver-grey. It had no movement, no apparent depth, yet seemed endless, hanging sullenly just above him. He felt that if he climbed onto the roof of the annexe, he could reach up and scratch her name into its icy frostiness. He paused for a moment, and a few snowflakes floated silently to the wet ground and disappeared. *Come on, it's cold out here.*

He entered the kitchen and felt the warm air surround him. He took off his black woollen hat, hastily smoothed his hair flat, wiped his glasses on his scarf and placed the heavy book and battered sketchbook he was carrying onto the nearest worktop. He looked around. *Better take my shoes off. Place is spotless. Cleaner must have been.*

He took off his lumpy top coat, placed his shoes on their sides and padded into the house, books in one hand, leaving a faint trail of damp footprints.

'Sam, you there? Saman… tha.'

There was no reply.

He wandered into the lofty expanse of the hallway, stopped and listened. Somewhere above, he could hear music playing. It was jazz or something similar, but he couldn't quite make out the soloist. Ahead, the stained glass in the front door waited for sunlight to switch on its geometric green, blue and yellow pattern and he felt the coldness of the ceramic tiles striking through his stockinged feet. He moved to the foot of the stairs and looked up. Now, the music sounded like an invitation, something to share and he made his way up the stairs, cold feet enjoying the dark-red stair carpet, hand stroking and occasionally tapping on the polished handrail. At the top of the stairs, the same red carpet had spread out across a broad landing and on a low polished table, an old music system was playing; now the dark-brown notes and languid words of the blues sliding around him.

He stood for a moment, listening. At the end of the landing, the door to a bathroom was ajar and from it, mixing with the music, was the hot, wet scent of bathing. He moved to the door and tapped on it. There was no answer. He rapped harder.

'Sam. Are you in there?'

'Alex. Is that you?'

'Yes. It's me.'

Alex felt a tingle of excitement.

'Can I come in?'

She didn't reply immediately.

'Just a moment… OK. Come in.'

'Hallo.'

'Hallo.'

The room was big and bright with many of the original fittings accurately reproduced. Around the white tiled walls swam a frieze of fishes, which Alex recognised as copies of William de Morgan and hanging from a tubular chrome radiator were large, fluffy white towels. In the centre of an expanse of black tiles stood a very large white roll-top bath with claw feet and in it, head and one hand showing, lay Samantha covered up to her chin by thick white foam. The room was a study in black and white and silver, the only colour being Samantha's deep red fingernails and auburn hair, darkened further at her nape by the water and tied up by a red bow into a small pony tail. A thick fragrance filled the room.

'What a glorious smell. What is it?'

'Lavender with sweet basil and jasmine.' She watched him. Alex took in a deep breath.

He sat on a nearby chair and placed his books in his lap. He felt strangely shy, as if he really shouldn't be there and now that he was, uncertain about how to act. Inside him, his feelings fought each other over the proximity of Samantha lying hidden in the warm water and the beautiful aesthetic of the scene in front of him and his huge urge to record it.

'So now you've seen me at my worst.'

'Hardly. You look great.' He was tempted to add 'what I can see of you' but thought better of it. 'And what a wonderful room.' He stroked one hand through the hot, damp air to embrace the scene before him and his sketchbook tumbled to the floor, spilling out loose drawings.

'Oh, what are they Alex? More drawings? How exciting.'

She leant to one side to look over the bath's edge and her opposite shoulder rose from the water, smooth and pale and shining wet.

'I brought them to show you. Just been practising.'

'Can I have a look?'

'You'll get them wet. I'll hold them.'

She smiled at him.

He stood and sat carefully on the edge of the bath, ignoring the dampness now seeping into his trousers. She sank back down up to her chin and both knees now appeared shiny in the soapy water. She wondered how long the thick bubbles would last before her body would gradually become revealed. Like a wet strip-tease and she knew that right now, she didn't care.

Without any make-up and with her hair tied up, her face was less soft, a little older, a little darker and yet her eyes shone as she looked at each piece that Alex held before her. She said nothing but smiled occasionally as if seeing favourite family members. Alex watched her reactions closely.

'They're wonderful. You're so talented you know.'

He said nothing; put them safely back into his sketchbook and picked up the large book he had also carried.

'I wanted to show you this.' He held up the book so she could see the title.

'Impressionism. Oh, I know about them. Well… a little.'

He had marked a page with a strip of white paper, and he opened the book at that place. The strip fell out into the bath water. Both ignored it.

'There. What do you think?'

He held the heavy book close to her, trying to control the trembling in his hands. She noticed. He readjusted his hold, now balancing the book on one thigh. 'That's better.' She looked closely in silence, face still, but inside she began to tremble. She read the title aloud, as calmly as she could. '"After the Bath. Woman drying herself". By Edgar Degas.' She smiled teasingly up at him. 'And you haven't told me his dates.'

'Yes… well, I'm trying not to.'

'Oh, I don't mind. I want to know. Really.'

She looked at the page again. There was a long pause. Somewhere, Alex could hear a clock ticking.

'It's beautiful, really beautiful and… unexpected really.'

'Unexpected?'

'Yes, this woman, alone in her bathroom, even though Degas…' she looked up to make sure of her pronunciation, 'even though Degas was there as an observer, the artist, at a very intimate moment and yet somehow his drawing is so… honest, so candid. He's not a voyeur, is he. It should be erotic, but it isn't, is it? I've never seen anything like that before. Never thought about it.'

'It's a common theme in the history of art. Rembrandt. Gaugin. Renoir of course. Ingres certainly. Even female artists like Mary Cassatt. But this is my favourite… as well as Bonnard of course but for different reasons.'

She listened and then returned to the picture. She raised one arm and carefully placed a single fingertip against one corner to hold the page flat. Alex imagined that pressure against his thigh.

'It's very beautiful. Is that because she has her back to him?'

'Maybe. Women's backs can be very beautiful of course.'

He closed the book but continued sitting on the edge of the bath.

Outside the music had come to an end, leaving a heavy silence. She looked up at him.

'Water's getting cold.'

'More hot?'

'No, no thank you. I need to get out, otherwise I'll look like a prune.'

Alex remained where he was. 'I'd like to draw you again.'

'OK. That'll be good.'

'No. I mean like this.'

'Like this?'

'Yes. Like Degas.'

'Oh.'

'Do you mind?'

'Well… I don't know. I do need to get out first, before I get cold. Get dried. Can I do that?'

'Of course. I'll wait outside… shall I?'

She looked away, towards the towels, uncertain as to what her face might betray. When she spoke, she did so softly.

'Why… why don't you fetch your drawing materials?'

'Really? Well… OK. That's… that's great. Excellent. Well, OK won't be long.'

He stood and his hand moved to the cold damp patch on his seat.

'Don't rush. I need some time to pamper myself.'

Alex pulled the door to and tried not to run down the stairs. His mouth was dry. Certainly, the opportunity to follow that long line of eminent artists excited him immensely and through his mind ran many possibilities and poses. Maybe even a painting. A large piece to rival Twombly? In the style of Bonnard? A dialogue with colour. Samantha as *baigneuse*. He was sure he could do it now even though he had avoided it in the past. Found intellectual excuses and bombast to disguise his inability or maybe it was to cover his lack of confidence or fear of failure. That wasn't occurring now. Maybe the process of ageing or maturing had put all that nonsense into perspective. And being with Sam made it so different. She believed in him. And then there was her body of course. Lying naked in that hot, soapy water. So close to him.

By the time he reached the annexe, he was breathing heavily and was forced to sit down. *Calm down old son. Calm down.* He took a very deep breath and thought about the drawing. *Well, not pastels. Don't have any. Maybe coloured pencils? Shall I take my drawing board? No, just the sketchbook. Just a few exploratory sketches. To begin with. More later maybe.*

He returned to the foot of the stairs, equipment in a large supermarket bag. Samantha had wanted to buy him a proper box for his drawing materials, but he had declined, feeling uneasy about her continued generosity. As he turned to climb the stairs, he heard more music coming from the landing above. The brisk, bright beat of brass and a plaintiff crooner but not so loud this time.

On the landing he stopped, realising that his heart was beating quite strongly. *Maybe I came up the stairs too quickly?* He waited, took two deep breaths, noticed the bathroom door was now open, wider than before and called out.

'Can I come in?'

He pushed the door and cautiously peeked in. Samantha was standing in front of a mirror wearing a long dark-green silk robe, tied by a belt, brushing her hair. She had dried herself quickly and hastily rubbed cream into her body, feeling vulnerable all the time. *He'll be back any minute and find me starkers and rubbing skin lotion into my bum.* Quickly, she had slipped into the safety of the robe but now felt uncomfortably hot. She opened the collar slightly, then realised the bath had not yet been emptied and damp towels lay on the floor where she had dropped them.

Alex stopped and took in the scene. Noticed how tiny her feet were. Felt the room warm and sultry with the scent of lavender still hanging delicately in the air. *It's like an erotic greenhouse.*

'You don't *mind* me brushing my hair?' She spoke to him in the mirror. 'I know you probably want to catch the essence of *woman stepping from bath,* but, I still have to look good. Sorry.' She continued brushing.

'That's OK.' But it wasn't really. He had pictured her at the moment of rising from the bath, hearing the liquid rush of water releasing her, seeing her lower body flushed by its heat, standing slightly unsteadily, skin shiny, hair still dark-wet and curling, one pale leg tentatively seeking the bath-side mat. Not as Aphrodite, not as Botticelli's slim, coy Venus, but as an unfeigned, fragile, living and breathing human being with drops of spilled water shining on the floor and damp footprints already fading away in the surrounding warmth.

He sat on one of the chairs, opened the sketchbook, took an old fountain pen from his bag, unscrewed the cap and made a few marks. Samantha kicked a loose towel out of sight. Satisfied, he stopped and watched her. There was no sound except for the brush pulling through her hair. He stood and placed a second chair next to the bath. Samantha watched the movement in the mirror. He sat down again, feeling calmer now. Prepared.

She half-turned. 'So, do you like Sinatra?'

The music came to an end.

Alex said nothing but continued to look at her. She fiddled nervously with the belt of her robe under his gaze.

'So, how do you want me?' If the question was at all provocative, he ignored it.

'I'd like you to sit backwards on that chair.'

'Backwards?'

'Yes. With your arms over the back. The chair back. Can you manage that?'

'Like this?'

'Yes. That's good but I need to see your back. Can you drop the robe slightly?'

'Like this?'

'I need like to see *all* of your back. As in the painting.'

His voice sounded calm and authoritative now, as he watched her carefully pull her arms free and the robe dropped, silky folds catching the light. Her delicate skin was unblemished apart from some darker markings at her shoulders and her body rose palely from the green at her waist. He was immediately struck by the fragility and beauty before him but also by its inherent strength. Before him was a feast. A feast of light and colour and tone and form.

Samantha waited. As the robe dropped, she had felt a huge weight lift from her, as though she had just freed herself. That was so strange. How could such a delicate material, a material that stroked her skin so lightly, have also been so constricting? So heavy? But now, free, she became acutely aware of her own body, her upper body, her back becoming alive, almost glowing, almost singing under his gaze, as it had in her bedroom. As it had before the moon. She felt her milky skin ripple and twitch unseen, as she imagined his eyes sliding over her and she waited, wanting to be touched again. To feel the magic of his strong, long fingers on her. Making her complete again. Making her whole again. *What on earth am I doing? An old lady pretending like this. Just keep still.*

Alex drew rapidly, almost feverishly, pressing the pen nib to achieve different marks as he strove to understand and capture the image before him. He turned over to fresh pages rapidly, roughly with a crash as though there was not a second to be lost. This was no leisurely observation but a madcap dash, a manic sprint until finally like an athlete falling through the tape he stopped and slumped in his chair.

'Sorry Sam. Have a rest.'

Samantha pulled the robe back around her. It felt unwelcome. She stood, stretched and turned towards him, one slim leg briefly appearing and then being hidden again.

'What are you doing?'

Alex was tearing pages from his sketchbook and laying them on the floor, where some began to soak up the wetness there.

'Need to see them all. Side by side. Come and have a look.' He saw the look of surprise on her face and laughed. 'Can't ever afford to be precious you know.'

He pushed the chair back and they stood side by side. He could still smell the fragrance of the bath on her.

'They're so…'

'So what?'

'So… different. No, that's not enough. So… direct, so immediate. They're exciting Alex.'

He smiled and wanted to put his arm around her. This innocent child; honest and open. Not afraid of awe. Excluding any pretence at false sophistication.

'How do you do that? Draw so furiously – I could hear you – and yet so accurately and it's me and it's part of my body I hardly know and I look good. Almost young. Don't I?'

Tears began to form in her eyes.

'Hey. Don't cry. Come here,' and he laughed and took her into his arms to comfort her but she reached around his neck and pressed a damp face against his chest. They stood for a moment in silence. Alex could feel the softness of her body through the thin robe, stroked a comforting hand over her back but instead of comfort, felt his fingers slip sensuously across the silk. The drawing had devoured so much of his pent-up energy and anxiety, so much emotion had flowed from him onto the paper, leaving him strangely quiet.

'Sorry.' Samantha moved slightly away, wiping her eyes with one hand. 'Bit silly.'

Alex bent forward and placed his mouth on hers. For some reason, he expected her lips to feel tight and mean, reluctant or even for her to resist, move away, wrap her robe tighter around her… but she didn't. Her lips felt full and hot and open, drawing him in and her fingers grasped the back of his neck, pulling him to her. His right hand slid over her robe until it gently cupped her left breast through the material. She pulled apart.

'Sorry.'

'No.' She moved her robe away and placed his hand on her naked breast. She looked directly at him, saying nothing. He noticed a red flush around her neck and her lips slightly apart. In his hand, her flesh felt slightly clammy, but he instantly knew the unique feel of her breast, a woman's breast and the urgent pressing of her nipple against his palm. He stood quite still, holding on, uncertain as what to do next, a teenager again in a dark Saturday night dance-hall alleyway.

'Let's go to my bedroom. Let me go first.'

*

In the dim light of the bedroom, Alex stood naked, except for a pair of rainbow-coloured socks, afraid that trying to remove them elegantly would require the skills and athleticism of a Herculean stripper, skills he knew he did not possess and more importantly, might disturb what he hoped was throbbing impressively from his loins. With difficulty, he resisted the temptation to reach for reassurance or stretch for appearance. Behind him lay a heap of mangled clothing and a pair of shoes, still laced.

Samantha had already slipped into bed, and now watched, duvet pulled up to her chin. She had wanted him badly but had never seen his naked body before. How odd, she thought, to desire someone physically whose daily appearance normally consisted of an old pair of jeans, a crumpled shirt and sometimes that day's stubble, without knowing what lay beneath. Now however, she looked with pleasure and some relief at the object before her. Although not yet fully extended, it had, long ago, been cut into a thing of beauty and elegant proportion. That was clearly evident and seemed so appropriate for him. Obviously, your career could relate to your physical condition and she thought of athletes, so why not an art historian? Suddenly an insane thought entered her head, forcing her to raise the duvet further to prevent what could be a disastrous giggle. Weirdly, she suddenly saw him in her mind, standing there, giving a public lecture on the aesthetics of his own penis.

'You alright Sam?' He sounded rather breathless.

'Oh yes.' She spoke through the material. 'Come and join me. Don't forget your socks.'

She lowered the duvet slightly as an invitation.

He arrived with a crash which made her start and the bed bounce, afraid that any delay might cause some hydraulic failure, and pressed his body hard against her, free hand finding the smooth coolness of her flank and back. Their mouths met.

'Wow. Welcome, Captain Kirk.'

'Captain Kirk?'

'Yes. Landing on planet Samantha with your impressive space ship.'

He laughed and she reached down for him. The laugh was replaced with an inward gasp and he pushed firmly against her shoulder, turning her backwards. *What now? What about…* He stumbled over an open leg, trying not to kneel on her and crouched on all fours, looking down, waiting, watching her eyes. She smiled and closed them. He looked down and approached his ultimate destination. *Quickly before I lose this. Captain Kirk approaching docking,* but his arrival did not trigger any electronic swish of opening and instead he crashed into soft but unyielding flesh. He wriggled for a while, blindly seeking entrance, fearing that his sleek craft might metamorphosise into jelly at any moment. She reached down to guide him and her touch energised him again, but without success, and his supporting arms began to tremble, sweat prickled his face and he slipped away.

'Sorry Alex. Sorry darling.' But he didn't hear her.

He rolled away, lay on his back and looked at the ceiling. Part of him felt strangely relieved.

She reached for his hand and cursed herself for not thinking. This old lady.

'Sorry, needed a little help.'

'Help?'

'Yes. Should have bought some lubricant.'

He turned towards her, concern on his face. 'Oh, I didn't realise.'

'Probably a bit nervous and you are rather big.'

'Oh yes.' He grinned at her, more reassured now, then they both lay back, covered in their own thoughts. It was Alex that broke the silence.

'There's some butter in the fridge.'

Samantha let out a wail of nervous laughter, breasts shaking. Alex sat up on one elbow and watched her.

'Alex James. You are crazy.'

He nodded. Uncertainly.

*

Alex woke at dawn, knowing *exactly* where he was. Even in the semi-darkness he sensed the extra space around him, smelled *her* room, felt how *this* mattress yielded beneath him. He moved carefully onto his back. Next to him, Samantha also lay on her back, duvet pulled down as the warmth of the room covered her. He could see her profile outlined in the shadowy light; her neck, shoulders and breasts uncovered. He listened for her breathing, but there was no apparent sound and despite the closed eyes, he wondered if she was really awake, uncomfortable about making contact again. Delaying that moment. He really couldn't blame her. Very carefully, he felt down under the warmth of the duvet, but everything was sleepy. Switched off. *Oh shit. How could I? Or couldn't I, that's more like it? Captain Kirk? More like Captain Useless.* He looked across at her. *She is so delicious. So still.* He wondered what thoughts and images and feelings were moving through her mind right now like animated postcards; drifting away, stopping, coming back. Maybe some of him.

He turned very carefully until he was facing her, his head still on the pillow, and began to study her breasts, lying still, each round and smooth, forming magically out of her body, with each centre point gradually receiving their true colour as the light strengthened. From where he lay, they were twin islands rising in perfect symmetry out of a pale, calm sea, or maybe the soft, sensuous shapes of the desert except those shapes were never semi-spherical, always shifting and only smooth from that biplane winging far above. He looked again at the centre of each island, now soft and sleepy and yet he knew that his tongue and lips might raise them until they stood as magical monuments. Monuments of a timeless order, one that had never changed, would never change; a symbol of need and desire and beauty and womanhood so loved of art and poetry, certainly poetry and he thought of Robert Herrick's Julia, all that time ago. *What, seventeenth century? 'A red rose peeping through a white… or else a cherry double graced within a lily centre placed… a strawberry shows half drowned in cream.'*

Laying as she was, they seemed so young, almost boyish and he wanted to slide a single fingertip slowly around their base, feeling their warmth and perfect smoothness, but didn't dare. *Bet I snored as well. That would just about finish it.* Very slowly, he sat up, pushed the duvet away and swung his legs over the side of the bed.

'You alright?' Her voice sounded drowsy.

He turned. Her eyes were still closed, and she didn't appear to have moved. *No. I'm going to run away and hide somewhere. A monastery maybe.*

'Alex?'

Her voice sounded slightly more anxious and he knew that at any moment she would open her eyes and reality would return.

'It's OK,' he whispered. 'Just need the toilet. You sleep. It's very early.'

'Alright. Come back soon. I need you to hold me.'

You do? He stood and remembered he was naked, looked around for something to cover himself but his clothes seemed to be strewn on the floor. He looked back at Samantha whose eyes were still closed but now she had quietly pulled the duvet up to her chin. Silently, he picked up his glasses, fumbled them on and crept from the bedroom, slightly hunched, hands clasped before him.

He pattered to the bathroom he normally used, quickly pulled a navy-blue robe from the back of the door and put it on, tying the belt firmly to him, feeling reassured by its soft covering, even though he was completely alone. He stood and looked into a long wall mirror. Saw this elderly man who he barely recognised, pale skin contrasting against the dark material.

'Who the hell are you?'

The flesh above his eyes seemed to be slowly sliding down over his lids and now rested in a puffy, creased, dangerous sort of way as if any moment it would give way and collapse like a fleshslide and cover his eyesight. He raised his mouth in an exaggerated and toothless grimace and the flesh below collided with that above, producing a pile-up of sausage shapes at the corner of each eye.

Oh, that's horrible. No wonder old people don't smile much. Not because they're miserable. Just trying to keep it all taut.

His ears looked the same as ever as did his mouth, although he noticed two creases at each corner. One up. One down. *Happy up? Unhappy down?* His happy up crease did seem bigger. *S'pose that's something.* From his sideburns, short hairs pointed outwards and downwards like silver spikes and on his forehead, he could see under and through the sparse hair as if he was looking into an open coppice of young saplings.

He tugged at his belt and let it fall away, opening the robe and exposing his nakedness. He had never been very athletic, preferring the spiritual pull of the arts but surprisingly his body seemed almost acceptable, if a little flabby. True, he had always eaten sensibly, never smoked and the kick of alcohol and its attendant pounding nausea had been left behind a very long time ago… ever since… although he was beginning to enjoy it again now, in moderation, with Samantha.

The silver-grey of his head seemed to be slowly descending onto his chest where the hair was also beginning to curl like an old sheep, although on his belly and pubic area it was still quite dark. It was as if the ageing process had started from the head and was now steadily creeping southwards. *Makes sense I s'pose. Seeps out of your brain – lose your memory – then downwards – poor eyesight, can't hear a thing, teeth fall out, flesh collapses – then creeps across the shoulders – mottled like some old tombstone – onto your chest – wonder what the silver-grey equivalent of rusting is? – clogs up the heart and lungs and then a mad dash to your cock.*

He looked down and then held himself in his right hand. It felt familiar, warm and flaccid. He spoke, like a shepherd addressing an old, faithful but now slightly lame sheepdog. 'I know it's not your fault. It happens and I suppose I knew it might, but such timing.' And yet, in his brain, he also knew that he had been almost suffocated with a raw passion that had spread around him, tingling and pulsating. He had felt her smooth, warm flesh, stroked her pale skin, tasted her hungry lips, felt her body straining against his. He turned to the toilet and began to pee as quietly as possible. *So why couldn't you…? Bloody mind of your own.*

'Alex. You OK?'

He flushed the toilet, washed his hands, quickly brushed his teeth, tied his robe around him and walked back to the bedroom.

He perched on the edge of the bed, facing away, for the morning light was strengthening now.

'Are you alright?'

Her voice sounded soft, maybe concerned?

Is that really softness? Maybe it's gentle accusation. No not accusation. She wouldn't accuse, would she? No. Just glossing over. Pretending it never happened. Well it didn't. I know. I know. Or disappointed. Is that disappointment?

'Don't you want to come back to bed?'

Oh dear. This is the moment. He turned, struggling for words, stopped and laughed out loud.

'Sam. Your eyes.'

'What? What's wrong…?'

She sat up, clutching the duvet to her, and turned towards a bedside mirror, involuntarily exposing most of her back, pale and slim, with just a glimpse of the swelling of her buttocks.

'You look like—'

'A panda. Yes, I know.' She hastily wiped around her eyes with a tissue.

'It's your fault.'

'My fault. How is it my fault?'

'You shouldn't be so passionate.'

'Passionate?'

'Yes. It's all that creative temperament bubbling away. Don't even give a girl a chance to get ready. Dragged me into bed from the bathroom. Is that better?'

He sat surprised. *Is that what happened? Not what I thought. I thought… never mind.* He grinned. 'Would you like a cup of tea?'

Samantha waited until he had made his way to the kitchen and then fled to the bathroom where she attempted to tidy her face and hair, quickly refresh her mouth. She stood at the open door listening for sounds of him returning and then slipped back into bed and sat up, breasts covered, then uncovered and finally re-covered, waiting breathlessly. Alex returned carrying a tray with two cups.

'Thank you. That's very sweet of you.'

'My… er… pleasure.'

He felt for her legs under the duvet and sat on the edge of the bed nearest to her, but towards the bottom. He said nothing. She sipped her tea and then held the cup between her hands, looking at him curiously. *What a dark horse you are. What a wonderful surprise you are.* She had been completely taken aback and slightly overwhelmed by his passion and directness. So fierce, so total, so open, like some wild animal, an erotic wild animal. Yes, that's how she remembered him, from all that time ago. An erotic, wild creature. Roaring, powerful, devouring. *Oh my God, a panther.* It had scared and excited her in equal measure. She *had* imagined that he would have been more considered, more measured, concentrating, as she had seen him when immersed in his drawing but no, he had wanted to take her. That was the only word that fitted. She had tried to respond but had found herself torn between powerful, almost primitive urges from somewhere deep within her and decades of control and restraint. *Damn control. Damn restraint. If only I could. Oh dear, those words. I need to spit them into the eye of the world. Take me Alex. Take me hard. That's what I want.* She had wanted to shout that aloud but couldn't. It had stuck in her mind, never even reaching her mouth. And of course, she had forgotten the lubricant. How stupid. *I should have known.*

She looked at him, sitting quietly on the edge of the bed. *Maybe he's as befuddled as I am? Maybe he is thinking that I'm not enough for him? I couldn't bear that. Do something Samantha.* She put the cup down and pulled the duvet down a little on his side.

'Why don't you take that robe off and get…' she wanted to say naked but couldn't, 'close to me.'

The words surprised him. Surprised and aroused him. *She still wants me.* He smiled, not totally certain, slipped the robe off his shoulders with his back to her, let it fall to the floor and felt his flaccidity begin to swell slightly and tingle with interest. *Good boy.*

The bedroom was pleasantly warm and so the heat from her body surprised him as he rested one hand on her waist. They lay close, facing each other.

'Sorry about last night.'

She drew back in surprise.

'Sorry for what? Last night was lovely.'

'Yes, but I'm afraid I couldn't… well… perform.'

'Perform! Oh Alex. You are daft.'

The swelling reduced slightly.

'You're not a seal in a circus. Typical man. And it was my fault anyway.'

She gently stroked his cheek with the back of her fingers, feeling more certain.

'You are a wonderful, funny, clever, talented,' she shook her head slightly, 'oh-so-talented, kind, thoughtful man who makes me feel so good, so young again, and that's what's most important. The rest will follow. Feeling your arms around me made me feel… whole again and …wanted. Nobody has ever done that since… well, for a very, very long time.'

He felt tears beginning to form in his eyes.

'I thought…'

'Oh, sweet Alex. Of course I want you. Always have.'

Their bodies moved together, arms wrapped around each other and Alex pushed one thigh against Samantha's legs, which opened and closed on him. She reached down for him. More an act of affirmation and comfort. They lay eye to eye. Mouth to mouth. Breath to breath. Quietly for a moment. Almost afraid to speak. Afraid to trust their feelings. Uncertain of what to do next.

'Touch me Alex. I love it when you touch me. Stroke me. Please.'

'OK. Turn over.' He knelt with some difficulty on the soft mattress and then pulled the duvet back. She felt an instant tension as he uncovered her, felt the temperature change but lay still and waited. He waited for a moment, taking in her slim but strong back, mottled at the shoulders, that he knew so well from his drawings, saw it swell into her hips and her soft creamy buttocks, then the back of her thighs, marked here and there by the odd red-purple blemish. He knew that her shape would have changed over the years, as his had, but the thought of quietly exploring her, inch by inch, excited him.

She felt his fingertips slide lightly from her shoulders and trace their way slowly down her back, either side of her spine, then out across her ribs, finding the very outline of her breasts, taut beneath her and then back again. Relishing. Communicating silently. She closed her eyes and took a slow breath through her nose. He felt her relax. His fingers continued. Over the hardness of her lower back and then across to her hips and up onto the globes of her buttocks. So smooth. So cool. Soft. They brushed across their tight crease and then rested just between for a moment. She hardly dare breathe at this unexpected intimacy and for fear he might stop. His fingers moved on to one globe and then his full hand followed. Stroking. Squeezing. Stroking again.

'You feel so, so good.'

He lowered his head and rubbed his stubble across her. She stiffened in surprise, then relaxed. 'Do that again.' He did.

He looked down at her, tried to imagine her way back then, when he had not known her. When she had probably not even really known herself. Imagined watching her from behind, crossing a room, climbing a stairway. Her chattering bubble beauty, bouncy, smooth as river stones, flesh milky pale and as untarnished as a fresh dawn, tautly flowing, swaying, speaking sensual slink, whether she was aware of it or not. And now? No doubt the hot noon sun of her youth had moved on into a more relaxed afternoon, into a broader, softer vista like snow fields dipping into a fold and out again but they were still her. Still hungry. He imagined her now waiting for him, fully shaped, confident, her wanting to kneel on the edge of a crumpled bed, away from him, head bowed, urgent and needy. He suddenly realised she was still talking to him and he swallowed hard.

'Is it the artist that makes you want to stroke me?' Her voice was slightly muffled, breathing slightly more noticeable. 'Explore me with your hands; the same shapes and textures you do with a pencil. Understand my body?'

'Maybe. I just love the tactile feel of you. How it changes under my fingertips.'

'Hope you never get bored with it?'

'No. Never. It's magic.'

Magic. How wonderful you are. He ran his hands gently along the back of a thigh, down the fullness of her calf, quickly pushing the duvet to the floor, before running a fingernail down the sole of one small foot. She jumped.

'That's not fair.' Her voice still sounded muffled in the pillow, almost sleepy.

He smiled to himself. His fingertips now retraced their slow exploration, this time deliberately stroking the blue/red threads behind her knee, determined to include them before pushing between the backs of her thighs. She wondered if she should open her legs slightly for him. But didn't. Over the smooth, cool globes that formed the frontier between upper and lower and onto the tight strength of her lower back. He stopped and then very carefully ran his very fingertips over her shoulders, feeling the tiny blemishes left by the sun and wind and time that made her who she was. A human patina of priceless experience. He leant forward and kissed the back of her neck. Samantha felt like purring.

'Turn over now. Face me.'

His voice sounded soft and yet commanding. For a moment she felt a familiar fear and was prepared with a negative reply. But instead she turned and lay naked before him. Still nervous, still vulnerable, her eyes still searching for any look of criticism. *Not this man. Please.* Alex sat back on his haunches and smiled at her. It was a smile that included her, all of her and to her surprise she reached up for him, pulled him down towards her and placed her lips gently against his. It felt strange, she had not been used to taking the initiative. In the past, she had lain quietly in the darkness. Waiting. Ready to follow and utter the sounds that the man had wanted. Rarely had they jumped from her mouth without warning. Surprising her. Now she felt Alex's lips, hot and soft and an excitement welled up inside her. So wanton. So powerful. *Now I can do what I want and he will let me.*

He smiled and looked at her slim body. Almost skinny. Too much worry. Too much stress maybe. Too much past. Her small breasts were not so firm now but her jutting nipples were once again young and bursting with sensation and need. Her thighs stretched before him were smooth and strong and her legs were almost faultless and seemed somehow to have escaped most of the pink-purple ravages of time. More than his had done. The darker hair between her legs showed a simple, dark, vertical smudge, slightly apart, on a soft mound that disappeared beneath her. Running down her belly she carried a single white scar hardly seen against her milky skin.

She never mentioned it but much later when he kissed her there, her eyes had filled with tears.

'You've shaved.'

'Waxed.' She raised herself onto both elbows. 'Is that OK. I've never done it before. Do you mind?'

'Of course not.' She fell back onto the pillow, relieved. 'It was so exciting doing that. Things that real women do. Modern women do.'

'You're certainly a real woman Sam.'

'It will grow back if you prefer.'

He shook his head and tried to stifle a yawn. 'Do you want me to trim, shave, whatever it's called. Does it have a name? Brazilian or something.' He yawned.

'Come on. Back into bed. It must be very early.'

They pulled the duvet back over them and settled down, Alex now lying behind her. He cupped his hand over her right breast, feeling the acquiescence of her nipple in his palm. He squeezed once or twice, trying to maintain the intimacy that had stirred them earlier, but sleep began to overtake, and in his hand, the soft sensation of her breast slowly disappeared into no more than body heat.

*

Alex woke later. On his back. He turned eagerly towards Samantha but only a creased pillow looked at him. He rolled slowly over again and thought towards the ceiling. *Why isn't she here luxuriating with me in this warm, crumpled, rumpled scene of human explosion? This bed should have police tapes around it. I need to fill my hands with her soft body again.* He looked back towards her pillow. *Interesting how plump, fat pillows invite you to empty a waking day into them and then the next morning leave evidence of the night's twists and turns and torments. Wonder if you can read pillows like palms or crystal balls? Wonder what hers would say? How about mine? Wonder where she is now?* Somewhere below came the faint sound of cutlery and ceramics meeting marble.

He swept out of bed, sprung upwards, swayed slightly, placed one hand on a dressing table and then made his way towards the shower.

'La dee da da da dee, da da da dee do do.' Alex stood and watched the water cascade down, reluctant to step inside its force and wash her away. He cupped his hands and offered them, watching the water bubble frantically, listening to its liquid slapping. Satisfied, he stepped forward, lowered his head and gasped as the hot spikes struck him, flattening his hair and running off his nose and chin. He turned, felt hot drumming on his shoulders, easing them, and closed his eyes. He felt unusually in touch with his body, his flesh aware and alert... almost wicked. He turned again and allowed the stream to gush over his belly and thighs, tingling and spreading a hot glow, making him feel full and potent. He looked down, reached and stretched himself. *That looks better. Amazing how things can change. One minute a limp scrap and now... well not exactly roaring... not yet King of the Jungle... but certainly looking around. Full of that knowing buzz. It's right what they say... use it or lose it.*

He slipped on a fresh T-shirt, relishing its crispness against the freshness of his body and contemplated his pair of old jeans. *Shall I wear just them? Nothing underneath.* He slipped them on, feeling the rough material grasping his body, feeling daring and barefoot made his way downstairs.

'I'm in here. In the lounge.'

Samantha was sitting on the long settee, a large envelope opened beside her. He bent forward and kissed her lightly, almost formally on her lips. Both realised at that moment that the single kiss was a form of confirmation, a seal on their relationship. Neither commented.

'I've bought us a present.'

'You have?'

'Hope it's OK. Oh dear, I'm not so sure now. I feel slightly embarrassed.'

'What is it Sam?'

She turned and picked up a book beside her.

'I bought this.' She turned the book so that he could see the front cover. He leaned forward and squinted.

'Sorry. Can't see without my glasses and I don't know where they are. So, what does it say?'

'*Tantra Explained*. It's extraordinary.'

'Tantra? Really?'

'Yes, and I actually went into a bookshop and asked for it. Thought I might be embarrassed but nobody turned a hair. How times have changed.' She looked at him uncertainly. 'Do you want to have a look?'

'When did you buy this?'

'Oh, quite recently.'

He took the book and started to skim the pages, occasionally stopping to look at her with raised eyebrows. She continued, trying to deflect her discomfort, filling the silence. 'You must have had similar difficulties when you were younger. Getting hold of things. Like condoms? That must have been embarrassing? Wasn't it?'

He stopped skimming.

'Condoms? You mean French letters… or Johnnies. Rubber Johnny. Lawrence's fault. Well, you really had to go to a barber and get a haircut. Not something I did very often of course and then as the barber finished, he would whisper discreetly in your ear – *something for the weekend sir.*'

'Only the weekend?'

'Yes, I know. Well the English only did it at the weekend apparently or at least only admitted as much. Saturday night after the pub and Sunday morning after a lie-in and because there was nothing else to do.'

'And what did you say?'

'Just a packet of three please.'

'A packet of three?'

'Yes, and then he would put the offending article into a brown paper bag to hide it from sight.' Alex sat up and began to laugh at the thought. 'Yes, and worse than that, my local barber was in the gents' toilets, right at the end and unusually he was a keen amateur artist, so you passed the urinals, took in the paintings, got your little brown paper bag and walked out again, all to the aroma of that day's urine. It was a strange sensory experience.'

They both laughed and sat for a moment, reflecting.

'So, why tantra Sam? Bit bold isn't it?'

She felt her cheeks redden. *Knew I shouldn't have done it. Just seemed so adventurous. For me. Thought he would be pleased.*

Alex became aware of her discomfort. 'I expect it's very interesting though, isn't it?'

'Oh yes. Extraordinary.' She smiled sweetly. *And now I've gone to all the trouble of getting it, you're going to hear this, whether you like it or not.* 'Listen to this. You'll like this.' She took the book from him, found a page turned down and started to read. '"Women's breasts are the gateway to true sexual pleasure and bonding between the man and woman. If the clitoris alone is given attention, the results will be unsatisfactory if exciting. The woman cannot become fully and deeply involved because her genitals are of less importance. Her breasts and nipples must first be lovingly aroused so that she is both physically and mentally ready."'

'What? Less important?'

'That's what it says.'

'Who wrote that?'

'Not sure, except it comes from the fifth century AD. In India I think. I'm surprised you never came across it before, with your arty hippy background.'

'Mmm. Anyway. So, a woman's breasts and nipples are the key to pleasure. Well, that does explain a lot. Is that why I like them so much, your breasts?'

'You do? You never said.'

'Didn't I. Well, we've only just met. Me and your breasts I mean. Of course I do. In fact, most men do I guess, like breasts I mean, not yours, although I'm sure they would.' She smiled at his nonsense. He continued. 'So then, is that attraction really some deep-felt primeval understanding that all pleasure initiates from them? Something that, intuitively, men know. That's why we have a need to fondle them but have forgotten why?'

'So why *do* you fondle them?'

'Why? Well because they look so tactile – like stroking a horse's flank or a cool piece of marble – you know, this urge to touch *and* because of their feel. Soft. Warm. Smooth. And the contrast. The hardness.'

'Hardness?'

'Yes Sam. Your pert nipples.'

'Oh that.' She felt both embarrassed and elated.

He sat down, next to her. 'Is there more?'

'Loads. Listen. "True sexual beauty has nothing to do with physical looks. It is a quality that shines from within us."'

'Well, thank God for that. Means us oldies can join in then, wrinkles and all.'

'It gets better for us old 'uns.'

'It does?'

'Oh yes. How about this? "The human body is designed to have sex for many hours without great physical effort and without seeking any pre-determined goal. Orgasm is then by choice and not through habit."'

'Hours? Hours? How on earth do you do that?'

'Think we've already started. Have you ever had a conversation like this with a woman before?'

'Not really. No. How about you and Henry?'

'Unthinkable. No wonder we drew apart. And at times I didn't really know why, just some deep-seated dissatisfaction. He was kind and generous and hard-working and sexually potent, but sex happened as soon as he was ready and I was left struggling to keep up. I never faked it – well not really – probably made the sort of noises he might expect but I was left unfulfilled and never knew why. I thought I was doing what was required of me. What he wanted.'

'I suspect that most women would recognise that. And, I guess, from what you are saying, it also means being rather vulnerable.'

'Oh yes. You *have* to open your soul to the other person. And, be prepared to show all sides of your make-up to each other, both masculine and feminine, which we both have apparently – that's what it says in the book. And trust them. I realise that now. There's a lot about that in here. The need for polarity. That's what they call it. The balance of the masculine and feminine. Even the need to relax and find time. Time to smell the roses.'

'So, is tantra just about sex then?'

'No, I don't think so. Not really. It seems to be about transforming sex into some glorious, blissful experience that connects you somehow with your body again rather than your mind. It's sometimes called "sacred sexuality". A pathway to enlightenment.'

'Now that does sound a bit hippy.'

'Maybe. But it's been around for a very long time and you would be the perfect person.'

'Me?'

'Oh yes. In tantra, sacred acts included eating, dancing and creative expression… like drawing and painting, like being an artist.'

'Really?'

'Really.'

'So, I could be a tantra god then. Well, how about that. Anything else to assault my feeble struggling brain?'

'Your brain is far from feeble Alex but since you ask… how about this? "A man's ejaculation cannot really be called an orgasm. An orgasm is where the body can no longer be felt as a physical state, instead it reverberates with light and colour and electricity."'

'It does?'

'I don't pretend to understand it either Alex, but I just know there is something there. I can feel it when I'm with you. You seem to release me. And it will be an adventure. Our adventure.'

She sat up, eyes shining.

'Will you come with me, sweet Alex?' She reached and touched his hand.

'To where?'

'I've been doing some research on the internet.'

'That's brave of you.'

'No, I've found a festival. A tantra festival. In London. Shall we go? Shall I get tickets?'

'I don't have to dress in robes and chant, do I?'

'No, of course not. There's a whole section for beginners. There's obviously no pressure on you to do anything you don't want to. No nudity. No intimate touching. What do you think?'

He looked at her. Her fervent anxiety. His inner surprise and growing excitement. 'OK. If it pleases you.'

'It does but I want you to go with an open heart, not just to please me.'

'I will. Promise.'

'OK, then you'll need to read this. Some of it will blow your mind,' and she handed him the book. Something fell from it. He bent to pick it up. It was a pale pressed flower. Once it had been alive and as yellow as the sun.

'You kept it.'

'Of course. I usually keep it in my diary, but it feels more appropriate in there at the moment. It's important. Was given to me by a god.'

8

Tantra

A LEX AND SAM climbed step by step out of the Saturday crowd swaying in the rush of the Underground below and arrived into what appeared to be a Sunday. They stopped for a moment, surprised at how empty and peaceful the streets were. This part of the city was given to the practise and learning of law, and large, thronging stores and social housing had shied away from such earnestness.

The young man was stacking shelves, probably thankful for the opportunity or glad for something to do. A solitary Asian customer was picking silently through the products. The man had no idea of their destination although it turned out to be less than a hundred metres from where he stood, but yes, this was the right road. Maybe, thought Sam, he came in every day from his small, overpriced bedsit, walked the ten metres from the Tube exit, raised the rattling shutters of the shop and felt no curiosity for the strange world of wigs and gowns that centred on this neighbourhood.

They began to walk, hand in hand, along a nondescript road lined with large plane trees whose roots had stretched the tarmac, causing it to rise and fall in places, like a tarry wave. Beside them, a long, forbidding wall coated with the grime of age and pollution stretched away to the next intersection, where a red double-decker bus travelled briefly from right to left across their vision. At intervals, doors and gateways resolutely barred any entrance.

'What does it show on the map?'

'No map. Just written instructions and we seem to be there.'

They looked around in the hope of salvation.

*

The young woman pulled an earphone from one ear and held it between pale fingers tipped with bright green polish.

'Sure. Just up there and turn right. Can't miss it.'

She smiled at Alex. A friendly smile to help an older man and his wife.

'Thank you.'

'My pleasure.'

Her accent had the youthful softness and confident honey drawl of the Southern States and for a moment Alex felt uncertain. Maybe it was a bad idea after all to attend a tantra festival. They had talked about it and laughed at their daring, scoffed at their contemporaries and smiled at the soft-focus images and white doves that had accompanied the advertising but now…

They turned into a broad enclosed walkway, with cool cobbles at their feet and emerged into a large courtyard and garden painted in sunlight. To their right hung a banner, announcing their destination. To Alex, its purple material felt fluid, satin and shimmering; at odds with the surrounding buildings. They stood, solidly right-angled and unbreachable with their neat, almost endless lines of white-pointed red brick, held tightly at regular intervals by cathedral-like buttresses that added an extra ecclesiastical respectability.

On the few steps leading to the main entrance sat or lounged a small group, apparently preferring the sun's warmth to the opening ceremony. They could have been any group – waiting for the stalls to open, spilling out from a hot, noisy party, sitting in a green park.

'They look normal,' whispered Alex with some relief.

As they stepped inside, the atmosphere abruptly changed to one of chaotic animation. To one side, long queues of people looked down at them, whilst waiting patiently on a long, dark-brown staircase. Others slipped past each other on their way to various rooms and at their side, a young man with a struggling beard and dark, keen eyes, attempted to explain the logistics. The air simmered with smiles and an itchy pent-up energy.

'Come on Sam, let's start in the main hall. Starts at eleven. Five minutes.'

'What's it called?'

'Er, awakening multi-orgasmic potential in men and women.' He looked at her and grinned. 'Can't believe I just said that. Come on before all the seats go.'

Inside, they found two adjoining seats. Around them, the hall had over many centuries acquired a deep brown coating of honour and tradition. The walls were encased in stiff wooden panelling on which coats of arms sat proudly and the roof, supported by heavy black beams and on intimate terms with heaven, soared upwards to a cheese-coloured ceiling from which hung clusters of lamps, dusty with tradition. On the walls, stained glass figures looked quietly and soberly inwards and the whole hall seemed to wait ponderously and rather uneasily. In the middle of the floor stood an open stage, behind which hung another large purple banner. To Alex, it looked like the broad slash of a huge disrespectful paintbrush. He smiled approvingly.

They both looked around. The hall was full, with many people sitting on the floor in front of the stage. There was an air of expectancy. Sam and Alex leant towards each other. Uncertain conspirators.

'How you feeling Sam?'

'Nervous. And excited. Don't really know what to expect.'

'No, but we're not the only old 'uns here.'

Dotted around them were glimpses of silver and grey and the occasional tanned bald patch. The expectation was becoming palpable.

'Like waiting for a controversial play to start.'

Everybody sat, curious, willing to learn, wanting to understand, hoping for transformation and enlightenment, each feeling that same life force sparking within them, regardless of age or gender or race or nationality or upbringing or culture or shape or size or looks. The same vibrant dynamo had drawn them all together, and now they waited.

A loud, metallic voice suddenly crackled around the room and heads lifted. From the front came a ripple of applause for the man now sitting centre stage, legs crossed. Open-necked and silver-haired with a modest beard and moustache and wearing soft clothes, Alex recognised the comfortable air of an academic about to give a lecture. Samantha leaned forward. Alex clicked his pen into action.

'Welcome to you all.'

He smiled broadly, displaying perfect white teeth. Alex clicked his pen twice in irritation. Samantha felt the waves of relaxed sensuality from twenty-five yards away.

'This is a path of many steps, not a goal. Biological orgasmic state is quite different from a spiritual state – the multi-orgasmic state which we are all capable of. So, become self-aware. Become exotic beings. Understand your own sexuality. Be honest with yourselves. Do not impose values on yourselves determined by others. We are all different with differing levels of sexual need and drive. Find out who you are. Look within. Inner awareness is a more delicate phenomenon than the thinking process.'

A ripple ran through the audience and many turned to smile and nod to their neighbours.

'We all have both masculine and feminine traits within us. Recognise, accept and value them… especially you men,' and he waved an arm across the width of the audience and smiled even more broadly. 'Yes, *you* have feminine traits as well. Do not ignore them. Embrace them. You need to achieve polarity – the perfect balance of masculine and feminine within each of you.' He stopped to look down at his notes. 'Store energy. Do not waste it. Men… do not ejaculate.' He paused, waiting for the inevitable buzz to die down. 'I have not ejaculated for decades.'

There was a collective gasp. Alex turned to Samantha, eyes in disbelief. Slowly the chatter died down.

'You only need ejaculation for making babies. No more.'

Somewhere somebody clapped. He nodded in that direction and waited.

'Women…'

The audience now sat in total silence.

'*You* are the centre. *You* are the engine. *You* are the initiator… not the man. You must start by exploring your own eroticism. Be positive not passive. You must initiate without fear, then you can teach the man. Men like pleasure but not too intensely. Women are the opposite so it is the woman who can teach the man but remember,' and he wagged a finger towards the audience, 'men cannot enter if they are afraid of the magic.' He waited until the buzz died down. 'You know, men and women are programmed to live happily together for two to four years. After that hormonal changes push them apart. With this, believe you me, you will be together forever. Multi-orgasm is very different from normal orgasm. With repeated normal orgasm, the climax lessens every time, you grow physically weaker. With multi-orgasm, the climax increases every time and will last far longer. Believe me your organs will know what to do. They understand.' He turned an ear towards the audience. 'Sorry? How long? Maybe six to seven times longer and will feel completely different.'

He stood and smiled at the audience.

'Unclench your mind. Grow from within. Breathe into your belly. Become a gourmand of pleasure. Thank you.'

The audience erupted into cheers and wild clapping and a great deal of smiling.

*

'You wouldn't imagine for one moment that this was here.' Alex balanced a portion of curry on his plastic fork. 'Like a green oasis surrounded by mucky fortress walls. It is real, isn't it? Not some sort of weird tantric mirage.'

They sat in a very large open garden, feeling the pale sunshine on their faces, surrounded by imposing buildings. It felt strangely big and open in the crammed city.

'What did you think of that then Sam? Rather mind-blowing.'

'Yes, but all based on his experience.'

'Presumably. So how do you manage it then, this multi-orgasmic state? What on earth do you do? He didn't tell us that.'

'I really don't know.'

They both sat thoughtfully.

'So, what shall we do this afternoon?' He wiped the corner of his mouth. 'There's loads to choose from, not that I understand it all and have you noticed the names of the – what would you call them – the presenters? Angel. Breeze. Sky. Nothing normal. Surprised there isn't one called Vagina. Anyway, open mind, eh?'

Samantha had opened the programme and folded back a page. 'How about this? It's about the ritual of meeting people, being attracted to them and then being open and honest and giving. Does involve some activities but nothing of a sexual nature or involving nudity – so it says. Shall we go?'

*

The room had been cleared, apart from a few wooden chairs gathered around its edges and was already quite full, mainly with young people. Those without seats stood patiently or sat crossed-legged on the floor. Against one wall was a small platform on which stood a slight woman dressed entirely in black. Her glossy dark hair hung to the middle of her back and behind one ear sat a large red rose-like flower. She regularly checked an oversize watch secured to her left wrist by a pink strap, and eventually tapped the microphone next to her and spoke into it.

'Hokay my name ees Willow.' She smiled, displaying more perfect white teeth. 'Welcome to you all. I theenk we start.'

For some reason, Alex felt a pang of anxiety. He looked towards Samantha, but she was already engrossed.

He heard the words echoing around the room – how people normally behaved on first meeting – with reserve and caution – how defensive they could be. How much potential could be lost.

'So, I want you to relax with some music. Just dance on your own or with your neighbour. Doesn't matter. Hokay?'

The music was modern and lively with a strong beat and all around, people threw themselves into its rhythm with little hesitation. Alex felt the music coursing through his body, but suddenly, his feet and hips and arms felt clumsy. Beside him, Samantha swayed with a serene smile.

The music stopped abruptly to be replaced by a heady buzz and a battery of smiles.

'Hokay. Now you meet everyone.'

The buzz increased.

The perfect teeth gleamed.

'Now you make two circles. One within the other. That's eet. That's right. Now one circle moves like the clock and the other against the clock. Hokay? Now leesten. Very important.' She clapped her hands. 'As you walk, you look everybody in the eyes, you smile – beeg smiles – you say nothing. Then when we stop, you make groups of three persons. Three persons you like. Three persons like you. You got it?' The smiles said so. 'Hokay, start walking.'

Alex felt confused and the first moments of panic and self-doubt started to stir in his stomach mixed with the strange pleasure of the eye-to-eye contact that moved past him. How should he react? How did he look? What was his expression? Was he attractive? Interesting or just old and boring? *But I have achieved so much*, he wanted to shout but of course couldn't.

A young Japanese woman, petite with raven hair and red lips wearing a figure-hugging dress looked him directly in the eye as she strolled past. The look wasn't shy or uncertain or even flirtatious. It was open and searching and relentlessly silent. Alex felt heat run up his neck and he looked away. No words. No words to hide behind. No clever words from him to disarm her, to affect her expression, to mollify that stare. No tell-tale tic or flicker or dilation from her. Just a young woman whose body and mouth he desired but whose eyes kept him a thousand yards away whilst they swept his very soul. Finding what? She walked on, followed by another and another. He felt increasingly naked and unsure and his body, he knew, must be rough and limp and wrinkled and stained by the years. Sam glanced at him, concerned.

'Hokay.' From somewhere came the voice of Willow. 'Now start to form into your small groups. Yes. Groups of three. That's eet. Find each other. Now tell each other of your dearest ambition. Be honest.'

Alex and Sam stood and watched as groups formed around them. Young people merged together with consummate ease, smiling deeply at each other and holding hands, until just a few older people stood, uncertain as to what to do next.

For Alex, they were old memories. From a very long time ago. But they were still not affected by the mollifying softening of distance and time and experience. They simply flew at him, still potent and mouth-drying and slapped into his fragile mind. Back then, way back then, it had been a strange, powerful sensation, which at the time had no name or understanding. Not yet desire – too young for that – yet strong enough to make his heart beat faster. Children still dressed in short trousers or frills, becoming aware, some more aware than others, with all the outward innocence of childhood but uncomfortably heated inside. Playing nervous party games or concentrating on a clumsy dance, fingers trembling. Sometimes face to flushed face and sometimes dancing in a line, holding on behind, so your embarrassed looks could not be seen. And, it was allowed, because for a while, the grown-ups had changed the rules. Today, you *can* be together – boys and girls – and talk (if you have any coherent words) and smile (if you are able) and be together (if you understand why).

He could see the adult faces back then, strangely different, flushed from a glass or two of sherry and smiling their consent, maybe wishing they could join in but now it was far too late for them. The men silently watching, sipping their drinks too frequently, their pale eyes dark, recalling that precious time before their own potency became corroded and uncomfortable and then lost. Now thinking the forbidden. And grannies and mothers and aunties now varicosed and empty, sighing and longing for that soft, smooth world and the hope of better things, of true love, bewildering romance and perfect words. And there you are, a child, dry mouthed, heart bumping, not daring to move your hands and fingers for fear of affront, or for fear of losing your grip on that precious moment, in this whirling wild dash of a party game. And there, against your fingertips, the sensation of materials from a foreign world, a world of delicacy and lightness, of gossamer and perfume. Such wonder. Such wonderful things to know and he didn't know. Will he ever know? And he stood aside in his rough clothes, awkward and gawky, without words, in his little boy party uniform. Rough boy. Silly boy. Outside boy. Left outside boy. Not chosen boy. Tears filling his head like rocks.

And so, he had learnt on his own, that most dangerous of activities. Never taught or instructed or guided or advised but simply learnt as best he could, soaking up rumour and half-truth and exaggeration eagerly – any titbit was a feast – and then eventually practising as an adult, without skill or understanding or sympathy or real knowledge, sipping life too frequently, thin sips, never realising that it could be taken in huge draughts until one day, it began to come to an end. So soon? Time to slow down, ease off, forget the visceral power of youth, put such wonders to one side, slip away, taxi downhill. You've had your chance and you're still not wanted. What? You didn't know? Too bad. Too late now.

'Let's go Sam.'

'You alright Alex?'

'Not sure.'

'Look at them Alex.'

Young people, male and female were sitting on the floor, holding hands, talking and listening. In one corner, a couple, strangers until now, hugged each other; not briefly in greeting, but with the intensity of lovers about to be separated by a desperate war, a return to the Front.

Alex and Sam watched entranced but invisible, outsiders, aliens from another planet and yet this was also *their* planet, the place they had struggled and marched across for many decades, trying to understand.

Nearby the young Japanese woman sat, legs tucked under her, dark hair now falling around her face, trying to hide her tears. Her partners – one young man, one young woman – complete strangers until now, sat with her, holding and stroking her hands, mouthing gentle words.

Alex had journeyed through life to this point and yet he knew that part of him was still at the beginning. He thought of Rachel and Jak and Georgia and then out of the corner of his eye he saw it again and glanced nervously into its black glass surface. Now it was so smooth, but reflected nothing around him, save for his own dim, uncertain reflection. He shivered.

It was the pressure spreading from his fingers that made him realise that Samantha was gripping his hand tightly. He turned and smiled into her concerned eyes.

'Shall we go?'

Alex and Samantha stepped silently out of the heady buzz that had surrounded them for most of the day and re-entered the outside world as if crossing the border into another country. Hand in hand, they retraced their steps along the dingy road until they reached the tiny shop which was now dark and closed, stopped and faced each other uncertainly.

'Well, I don't know about you Sam, but I need a drink after that.'

'A pub?'

'Can't see one. Oh, look a coffee will do. OK with you?'

The coffee shop was empty apart from an elderly woman hunched over her cup and an Eastern European waitress who greeted them with a warmth at odds with the brash, plastic emptiness of the interior. Alex thought of Edward Hopper but said nothing, his attention elsewhere.

'Well, what do you think Alex? About tantra?'

He continued to stir his coffee for longer than necessary. His face looked troubled.

'I don't know. I was amazed and confused and a bit… annoyed.'

'Annoyed?'

'Yes.'

'Why?'

'Well… how did I get to this late stage in life without knowing about that?'

'So, who are you annoyed at?'

He sat up. Dropped his spoon noisily and leaned back.

'Well. Me I suppose. How could I not query my life? Look for alternatives that were staring me in the face. Me, who's supposed to be creative and free thinking. And all those young people…'

'What about them?'

'Well, they already know. They have the rest of their lives ahead of them. Bastards. You know, I felt old and stupid and out of control.'

'Oh dear. Was that the afternoon session?'

He looked away from her gaze. 'I found that so difficult.'

'You looked terrified.' She spoke gently.

'I felt like an eight-year-old again, not chosen for the football team. Left out of the gang. Not wanted. Excluded. It was horrible because it was so real and unexpected. And *so* close to the surface. Just when you think you got things sorted. After all this time.' He looked away again.

'Yes, but it wasn't just us.' She smiled at him. A soft, discerning, disarming smile. 'I'm sure we'll survive.'

He looked back at her and sighed. 'Yes. Expect we will. Just felt like an old man aged eight.'

'Oh Alex, you are not an old man. Old men don't go to tantra festivals. Men young at heart do.'

He looked around. The blonde waitress was busying herself wiping tables that were perfectly clean and the elderly woman seemed to be more hunched than ever over her now cold coffee. *She could have died and nobody would notice until closing time. Like Fiona could.* He wondered how his mother was. She was very elderly now and not too well. He should go and see her again soon. Before it was too late.

'What did you write down? I saw you scribbling furiously.'

'Loads of stuff, Sam. So many sentences. Like orgasmic bombs exploding in my brain.'

'Did you get that about the two different types?'

'Of orgasm? Yes, I think I understand it, but I have no idea how to achieve it – the multi-orgasmic form that is. But he did say it took a lot of practice.'

'Yes, he did.'

'But I did understand the bit about chasing the biological orgasm. You know, the normal one. I think we all do that and worry about it because we've been so conditioned. The man to show his dominance and virility, the woman to show her passive position. You know, lay back and think of England.' Samantha took a sip of her drink before continuing. 'So, tell me about your bombs.'

'Well, how about "breathe into your belly". How do you manage that?'

'Like a musician or singer maybe. Don't they use their breath to express their inner self? But I suspect it's more metaphorical than that.'

'S'pose so. You seem rather excited about it all, Sam.'

'Well, I found it very liberating, that's for sure, and you know, so many things fell into place. Things that I seem to understand intuitively. Things that like you, I had never thought to question before. Isn't that sad?'

'Go on.'

'Well, the woman's role for example. Woman as the centre of pleasure. He actually said that women always know what to do. It's in their make-up. It's the man's job to follow, to pleasure the woman. That turns the whole relationship thing on its head.'

'You mean men have hijacked it?'

'Yes, and to everybody's disadvantage apparently. Do you remember this? It's from the tantra book I bought.' She opened a black notebook and thumbed through the pages. She looked up. 'Listen to this. "She cannot become deeply sexually inflamed because her genitals are of secondary importance as far as her inner body polarity is concerned. Her breasts and nipples must be engaged and her heart warmed first. When that happens prior to penetration, the readiness for sex is there both physically and psychologically. The man will immediately sense that the woman is with him, moving in rhythmic unison, with a feeling of oneness. He won't have to fight for love and she struggle to give it. It will be a true sexual union."' She looked up, unconsciously licked her red lips and smiled.

'You brought that with you?'

'Yes. Thought it might be useful.'

'And is that what you want, Sam?'

'It will do for a start, my sweet.'

'OK Goddess. Your desire is my command.'

They failed to hear the waitress's cheery goodnight as they left, hand in hand.

*

Alex watched Samantha from the bed, as she sat at her dressing table, one slim leg projecting from her green silk robe. He recognised it from his drawings in the bathroom. Wondered if it was some sort of message. It felt like a long time ago now and he realised how far they had come. He noticed a small bruise just above her knee and wondered how she had got it and then how her small feet were roughened and reddened either side of her toes. *People see that and all the other blemishes as faults. Imperfections. But they are her journey. Her experiences. Bit like that old oak table downstairs. Full of cracks and knot holes and covered with age. And people love that in a table. But not when it comes to each other. How fickle. How strange.*

'What are you thinking?'

She was watching him from the dressing table mirror.

'How gorgeous you are and what I'm going to do to you when I get you in this bed.'

She stood up and faced him, inwardly uncertain, her eyes never leaving his, then dropped the gown behind her and really for the first time, stood before him, completely naked, flaunting her insecurities, trusting him. He felt his face tighten and he held out a supporting hand.

'Come on.' He patted the bed. 'We've got lots to talk about.'

She climbed in beside him and felt his arm around her shoulder.

'What an extraordinary day. Certainly made me stop and think, although I still feel rather confused. But maybe that's good. Anyway, it's given me an idea Sam. So, come and join me. Here, between my legs. With your back to me.'

'Really?'

'Yes. Come on.'

She clambered awkwardly between his legs.

'I can feel him. I won't hurt him?'

'No. Let me tuck him out of the way. There.'

'This is cosy.'

She leant back against his chest, felt his warmth, her hair just above his chin, where occasionally it brushed his mouth and cheek in an itchy kiss. Over her shoulder, he could see the length of her body, down to her red-painted toes. Her nipples seemed darker and were already pointing in anticipation.

'They're bigger now than I remember.' He ran the fingertips of his right hand delicately across, in a slow glissando, feeling their tip spring back each time.

'They've had a lot of attention.'

She nestled against him, turned her head to one side and he knew that she had closed her eyes.

'This is *so* comfortable.'

'I love your tits.'

She smiled to herself. He had said that so many times now; but she was always delighted and surprised.

'Pity they're rather small, Alex.'

'Not important. Anne Boleyn was small apparently, but she did OK with her little duckies… for a while at least.'

He reached around and filled both hands – fingers and palms delighting in that unique softness. He held her quietly for a moment, without moving or speaking and then opened his hands and cupped beneath her, feeling their weight, their measure, before squeezing them against her, his large hands containing her, nipples almost peeking, dusky pink and firm, between his long fingers. Now, they moved, high and round and compact, like the limit of some décolletage; the gypsy girl who caught the eye of Frans Hals, and now, as he re-opened his hands, a bare-breasted Tudor courtier or maybe Renoir's Gabrielle or now, partly hidden, she became *une Parisienne*, whose eighteenth-century nipples, barely covered, might appear *'par hazard'* from a deep breath or a sudden calculated dip of her body.

He began to feel her body roll in unison with the movement of his hands and fingers. He held her, firmly and confidently, and as he moved her soft flesh upwards again, a first shiver slid deliciously down her body and disappeared into her. She gave a little start, a little short sigh. It was very tiny, but he noticed and began to stroke upwards, with the sides of both hands, a finger just catching her, there and there, as if by accident. She jumped and shivered again, and again, and her composure began to drift away, behind closed eyes. Sunny open fields; hot saturated dunes; warm, wicked zephyrs whispering her flesh alert. His fingertips were now flickering across her, one after the other, catching, surprising, taunting, and then suddenly, he stopped, felt her relax, almost in relief, and his large hands held her again, gently moulding.

She waited, silently, knowing that soon his fingertips would reach for her again, but his palms left her body, left her untouched for a second and she held her breath and waited tensely. Then, and with no warning, she felt his fingers begin to roll very gently, gently; now stronger, sending a fusillade of shocks ricocheting downwards, rippling onwards, along mysterious channels, then bursting powerfully inside her. Her body rippled; lime-sharp alert, pushed back against his, her own hands opening and closing, stretching like a cat, head moving slowly left to right; right to left. Telling him. Without words. He the conductor, now orchestrating this symphony in sensuality and sensation. Now tiny notes; pianissimo, drifting gently; now jumping suddenly, sforzando, shock after shock racing down her body, collecting in thick hungry pools, darkening her blood; now building, building, forte; and then once more, da capo. Oh, no more. No more.

She moved her hand and began to stroke strongly between her legs. He watched, excited by her unexpected abandon, now himself pressing stiffly against her hot back. He remembered and began to roll his fingers constantly, vigorously, feeling her reaction. *Jesus Sam. Jesus.* Nothing else would formulate in his mind.

Samantha thought she was moaning; her breath was coming so quickly. There were no words and her thoughts collided madly. *Don't stop Alex. Please don't. Don't stop. So wrong* as she struggled in desperate need, fingers still stroking, strongly, accurately, faster and then suddenly… stop… body raised rigid, words strangled, no breath for an eternity, then… a long rasping gasp of shivering release, head rolling, now mewing tiny sounds. Alex continued to gently stroke and squeeze as she drifted away.

Alex sat quite still, not daring to move, hands still holding her, amazed at what he had just witnessed. This other Samantha. This other woman, so charged with passion. She appeared now to be unconscious or asleep, but he knew she had simply retreated to some inner private world, a long-neglected place. They remained still for a long time. Slowly, he realised that the sound of the bedside clock ticking had returned.

She fell from his lap and lay on her side, across his thigh, one arm stretched out, eyes still closed. He looked down at her slim, worn body and noticed a line in her hair, near the scalp, where her hair had parted, revealing a light pink where the colour had retreated towards white. How ironic that nature should remove the bright colours of youth, leave the marks of toil and endeavour and yet inside her throbbed a nuclear reactor, hardly used.

'Alex. Can't move.' Her words were mumbled, as though she was talking in her sleep. There was a long pause. 'What about you?'

'Me?'

'Mm.' She opened her eyes. 'You. You must want to, now… don't you?'

It had been a public library, rigid with silence and musty with the odour of old print and paper. Around him, he had sensed knowledge and understanding stacked there, and had felt at home, although daunted by the millions of words that lay dormant, waiting to be sparked into life. In the middle of all of this, he had found it. Maybe by chance. Maybe by fate. He didn't remember a lurid title or cover but it *had* opened easily to *that* page. Perhaps he had been guided there by other needy eyes and fingers who had read and then re-read, so that now it opened readily for the next hungry soul. Many of the pages were still crisp and clean but this one was limp and slightly grey in one top corner. He had come back to the library many times to change schoolboy books but also anxious to find and read this passage again and again. His heart had thumped at the prospect, had felt dismayed when it was missing and had felt hot and strange and certain that he was being watched, embarrassed at being caught, incredulous that such sentences existed, reassured that they did, that maybe he was normal, and always returning for his next fix.

Now, he had little memory of its content. Now, it would probably seem very mild but back then that limp page had been so sexually charged; a red-hot phallus, burning like a beacon in a grey repressed world. Much of it he had not understood but one phrase had stuck with him. *'He would play her like some exquisite musical instrument and satisfy her.'* Then, as a schoolboy, he had no idea what that meant or how to achieve it, but it had remained in his mind for all those decades, waiting patiently, until now. Right now.

'That would be lovely, but at the moment, it doesn't seem so important. It really doesn't.'

She turned quickly and looked up at him, a look of surprise on her face.

'I thought it was *so* important for a man?'

'Well, it is incredibly powerful, especially when you are younger. Then it certainly took over my life. Was all I ever thought about. I just walked about following what felt like a permanent hard-on. It was an obsession that stirred me constantly. An all-consuming driving urge. I felt like a permanently on-duty pole vaulter. How I ever got anything done, passed exams, I'll never know. I suppose, looking back, I was lucky to have had that other powerful creative urge to help balance things and rid myself of so much bubbling energy.'

Samantha suddenly felt herself dancing again before the full moon. Felt that strange drawing urge. She moved and sat next to him.

Suddenly, Alex started to laugh aloud. 'You know, I can remember going to dances – ballroom dances. Don't look so surprised. We all did. Where all the girls arched their bodies away from you to avoid rubbing against this throbbing demon, which insisted on preceding you and which you couldn't control. That must have been a weird sight. All those pretty bums sticking out. And it ached.'

'With desire?'

'No. Bloody hurt.'

Samantha suddenly recalled wet, dreary lunchtimes at school, sitting in the gym, out of the rain, pink cheeked, waiting excitedly for 'the book' to be handed round. 'Read pages hundred and thirty-one and two. My God, wish my Terry was here.' Only she, like many others, didn't have a spotty-faced Terry and had to wait until the sanctuary of home and bathroom to rub the ache away.

'That's why tantra itself has started to make sense, Sam.'

'Go on.'

'Well, it's that same driving urge that compelled men to take over. To release that. Literally. For procreation, I guess and sanity.'

'Leaving women behind.'

'Leaving women behind. Well, until fairly recently. Certainly our generation. Which worried me, until now.'

'What worried you darling?'

'I think that what I'm trying to say is that although I want you all the time, I'm no longer that driven young man. My powers are beginning to wane as they do with everybody – well, every man at least – and you think, OK, that was fun while it lasted, and look around for your slippers.'

'And now.'

'Now, my hot babe. Now, I'm beginning to realise that I got it all wrong.'

'Really. Now I'm confused. So, what's changed?'

'What's changed? Well, now that frantic urgency has diminished, we are no longer being driven, are we? *Now* we can be in charge. *Now*, we have choice.'

'Choice?'

'Yes, I've just realised that I don't always *have* to come anymore. Unless *I* want to. Unless *we* want to. When you think about it, that was so selfish, wasn't it? Left you in second place. Remember what he said at the tantra festival? That he hadn't ejaculated for decades, and the audience's reaction. I don't pretend to fully understand but that statement alone must open up all sorts of alternatives and possibilities. Like just now.' He took her hand in his. 'That was amazing Sam, and I didn't even need an erection, which I must say is a huge relief. Never ever thought I would say *that*. But now I can focus on pleasuring you for example. Satisfying you maybe.'

He heard the word ringing jubilantly around that dark musty library in his mind. 'I never realised the enormous satisfaction, simply knowing that I can, that I have just done so. That was extraordinary Sam. It's such a privilege being allowed into your world. Being able to experience such a powerful and intimate outpouring. So amazing. Feels so close. So protective in a funny sort of way. I never realised it could be more than just a physical sensation. It was very moving.'

Samantha listened in silence transfixed by this unexpected outburst. She felt her emotions beginning to build unsteadily inside her.

'Oh Alex. I don't know what to say. I feel… well, rather embarrassed at my, well, you know, outburst. Sounds so out of control. So inappropriate. So young.'

'No. You are the Goddess. Exactly as they said.'

'Hardly. Not at this age Alex. Surely. Are you being serious?'

'I am and age obviously has nothing to do with it. I've realised that all those grey-haired old ladies, playing bingo and knitting bootees for the next grandchild, aren't watching afternoon TV after all. Oh no. They're all tuned in to a porn channel, sound turned down, vibrators hidden in the linen basket.'

She laughed. 'Alex, you are outrageous.' She squeezed his hand and they sat silent for a while.

'One or two people have told me how well I look,' she mused.

'I bet. The light in your eyes. The hint in your smile. The way you walk.'

She looked at him, still unconvinced.

'You know Sam, I'm beginning to feel like some innocent who, at an advanced age and after much study, has just realised that the world isn't flat after all, that I got it completely wrong and some vast, endless possibility is lying open in front of me, and I really don't quite know what to do with it.'

'We'll face it together darling.'

He sat quietly, aware that other issues would also have to be negotiated in this new non-flat world and wondered if he was brave enough to reveal his inner emotions, to be that vulnerable, to ask for that much trust. He turned to look at her. She would. She was brave. Braver than him. Maybe didn't know it yet. He remembered how he had struggled at the festival. Remembered how easily she had slipped into it.

'Have you noticed how erotic talking can be? Just words?'

She nodded. 'Oh yes. Love it when you talk to me.'

'Go on then Sam. Say it.'

'Say what?'

'You know. Say it in your posh voice.'

She looked at him, bemused. 'Say what?'

'Say fuck.'

'Oh. Why?'

'Just say it. Go on.'

'Do I have to?'

'Go on.'

She released a long breath. Then breathed in. 'Fuck.'

He smiled. 'You're not certain.'

'I'm not?'

'Like a child with a forbidden word. Slightly hesitant.'

'Might get my legs slapped '

'I like you to say it.'

'Why?'

'Excites me.'

'Gives me a thrill too.'

'Why is that?'

'Breaks the rules I suppose.'

'Yeah. Those long-ago rules.'

'You've changed so much Alex.'

'I have?'

'I used to think at first, that you were the wild eccentric professor spouting loads of crazy stuff to keep people away. Massing facts around you like a wall. Just emerging from time to time to hopefully want to fuck me. There. I've said it. Again.'

'Samantha. Really. See. See what I mean. You would never have used such language back then.' He laughed. 'And, I was never a professor. Should have been of course.'

'The language feels right. Honest and liberating and special.'

'Your parents would have had a fit… I don't hide away, do I?'

'Not now. You share things with me more. The pain and the anguish as well as the fun. That makes you a real man.' She paused. 'Henry would never do that. Poor stiff-upper-lip Henry.' For a moment, she looked lost. 'You know, I think Henry would have had a seizure, if I had ever taken the initiative. But you wouldn't Alex. Would you?'

He grinned. 'The thought makes me very horny. For some reason, it's very, very naughty.' His bare feet waggled at the end of the bed.

'Strange isn't it and rather sad. I was brought up to believe that was the man's role and I was supposed to lie back and conjure a shopping list and consider the price of tea. What a waste Alex. What a waste.'

'Same for all of us. Just products of our time.'

'But it makes me so angry. All that ignorance and segregation and control. We never stood a chance.'

'I know. Look at the disaster with poor Rachel. Treated like a criminal. I still feel so bad about that. Should have done more. Think about it all the time.'

'You did your best, my sweet,' and she squeezed his hand. They paused again.

'OK. Now you say it Alex.'

'Why?'

'Just say it.'

'Fuck.'

'No. Say it properly. Say it to me. As though you mean it.'

He leaned towards her. Looked directly into her eyes. Face set. 'I want to fuck you hard… here… now.'

'Oh Alex.'

'Do you like that?'

'Oh yes. Makes me feel wanted and cherished and attractive… and sort of complete.'

'Even though it's a swear word.'

'Oh, it's much more than that. It's so versatile for a start. Violent. Yes. Angry or dismissive. Exasperating or exciting. So versatile and strong. So meaningful.'

'Better than the L word then?'

'Much better.'

'Why?'

'The L word is so lazy. Simply brings things to a hazy conclusion.'

'Hazy?'

'Yes. Most people wouldn't be able to explain it to each other. So, it's an easy option. The deal is done. Contract signed. There is nowhere else to go. So, you don't have to bother too much.'

'Go on.'

'Without it, you have to develop and grow and work hard. Seek new levels. New understandings. New awarenesses. Never take each other for granted. Communicate all the time. Be honest. So, whenever you feel the L word bubbling up in your breast, you need to stop and think exactly what it is you are trying to say. Then, there is no limit.'

'Limit?'

'Yes. The L word acts as a handy limit but it's also vague and slippery and mythical and brittle. One moment, all-consuming and the next shattered into a million pieces. So really—'

'Really?'

'Really, I don't want to hear it.'

'No?'

'No. It would feel like a full stop.'

'The end of the sentence?'

'The end of the book. Nothing left to come.'

'You could always get another book.'

'Don't want another book. Want to keep reading this one.'

'You are amazing, Sam.'

'You let me be.' She reached and took his hand. Said nothing for a while.

'I need a drink. How about you Sam?'

'No thanks.'

Alex climbed from the bed and stood for a moment, his back to her, stretching, arms in the air. His naked body looked rangy and worn, pale save for the marks of the sun at the back of his neck and forearms and the occasional blue flecks that broke through the skin on his legs. She could see the brown patch on his crown where his hair had retreated and red points on each elbow as if the bone was trying to push through. That thought made her shiver and afraid for him and she pushed it away. Instead, she saw long, dark hair tumbling down strong flesh and with a pang of envy, knew why Rachel had wanted him so much.

She reached down and pulled the duvet back over her.

9

Exhibition and Edmund

'YOU REMEMBER FROBISHER STREET?' She looked up at him.

'Frobisher Street?'

'Yes, where the gallery was… is.'

'Oh, that Frobisher Street. Oh yes, of course I remember. Didn't we talk about it? I certainly remember *you* there.' He waved his hands descriptively through the air. 'Glorious cascade of red hair, pale smooth shoulders and milky white breasts. I remember that alright.'

'Well, that was then…'

'Oh, come on Sam. You've got lovely tits. I love your tits.' He sat beside her and ran one hand gently over her. She pretended not to notice.

'Well, if you could just concentrate for a moment.' He stopped. 'It's become much larger and quite important now, and what do you think?'

He shook his head.

'They've asked if I will loan the Twombly… for an exhibition… and I've said yes, and—'

'How did they know you had it?'

'Oh, I don't know. Henry I guess. It doesn't matter. Listen. Listen to the best bit.'

'Which is?'

'In return… for guess what?'

'I don't know Sam. A load of money?'

'No. Not money. For an exhibition of your work!'

'What!'

'Isn't that great news? It is great news isn't it Alex? You are pleased?'

Alex placed both hands over his mouth and stared into the distance.

'An exhibition. Oh my goodness.' The worlds muffled between his palms. 'I never thought…' He turned to face her. 'How did they know? About me?'

'I showed them, when they came here to see the Twombly. That was OK, wasn't it?'

He nodded.

'They were delighted Alex. Really enthusiastic. Very complimentary. And it's not for another three months so you've got loads of time. Are you excited?'

'Bit overwhelmed to be honest. I never thought…'

'And at the Frobisher…'

'Yes. Where it all started.'

'Is that where it started Alex?'

'Yes. It did for me Sam. Soon as I saw you there.'

'You sure that wasn't just lust?'

'Well, of course it was.'

'So why didn't you say something? Do something.'

'You were married remember and a rich bird to boot. Why should you be interested in a scruffy, drunken, rude pseudo artist like me?'

'Oh, I can't imagine. I really can't.'

'So, what do you think?'

Alex offered the two halves of a bedraggled cream-coloured suit hanging from his fingertips.

'Looks like you just found it lost in a corner.'

'Well, almost. It had fallen down the back of the wardrobe, next to my sketching boots.'

'Sketching boots?' She looked at his intense face and thought better of enquiring any further.

'Is that linen Alex?'

'Don't know. Is it important?' He looked from the suit to Samantha and back again. 'You don't like it.'

'Well it needs cleaning and pressing, *and* will it fit you?'

'Yes. I bought it just before I retired when I thought I was going to get the Head of Department job.' He paused, then grinned. 'I didn't.'

'And what is going with it?'

'I've got that shirt in a nice shade of Mafia black and the bow tie. You've seen that. You remember? You liked that.'

'You *were* walking around stark naked at the time except for that lurid bow tie.'

'Surprised you noticed it if I was naked.'

She giggled.

'I love it when you giggle like that. Like a naughty little girl.'

'I never used to.'

He handed the suit to her. 'You'll sort it Sam, won't you? Gotta go. Things to do.'

'What about shoes?'

But he was gone.

It had been a very busy time. Alex had worked day and night, finishing drawings and producing new paintings, organising framing, discussing publicity. Samantha became aware of his acute attention to detail, of his insistence that everything was done exactly to his instructions, heard him shouting at those that couldn't keep up with him and realised just how important this was to him. She also had the linen suit and black shirt cleaned and pressed and hoped and prayed that they would indeed fit, for he was in no mood for such trivial details. Of shoes, there were no sign. He never thought to ask what she would be wearing.

It rained during the day before the private view evening, leaving the air damp and uncertain and the streets rather empty. Alex constantly looked through the picture windows like a puppy dog wanting to go out to play but uncertain of the weather and sniffing for blue sky and some warmth. 'Alright for Twombly,' as he peered yet again through the window. Seeing the painting away from its normal berth had been strange; equally disturbing had been the notice thanking a Mrs S. Reagan for kindly lending it. Alex had felt a strange tug of jealousy at the link to her past.

During the preparation, he had occasionally left her side for a heated debate over some detail, which she barely understood but he always returned looking slightly sheepish and she had whispered encouragingly in his ear. She was also a little concerned but not wholly surprised at the number of attractive women who lingered at his elbow, drawn in by the enthusiasm and charm radiating from him. Not for the first time she saw the sexual magnetism that he possessed even if he wasn't particularly aware of it himself. Samantha, ever practical, had spent time with the press, ensuring that they were fully aware of his forthcoming exhibition.

'Come and sit down Alex. There's hours to go yet.'

Reluctantly he left the window, contemplated a large armchair, hitched up his trousers and delicately lowered himself, looking very uncomfortable. Samantha's eye was drawn towards the black and white trainers that he had decided would complete his outfit.

'Alex.' Her voice sounded alarmed.

'What's wrong?'

'Your trainers.'

'I like them.'

'You're not wearing socks.'

He stuck his footwear out before him. 'Oh no, I'm not. Must have forgotten.' He drew his feet back again. 'Doesn't matter. Too late now.'

She turned to reply but thought better of it.

*

They arrived at the gallery about an hour early, almost empty save for the assistant director and a gaggle of disinterested waitresses, wearing the obligatory black and looking for somewhere to have a smoke. The entrance was large, cool, geometric and echoed slightly. Even empty, it had a presence of its own and Alex walked around for a while, appreciating the concrete symphony in white, greys and highlight black, and the excited tingle it gave him, like a seaman looking out across the ocean or an aviator scanning the blue sky. *This is where I belong.* Around him, the blank white walls waited quietly and patiently and, as he walked, his footsteps clipped slightly on the polished floor. He stopped for a moment, stooped to touch its coolness and felt the urge to lie on his back to feel it seeping into his body. Samantha watched him and felt his joy. He turned and grinned at her and held out his hand. Together, they climbed the stairs to the smaller gallery on the floor above.

The door was tall and heavy and they both pushed it open, stepped inside and stopped.

'Oh Alex.'

'Do you like it?'

She shook her head, unable to reply. She had seen the drawings and paintings before, piled into a portfolio, taped to a wall, half completed, but now, they lined the walls, mounted and framed, perfect and complete. They both stood for a moment, hand in hand and in silence.

The ceiling slanted up at an angle, to the highest point, where clear windows allowed in natural light that flooded the white walls. Through the windows the sky was framed, appearing to be another exhibit. Above their heads, a series of lamps hidden behind large diffused panels offered a soft light that bathed the exhibits in a gentle embrace. Within this setting, the work waited and Samantha could see its quality even more than before. Alex had chosen a portrait of Rachel as the main feature for the publicity, even though he had also included several pieces of Samantha in the exhibition. She had felt thrilled and concerned at the same time. 'They are good enough, aren't they? The ones of me? You're not just doing it because…?' Alex quickly reassured her that only the best work would be exhibited, regardless of the sitter. The possible comparison between the young and beautiful Rachel and herself was no longer an issue in her mind. She had felt strangely comfortable.

'Alex. This is so exciting.'

'Let's hope they all turn up.'

'They will. They will. Rain's stopped now. Going to be a nice evening. A spectacular evening.'

Soon the first guests started to arrive, and Alex noted with satisfaction how the gallery staff swung into action, smiling, welcoming, offering a glass of champagne and a programme of the exhibits. Just inside the main entrance, Alex had placed an introductory panel outlining the background to the exhibition and his personal ethos, neatly printed and presented. He was pleased that his visitors were taking the time to read it. He was tempted to go and explain it to them but resisted. *They can always ask if they want to. That's what Sam would say.* Now the pregnant calm of the gallery was punctuated by an ever-growing buzz.

'Hey, Alexander, you old bastard. How are you? And who is this…? My, it's the beautiful lady. Never forget a face, especially one I've painted. So how did you two…?'

The man beaming before them was tall and gaunt, with long grey hair tied back in a small pony tail. A white collarless shirt enveloped him.

'Edmund. For goodness' sake. What are *you* doing here?'

The two men embraced with hearty back slaps. Edmund then turned, smiled at Samantha, took one hand, gently kissed it and still holding it, half turned towards Alex.

'I have no idea why such a beautiful woman should have anything to do with an old reprobate like you.'

Samantha gently withdrew her hand.

'And such a lovely dress; gorgeous colour; love the cowl back. McQueen?'

'Thank you. It's Ralph Lauren and the colour is… cranberry.'

'Sorry, still hasn't introduced us. Always was a rude bugger.'

'Samantha. I'm Samantha.'

'Of course. I remember now,' and he tapped the side of his head. 'I'm Edmund.'

'Yes. I remember you. The portrait painter.'

'Indeed. And what happened to my wonderful painting?'

'It's safe. My ex-husband still has it.'

'Ex… husband?'

Alex shuffled uncomfortably.

'Look, I'm going to circulate for a while. I can see some of my neighbours have just arrived. I'm sure you boys have a lot to talk about. Nice to meet you again Edmund.'

Edmund turned his head slightly and bowed. Then turned back.

'You lucky bastard. How did you manage that? Are you two…?'

'Manage what?'

'Samantha you idiot.'

'Oh, it's a long story. Come on, I need a drink.'

They moved outside to the small bar area for some more champagne and stood next to the wall from where they could look down to the entrance below.

'Hey, this is good stuff. Bit upmarket for you, isn't it?'

'Oh, Sam organised it all. Everything.'

'I'll say it again. You *are* a lucky bastard.'

Alex smiled thinly, raised his eyebrows and they both took a long drink.

'Anyway, I was thinking about you, you know, even before I heard of the exhibition. Great work by the way. You always had far too much talent. Not fair on the rest of us.'

'You did OK Edmund.'

He shrugged his shoulders. 'Maybe. No, I met someone. Quite out of the blue. Someone from back then. Busty.

Spanish. Italian extraction maybe. Guess who?' He grinned. 'Chased after you even when you were with Rachel. How is she by the way? Rachel. Do you ever hear from her?'

Alex's stomach kicked.

'No. Nothing. Not a word. She simply disappeared.'

'Tragedy that.' He placed a hand on Alex's arm. Both men were silent for a moment. Edmund took a sip of champagne. 'Great pity you know. Never even got the chance to paint her. What a painting that would have been eh? Wonderful body, well you would have known all about that of course.' He paused. 'Does Samantha know… about you and Rachel?'

'Well Rachel is over there on that wall. Yes, Samantha knows.'

They both stood in silence again, while the past plucked at their minds.

'You were so good together you know.' Edmund moved slightly closer, dark eyes soft with concern, voice lower. 'Apart from the rages. My God she had a temper. The fiery redhead eh?' They both smiled. Alex shook his head silently, anxious now to change the subject.

'So, who did you see? Not Stephanie was it? Sounds like her.'

'Yes, of course. Our Steph. Still a randy thing. Bumped into her in a bar in Wardour Street – beautiful barman, beautiful – anyway there she was, displaying most of her chest as she was always inclined to do. Not so nice at this age you know. Can't say she looked too well but asked after you in her own caustic way and I told her about the exhibition.'

'She's not coming I hope.'

'Doubt it. Not your best fan.'

'And she didn't mention Rachel?'

'No, old mate, not a word. Not a word.'

The two men stood quietly together, drink in hand, as they had done so many times in the past. Edmund finished his glass with a flourish and put both hands on Alex's shoulders.

'OK old chum. Great exhibition. Back to your Samantha before she thinks we've run off together.' His dark eyes twinkled mischievously. 'Anyway, I fancy a quiet tête-à-tête with that gorgeous creature,' pointing towards the gallery's young assistant director. 'Come and visit me. Same place. Been too long old mate. Promise?'

*

Many people came up to Alex to congratulate him. Told him of their own artistic ambitions yet to be achieved and those of their children and grandchildren and friends of friends. Somebody asked if he would give a talk at their school, a librarian enquired about a poster for the local library and a few wanted to commission him to complete a portrait but not too expensive. Alex calmly allowed such verbal flotsam to drift away, wallowing in the rosy thrill that came from showing his work to the world, albeit a small part of it, plus his old friend's praise and too many glasses of Veuve Clicquot. From time to time, he bumped into Samantha, who told him it was going quite brilliantly and that she had to dash to catch somebody else before they left.

Finally, Edmund kissed Samantha delicately on both cheeks, whispered in her ear, watched her nod a reply, waved vigorously to Alex, turned and was gone.

Alex sat down heavily and viewed the scene before him. The pristine order and expectation that had greeted him earlier had now lapsed into gentile disarray. Empty bottles were being noisily cleared away, together with the remains of any food, into black plastic bags, along with any remaining crumpled programmes. The polite smiles of staff had changed into the keen expression of home-going and a few were bold enough even to glance at their watches. The few guests still straggling said goodnight and disappeared onto the dark streets. *Just like fucking life. Starts off with such hope.* Finally, only Alex and Samantha and a few staff were left. She bent and took off her shoes, holding them in her lap.

'That was amazing Alex.'

'Yes, it was. Very successful. You must be very pleased.' The voice came from just across the gallery floor, from the red lips of the young assistant director, now checking the clear-up. 'The feedback has been very positive. I think there will be a lot of interest from the public over the next few weeks. Perhaps we should be thinking of a follow-up?'

Samantha beamed at both men.

*

'Can't sleep. There're a million thoughts running around my brain, madly, and… I think I'm slightly… pissed.'

'Not surprised, the amount of champagne you consumed.'

He looked across, a wry look at Samantha, sitting up in bed, glasses on, reading, wearing a white T-shirt. He could clearly see her shape through the material. He looked away. *Can't settle. Feeling really rather horny. That's Sam's fault. Her rear swaying through her posh frock. Lovely arse. Bigger now, different but better really. Not some neat, just off the production line, junior-type arse but a confident, self-assured, this is me, been around, arse. Bit like a veteran. At a memorial. Yeah, OK, old, grey, lined but still upright and carrying a chest full of bleedin' medals. Been there. Done it. And then there's*

Stephanie's tits of course. Now there's a bountiful memory. She didn't have any medals. Would have needed an awful lot to cover her. Never had a sense of proportion did Steph. Always a bit excessive. What a cow… Wasn't Sam amazing? Did all that for me. Just for me. He glanced at her again, emotions welling up in his chest. *Oh dear, that's the Widow for you. Too many glasses. Edmund's favourite you know. Good to see the old bugger again. Bugger. That's quite funny. My legs are jumping. All over the place. I'm going to have a headache. I know it. And I feel a bit yuk.*

'How many paintings did I sell?'

'None. They weren't for sale. Remember? But you did have four or five offers.'

'Oh yeah. That's right. What you reading?'

'The tantra book again. It's fascinating.'

'We're not going there again, are we?'

'Maybe.' She stopped reading and smiled at him. 'Don't you want to?'

Need the loo. Again. He stumbled out of bed, using the wall for support.

'You alright darling?'

'Yeah. Yeah. Need a drink.'

He drank the water greedily. Wiped his lips with a towel, moved to the toilet and splashed noisily. *Here I am. Fine figure of a man. Stark naked. With all of this.* He waggled his right hand. The acid reflux came up into the back of his throat. He swallowed uncomfortably, reached for the glass again, took more water, pulled the toilet seat down and sat heavily upon it. *She is amazing. Changed so much. Ironic, isn't it? When she was so much younger and beautiful… and she was, she really had less than she has now. Not money. Loads of that I expect. But the other day, when she was leaning back against me. My goodness.*

What an explosion. So exciting and I wasn't expecting it. It was almost scary. But I want more. Want to share more. And this is only the beginning. Wonder if I can do that? Be that vulnerable? That open? That sharing? He stood, took another sip of water, flushed the toilet and washed his hands.

Alex stood at the bottom of the bed, facing Samantha. His mind had cleared slightly and he felt more composed, even though his stomach was looping the loop. She looked up at him and removed her glasses. She was just about to open her mouth.

'Take it off.'

She looked at him curiously.

'The T-shirt. Take it off.'

She said nothing but pulled the shirt over her head. Her magazine fell to the floor. Neither reacted. He could clearly see that her nipples already knew what was to come.

'Slide down.'

He lifted the duvet at her feet, clambered beneath it, reached for the inside of each knee and gently moved them apart. He did this in one single movement to deny any query.

'Alex?'

He felt hot and slightly suffocated and burst upwards, shedding the cover and emerging red-cheeked between her open legs. He did not look at her, but slid his arms under her thighs, his hands appearing above her like a conjurer's trick. He reached for and found her, held her gently, between both thumbs and forefingers, changing his hold like an engineer adjusting a delicately balanced piece of fine machinery. She watched this theatre, intrigued now by his apparent expertise, never realising his inexperience and concern. He felt her tension and knew that words were about to arrive. Questioning. Maybe negative. He moved decisively and any words were choked by a shocked gasp, as he ran his tongue, strongly upwards, feeling a soft warmth, brushing the spiky hair that still just surrounded her. He looked up along the length of her body. It appeared to have become strangely rejuvenated, the years slipped away. *How odd.* His eye caught her eye. She looked surprised, mouth open slightly.

'Is this alright?'

She did not reply but lay back, closed her eyes, head to one side. Suddenly she was very tiny, seated with rows of others. A very long way above her towered a figure with dark, anonymous features, filling the ceiling. It was a woman, of that she was sure, for her voice was high and reedy and powerfully penetrating. All around came the smell of ink and chalk dust. Words whipped from the dark mouth like a hailstorm, each syllable leaving red pock marks on the faces of the children below. The Samantha child pulled her grey shapeless school skirt down to meet her long socks and squeezed between her legs as hard as possible to lose the hot abomination that lived there. 'Nice girls don't. It's not nice.'

She jumped as the tongue continued its warm, wet journey; as gentle fingers squeezed her in some sort of harmony. The dark figure popped like a fragile soap bubble. The sound reverberated down the long passages of her mind and vanished.

'God. Do that again.' Her head began to roll and her fingers now gripped the bed sheet.

He licked harder, in the hope that he might just repeat his previous success, but in front of his mouth was just a wet, warm softness within which his tongue could distinguish few features with any accuracy.

'No. Higher. Yes. There. Oh my God.'

Individual pods of pleasure had begun to burst open within her like a distant storm at sea; hot humid rumbles, some way off, flashing in the dark distance, arriving haphazardly at first, each leaving a spluttering trace, initially fizzling and going out, but now increasing in intensity, no longer dying away, but beginning to pool as one; some vermilion, some sour lime, some indigo, some hot pink, flashing and bubbling, like some insane technicolour chemistry set, with electric blue shocks now joining in, sizzling downwards, now one, now another, now both, trembling, like sacred synapses, deep inside her, a void begging to be filled, building, building, hot and itchy, knowing that it could overflow and with it would pour away her control; that it could overwhelm her, leaving her naked and revealed and she didn't care.

She began to shake her head from side to side, as if this might halt or deny the process but the tongue continued, struggling to breathe, struggling to swallow but unable to stop.

The storm arrived directly above her and crashed down with a fury; her body, unable to breathe, incapable of coherent speech, lifted in rigid torment, waited, waited and then cried out savagely and strangely, body moving frantically against the thick air, breath gasping, legs shaking, like a drowning soul in a hot, heaving sea.

Alex continued to lick, now to soothe, now to ease her return. Then he stopped. Samantha had moved onto her side and was lying, eyes closed, apparently unaware of the world around her. He watched fascinated as she lay completely still for several minutes, watched as her eyelids flickered alive, almost reluctantly, watched as she began to focus on him again.

'What have you done to me?' She looked away and closed her eyes again. 'How old are you?'

He wiped his mouth with the back of his hand and grinned like a naughty child. 'You were amazing.'

She wondered what he meant.

They sat upright, next to each other, against the bedroom wall, crumpled pillows plumped up and supporting their backs. Her perfume struggled slightly against the faint odour of perspiration. They both sat naked now, holding weathered hands but slightly apart, their bodies hot and slightly sticky. A curtain moved against a window, just ajar. Samantha wondered if the neighbours or people walking past would have heard them.

'We could have a shower together.'

She turned to look at him, imagining the naughty boy smile that would indicate more than washing each other's backs. It was there. She felt grateful for his words, for the small smokescreen that now partly covered her discomfort and confusion at the force that she knew now bubbled inside her, and which he could unlock. It had always been him. She did not know why or how, but it had been, she realised, since that night at the gallery, so many years ago. It had pulsed somewhere deep inside her, but she had missed it, preferring tradition and convention and rosy emotion to raw instinct. And now, she felt drawn to talk to him; found it strangely erotic and liberating. Her thighs still trembled slightly and between, she throbbed.

'That was amazing Alex.'

'Oh yes.' He spoke with the authority of the complete amateur.

'Some men wouldn't like to do that. Am I right?'

'No. I guess not.'

'Why is that?'

'Oh, upbringing, ignorance certainly, old wives' tales, a taboo.'

'Taste?'

'What? Bad taste?'

'No. My taste. Was it unpleasant? I always wash you know.'

'No.' He laughed. 'No, not unpleasant at all. Warm and wet and slightly salty but no more than that. Although you nearly drowned me.'

She relaxed but Alex knew she hadn't finished.

'Have you done that before. You know… cunnilingus?' She pronounced the word awkwardly, almost in two halves but felt aroused at using such words, even more so in normal speech. Wondered if she had ever spoken that word before, felt slightly embarrassed but also excited, waiting for his response. Maybe he would push the boundaries even further, say something even more forbidden and take her on with him. She felt her body begin to stir again.

'I did some research once.'

'Oh… research.' *That's not what I want to hear. I want your dirty, dirty stories. Of you licking half the female population. I'm not jealous. Don't think I'm jealous. I just want to be… me.*

'Yes. Artists like Paul Avril, French, born about 1850, illustrated *Fanny Hill* and *De Figuris Veneris* of course. And Egon Schiele I suppose and Giulio Romano and the Karma Sutra, although that's more of an instruction manual. Oh loads. I forget now.'

'And did they excite you or was it only academic?' She had meant the words to sound interesting, relevant but somehow they decided against that and lingered and prodded him. She didn't see him flinch, but she felt it and rubbed his thigh to make it go away.

His mother was sitting in the tiny garden, keeping the sun away. Big straw hat that lifted slightly with the meagre puffs of breeze. Sunglasses that hid her gaze. He had been holding his book with both hands, trying not to tremble in front of them because it had been so heavy. 'Oh Alexander, you are so clever. Isn't he clever Daddy?' His father, still collared and tied, red faced, desperate to be back at his manicured desk. 'Very, I'm sure. Pity he can't do more than just read.'

'Sorry Sam.'

'No. It was me. Sorry. Very rude.' She held his hand with both of hers.

'No, you're right. We've said it before, I do hide behind all that academic garbage. But of course, it defined me for a very long time, gave me my status, my position. Hard to let go you know.'

'Yes, of course it is, and I'm a little envious of that.'

'Envious. Why?'

'I was only a mother and housewife.'

'Only? My goodness. Isn't that extremely important? I would say so.'

'Yes of course. And I would never change from being a mother. Never. But I never did anything just for me.'

There was a silence. It was Alex who broke it. 'But do you know what is even more scary?'

She shook her head.

'I'm beginning to forget it, that academic stuff. Lose it.'

'No, you're just filling up with new stuff, that's all.'

'Well, that was pretty new.'

'What?'

'What we just did.'

'Really?'

'Yes. Truth is, I've never done that before… not really. Certainly not like that. I had no real idea what to do. It was really just lick and hope.'

'My goodness Alex, then you are a natural. That was amazing. I have never experienced anything like that before.'

'Yes. You were rather wild.'

'Oh don't. You make me feel really embarrassed.'

'Don't be. You are a most sexually potent woman.'

'I didn't know Alex. Not like that. I really didn't.'

'Then we are good for each other. We match. Thank God I walked into that shop.'

'Yes. Thank God. But it has to work both ways. I need to give you pleasure as well.'

'But you do. You've been brave enough and trusting enough to allow me into something that is mind-blowingly powerful and intimate and if I'm honest a little scary, and that is an honour and a privilege. We could both be at home now, separately watching late night repeats for something to do.'

'Then we need to add to our repertoire.' She reached across for him, held him, gently, firmly; something she often did, as an act of comfort or reassurance or affection; as you would hold hands in the park. She carefully laid him down and then regarded him for a moment, head cocked to one side, face serious. 'He is beautiful.' She looked up at Alex for a moment, then back. 'So beautiful. He is you. Always you. I love him when he is small and quiet like now and I love him when he is full and hungry.' She seemed now to be speaking to herself, quite dreamily, with Alex as eavesdropper. Her tone changed. 'So, this is for you.' She smiled at him. 'Just for you. Plump up the pillows so you are comfortable and can watch.' She turned back, her voice lower. 'I know you like to watch. So do I.'

Alex looked downwards. Before, the situation would have worried him, made him tense as he doubted his ability to perform. It could require a great deal of mental clenching and maybe a desperate need for fantasy plus a considerable degree of hopeful friction. Now, it didn't seem to matter. He relaxed and waited for her gift.

Very, very slowly, she ran one red-tipped fingertip along him, stopped and then bent forward with a series of tiny kisses, each punctuated by a word known only to her. The magic stirred him.

'I know you don't always come.' Her words had a strange, soft, hypnotic quality and were not meant for reply or debate.

'Sorry about that.' She ignored him and continued.

'And I know what tantra says, but *this*,' she stroked him again, several times, gently but more meaningfully, '*this* is a very, very, delicious cock; a special cock and right now, he needs a lot of attention.'

Alex listened. Intrigued at her words. Words he had never heard her say before.

She leant forward and licked with a soft, warm tongue. Alex jumped. She turned towards him. 'Did I hurt you?' He shook his head. She turned back to her dream. 'No, of course not. I wouldn't hurt my lovely, lovely cock.' She sat up, head to one side, eyes fixed on her stroking fingers, as if it were a sleeping kitten before her. 'Delicious cock. I love my cock.'

She felt safe. She had never been able to act like this before. In the past, she would have played the part determined by the man. It was for him to decide. For her to receive. There had been no sense of sharing or surrogacy. Alex watched fascinated at this strange, erotic ritual and gulped hard imagining what was to come.

She kicked the duvet vigorously to the floor, as if it were an irritant and knelt between his legs, breasts hanging like a she-wolf. He reached for them, excited by their jutting need but she gently pushed his hand away. 'This is for you. Lie still.' He laid back, eyes closed, feeling her hand holding him whilst a soft tongue continued to explore and wisps of her floating hair brushed his body, like a cloud of tiny fingertips.

The irony wasn't lost on him. Fifty years ago, this would have been all over by now. Blush faced. Apologetic. You simply refuse to believe that it will ever change and certainly not for the better. *Oh my God.* He thrust upwards with an involuntary gasp as her hot mouth finally covered him. He looked up but could only see the shape of her spine curving towards her gleaming buttocks, her hair shielding the steady movement of one hand and mouth.

He could hear words or parts of words, muffled, that he couldn't comprehend. Was she talking to him? He raised his head. He wanted to be logical, wanted to encourage, tell her the impact of her actions but her whispers – still primitive, mysterious, visceral – ignored him as she read his body, every quiver, every pulse, every shudder. Now, *his* control began to slip away, replaced with speechless sensation as every downward stroke issued showers of liquid sparks, followed by a return that went on and on. She continued. Now seeking, now lingering and teasing. Now stopping, waiting, listening to his breathing. Now encouraging with little sounds from her throat. Now waiting and then plunging suddenly. He realised that he could hear another sound, much lower, and realised it was coming from him and that he was now gripping the bedclothes in his fists.

'Lovely cock,' she whispered. As if it was the family pet. 'Lovely, lovely cock.' She stopped, but still held him, spoke urgently. 'Look. Look at him now.'

Alex looked up. Saw the glistening shape standing in her hand, recognised the need heavy in her face. He slumped back, unable now to control his upper body, his muscles paralysed with pleasure.

He wanted to tell her, but the words stuck at the back of his throat, would not form, lay there gasping. But by now, her mouth and fingers were so aware, gauging every change, every tremor, at the very congregation of his pleasure and now, she knew, the moment had come and her hand celebrated.

His body rose rigid, mouth open, eyes staring, hands pulling at mangled cotton and pleasure and sound poured from him, out of his control. He slumped back, ragged and spent, waiting for the hot ripples he knew so well to subside into a gradually diminishing pulsation, but she did not stop, did not even slow down, continued over flesh which was already on fire, where a billion nerve ends already screamed and scattered helter-skelter out of control.

Alex felt alarmed at the sensations now building and his body tried to push away, feet twisting a strange dance as they tried to escape the next unbearable red-hot razor wave to assault him. An erotic erethism. Where pleasure was screaming and tapping on the very shoulder of pain. He could stand it no more and reached for her arm. 'Stop. Please stop.'

Samantha lay beside him, head on his shoulder, his arm around her, his body still rippling, legs still jerking. His lower half gradually began to drift like some strange jellyfish at the whim of a warm, thick ocean. It might have drifted away had it not been for the hand that moored him. They lay there, not moving, not speaking; Alex empty of thoughts as the clock completed a full circle and then began another.

10

———

Bombshell

T HE DAY WAS bright and alert and full of expectation. In his breast, Alex felt energy bubbling like an itchy giggle looking for an excuse to break out and run loose. The reviews of the exhibition had been very positive in the local press and the gallery had phoned to confirm the numbers of people who had wanted to buy the work even though none had been for sale and to suggest further involvement. For the moment at least, Alex had become a local celebrity and although fame and fortune had simply not crossed his mind, now the idea seemed tempting. Samantha collected all the press cuttings, phoned all her friends and found herself beaming silently at him, much to his consternation.

'What *are* you looking at Sam?'

'Nothing.'

'For goodness' sake. They're only drawings.'

'I know.'

It was mid-morning when the phone rang.

'I'll get it Sam… Hallo.'

'Hallo. Is that Alexander James?'

It was a woman's voice, quite young he thought, but not one he recognised. He smiled to himself. *Another fan* and the itch ran into his mind and stood there, grinning, daring him. *Hey, it's that moment in the film when the shifty guy with tattoos and hard eyes says, 'and who wants to know?'* He resisted. 'Could be, but I suppose there *are* a lot of us, here and there… you know.'

'Yes, of course but I'm trying to contact Alexander James the artist. He would have taught. At a college?' The voice faltered slightly. 'Or maybe university?'

Alex felt a kick of curiosity. Fragments of faces zipped through his brain, trying to form, dissolving, reforming, but without success. 'Who is this?'

'Sorry to ask all these questions but it is important. Please don't hang up.'

Don't hang up?

'Are you selling something? If you are—'

'No, no. Not at all.' The voice dropped slightly. 'This is… personal.'

'Personal?'

'Yes. I …. just a moment please.'

There followed a long pause. Alex could hear indiscernible sounds. Rustling maybe, paper? Maybe just breathing? Suddenly and for no clear reason, he felt a pang of alarm.

'Hallo. Hallo.'

'Hallo. Were you born on Christmas Day, 1947? Were you? I really need to know.'

'What? What is this? Who are you?'

'Please. It's very important. Were you?'

'Well, yes, but why do you want to know?'

There was another long silence. For a moment, Alex thought she had gone but then her voice came back.

'I have something to tell you. Oh God this is not easy.'

'Is this about Fiona? My mother. Has something happened?'

'Your mother? Oh no. Not your mother. Well… sort of.'

'Sort of. What do you mean… sort of?'

There was another pause.

'My name… my name is Georgia… and I think I'm your daughter.'

'What!'

Around him the room suddenly reared up.

'I'm your daughter. Sorry.'

Alex stood speechless for a moment, trying to comprehend, then felt angry.

'If you think this is some sort of joke.'

'Oh no. Sorry. It's not a joke. Certainly not a joke. I realise this is completely out of the blue, but…'

Alex swallowed heavily. 'How do I know that…'

'Oh yes.'

He heard more rustling.

'Are you reading this?'

'Well yes. I'm so nervous. I might forget.'

There was another pause.

'I had a twin brother called Jak. We were both adopted. At birth.'

Alex pushed the phone away as if it might damage him further. He tried desperately to grasp her words, but they had already sliced into him, tearing holes in his mind. Any reason he might muster had scattered like startled fish in a dark, deep, icy pool. He tried to speak but the words stuck.

'Hallo. Hallo. Are you still there?'

'Yes. Jak.'

Memories slithered back. Memories and dreams that he had tried to forget. Empty grey corridors, hard seats, all bathed in screeching fluorescence. White coats pushing him away. The shivering stench of a dank alleyway and Rachel's anger, echoing shrilly. In his nostrils, the rot of fear and helplessness; in his mind, the awful magnitude. Trembling, he slipped slowly down the wall and sat hunched on the floor. *Jak and George went up the hill to fetch a pail of water. Jak fell down and George came tumbling after.*

'I'm sorry. I never meant to upset you.'

How could you, sweet Georgia.

'I'm OK. Just a bit of a shock. I never thought…'

'Of course. I'm sorry. Really am.'

'You know I often wondered. I really did. Thought there might be a vain hope. Maybe that's an excuse. Oh, I don't know.'

He spoke softly to the unknown voice in a strange, shared intimacy, as though the passing of most of a damaged life was immaterial, the pain of endless sleepless nights unimportant.

'Can we meet?'

'Well…'

'I've got some photos and a letter from my mother.'

'A letter?'

'Yes. From Rachel. Rachel Thomas.'

'Rachel?'

'Yes.'

'How is she?'

'She died. Yes, earlier this year I'm afraid.'

'Died?'

'Yes. Breast cancer.'

'No.' *Breast cancer. Oh no. No, that can't be, she had wonderful breasts. Some of the other girls had young pert breasts, perched high, almost uncertain, waiting to fledge. But Rachel's were full and heavy, meaningful, loaded with need and purpose, demanding strong hands.* He saw her for a moment, looking into that mirror, the one in the hallway; he, standing behind her, nose full of the perfume of her flame hair, his hands cupping the smooth, warm weight, she watching with that strange smile on her face – part curiosity, part desire, part pride. How could something so magnificent, so much of who she was – how could that – kill her? *I'm so sorry Rachel* and he bowed his head, covered his eyes, and breathed in and out heavily, just once. It seemed to take a very long time. He wiped a hand clumsily across his tense face and pulled the phone to him.

'Hallo. OK. Yes. Let's meet.'

'Are you sure?'

'Yes. I'm sure.'

'Thank you so much.'

Alex pulled a pen from his shirt pocket and wrote the details on his hand.

'You won't change your mind?'

'No, I'll be there.'

'That makes me very happy.'

He sat for a long time, looking into the distance and occasionally at the black scribble on his left hand. Eventually he hauled himself unsteadily to his feet. He felt very old and tired, but he knew where he had to go and silently he made his way to his studio. Inside he quietly closed the door and locked it. From the portfolio, he took drawings of Rachel, gently laid them on the floor and knelt before them. He knelt in silence for a long time, his thoughts churning inside him. Soon, sobs began to shake his aching body and tears pattered uncontrollably onto the young, hopeful images before him.

He knelt there for a long time, unaware of the world around him. It was the pain in his back and knees that made him move stiffly to the other side of the room, where he sat with his back to the wall, arms around his legs. *Georgia would be forty-eight now, same as Jak of course. Forty-eight. Such a long time ago and yet so fresh.* He tried to remember. Rachel had been angry. Very angry and her eyes had darkened fiercely in her pale face.

'You've got me pregnant.'

He had laughed. 'Wasn't only me you know,' but inside he was frightened.

'Well what the fuck are we going to do?' She always swore when angry or drunk and now when afraid. 'My parents will kill me. They'll make me give it away. They'll never speak to me again,' and she had turned away from him and wept.

How different things were then. The word 'bastard'. Such a terrible slur. A terrible weight to carry around with you forever, even though innocent. Now, it had all but disappeared. Rachel was right of course. She would bear the brunt of it. Slag. Slut. Whore. Vilified and shunned. Probably lose the baby. He would have to marry her of course. That went without saying. That was decided by others. *God, how many lives have been blighted by a shotgun marriage?* He remembered the feeling of total helplessness and loneliness as the world turned against them, because of their awful sin.

It was the interview that had been the problem. He couldn't say no, could he? Too good an opportunity to miss. And there *was* time to get there and back before… They had argued bitterly.

'If you're going to walk out on me now, don't bother to come back.'

'Don't be so ridiculous,' and he had left angrily.

It had been a relief to get away – he had to admit that. He had phoned her with the good news, but she had railed at him. 'Fuck you! Fuck your job,' and he had stayed another night. Better to catch the early train and arrive fresh the next day, wasn't it? But he had enjoyed the peace and freedom and the opportunity to think. Somebody had phoned the hotel. Rachel had gone into premature labour. Now she was asking for him. He could remember his panic, throwing clothes into a small suitcase, forgetting to pay the bill.

'First one sir? I'm sure it'll be OK.'

The staff smiling at his naïvety, some turning away because of his long hair and the gold ring in his ear and not on his finger.

It was grey and shivery when he slammed the heavy carriage door and looked for a public telephone. The hospital voice was remote and indifferent.

'Sorry sir. I cannot give out that information.'

'But I'm the father.'

'Sorry.'

'What the fuck is going on?'

He had slammed the phone down. *How dare they? Bloody officials.* Outside the phone box, he checked his change. Enough for another phone call or a bus to the hospital. He looked up. The sky threatened rain but maybe he could get there without getting soaked. And he needed to know. How was Rachel? Did he have a son or maybe a daughter?

He had recognised Stephanie's voice immediately. Stephanie with that hint of a foreign accent and chubby roving fingers and badly cracked nails; fingers that always held a black Sobranie. It was Stephanie who had sought him underneath that long Christmas table and stroked him to bursting point. But she wasn't Rachel and he had told her so after she had filled her mouth with him and then straddled him, eyes closed, in her tiny, cold flat.

'Stephanie. It's Alex.'

'Alex. Where the hell have you been?'

'What's happening? The hospital won't tell me. Won't let me in. How's Rachel?'

'I'm sorry Alex.'

'What do you mean?'

'I'm sorry but you should have been there.'

'What's happened Stephanie? For fuck's sake.'

'No need to get shirty with me. S'not my fault.'

'I'm sorry. Just tell me what's happened. Please.'

'You had a son.'

'I have a son?'

'Had Alex. Had. And a daughter.'

'A daughter?'

'Yes. She's named her Georgia. As you weren't here.'

'What do you mean had? You said had.'

'Taken into adoption. Both of them.'

'No. They can't. They can't do that.'

'They've done it. And she doesn't want to see you. Can't say I blame her.'

Alex lowered the phone and leaned his head against one of the cold glass panes.

'Hallo. You there? Alex. Alex.'

He could hear her voice fade as she turned to speak to somebody else with her. 'What? No. No. It's that wanker Alex.'

Her voice returned fully. 'Alex. You there? Alex.'

'Hallo.'

'You still there?'

'Yes.'

'Good, because I have a message from her. From Rachel, the mother of your children.'

'What is it? Tell me.'

'Fuck off, you useless cunt.'

The phone clicked dead and then fell from his fingers.

*

His father had often warned him of the dangers of mixing drinks. 'Beware the grape and the grain.' Nobody had warned him of mixing alcohol with anger, grief, loss and conceit. He woke the next morning in a grimy, piss-stained alleyway shuddering with cold and covered in vomit. He could only see through one eye and his ear throbbed where the gold ring had been torn away. Leading along the alley towards him was a trail of scattered red flower petals and crushed stalks. Before him, he could see the grey dawn and the occasional movement of early morning risers but felt no urge at all to join them.

11

—

Father and Daughter

THE PUB WAS empty as Alex entered, save for the young barmaid busying herself at the far end of the bar, who chose to ignore him. The interior was dark and brown except for the strong light flooding in through lead-paned windows and he stood for a moment trying to take in the mass of strange objects that adorned the walls and hung from the ceiling in a haphazard and apparently unrelated way. Normally, he would have chuckled and enjoyed their weirdness, but today his interest quickly evaporated. *Oh God, where shall I sit? What's the best place? Which door will she come through? My daughter. Which door…?*

He stood for a moment and then squeezed past heavy cast-iron table legs and sat on an upholstered chair. He sat quietly for a while, his nervous fingers finding and then slowly running over the metal studs that bordered the worn green leather seat, finding their coolness and regularity strangely calming. *Flick. Flick. Flick. Should I get a drink? Flick. Flick. I could certainly do with one. Flick. Flick. No best to wait. What should I drink? What would be right?* He looked across to where the barmaid was still checking something and continuing to ignore him. *Good. She's in no hurry.*

He realised he was sitting very upright and could already feel the tension in his back and shoulders. *Come on. Relax.* He looked around again. *Was this a good place to meet?* The pub was clean and tidy and interesting but empty and sad at the same time. It was as if it were trying hard to be jolly and welcoming but failing. All the signs were in place. Lights shone everywhere. Music played quietly in the background and nearby, an art deco maiden – young and confident in plaster – and draped in a simple flowing dress, thrust one hand clutching lit globes skywards, whilst at her feet, cherubs gazed on in electric wonder. To his right, a string of LED lights from some forgotten celebration still covered the doorway, and from the bar the illuminations from a pinball machine added an additional red, blue and green. On the walls, gilt mirrors of every shape and size reflected the light into dark corners. *But it still feels rather desperate. Like coming out of the dark magic of a cinema into the harsh afternoon sunshine of reality. 'Cos it's empty. It needs people. We all need people.* The barmaid was now glancing across at him.

It had been her idea. Georgia's. Somewhere near to where she lived and sort of neutral, where they could feel relaxed. Alex had readily agreed, happy not to have to make the decision, even though it had meant driving through the endless North London traffic. She had sent him a photograph of herself. Fairly recent, she had said and 'I'm the one in the middle'.

'I'll be wearing a red carnation and carrying a copy of the Times,' he had replied, but she hadn't laughed. He took the photograph carefully from his inside pocket and saw that one corner had already been bent back. He laid it on the wooden table top in front of him and tried unsuccessfully to smooth out the crease; to remove the damage; more damage. The round face of a middle-aged woman smiled out at him, and no matter how hard he tried, it would not change into that of a little girl. In front of him, a limp wallflower rested wearily inside a dark-blue nondescript bottle and he rested the photo against it.

What if I don't recognise her? What if she's late or decides not to turn up? Then what do I do? And what do we talk about? Do I kiss her on the cheek – my own daughter? Will she like me? He rubbed a hand across a damp forehead. *God, I wish Sam was here. She would know. Women always seem to know.* He felt uncomfortable in his jacket and for a moment wanted to take it off, hang it from the back of his chair, undo his shirt buttons and kick off his new shoes but he couldn't move and, in any case, Samantha had advised him on what to wear.

'Should I wear a suit? I do have one, somewhere. And a tie thing?'

'No Alex darling. It's not a job interview.'

'Bloody feels like one. Father required. Must be all seeing, all knowing, all forgiving – or is that forgiven.'

'Just be smart and relaxed.'

'I do have problems with *both* of those concepts.'

'No you don't. You're a fine figure of a man… when you try. But you will need a haircut and some new shoes.'

'New shoes! What's wrong with these?'

'Well apart from the fact that they have paint on them and shoelaces of two different colours? Nothing.'

'Oh Sam, I do wish you would come with me.'

'I really don't think Georgia will want to meet another woman in your life. Not yet.' And she had spoken her name, quite openly and normally, as though she had already met and accepted her.

Alex looked at his watch again. Ten minutes. He looked around the pub once more, at the original glass window panels, some broken and replaced with a slightly heavier frosted glass, at the large model bi-plane hanging from the ceiling, at the framed photographs of celebrities behind the bar that looked vaguely familiar, at the dusty sprays of artificial flowers and the worn oak flooring at his feet. Suddenly the door to the street moved and Alex's heart jumped. There was a slight delay and then through the half-opened door came a pram pushed by a young woman. In the pram a baby sat, looking around curiously. *My goodness, a mother, on her own, with a pram, in a pub. How things have changed.* Alex allowed himself a slight smile, leant forward, picked up his photo and replaced it carefully in his inside pocket. In doing so, he missed the middle-aged red-haired woman who came in directly behind the pram. Alex looked up and their eyes met uncertainly.

He had imagined this moment a hundred times, dreamed of little Georgia rushing sobbing into his arms, clutching him to her, instantly washing away the soiled pain of fifty years.

'Are you Alex?'

He nodded, the words he had rehearsed so many times left behind on some distant shore.

'Hi, I'm Georgia but you can call me George if you like. People do.' She held out a plump hand covered in rings.

Alex stood clumsily. Her hand felt cool.

'Hallo.'

He remained standing as she slid onto the seat opposite him and placed her bag on the adjoining chair.

'I think I need a drink.' She smiled nervously up at him.

'Yes of course. What… what would you like?'

'Oh. Vodka I think. With Coke.'

'Ice and lemon?' He felt pleased that he had remembered to ask and then moved to the bar, trying hard not to look back.

Georgia took a large swig of her drink, allowing Alex a moment to study her. He wondered if she had dyed her hair even redder for it seemed unusually bright and had the effect of pushing her naturally pale complexion towards the ghostly, like a sick patient wearing a Christmas cracker hat at the ward party. She looked up and realised that he was watching her.

'Sorry. Feeling a bit nervous.'

'Of course. Me too,' and she pushed her drink away.

She smiled. More broadly now.

'I was afraid I would be late. Have you been waiting long, Alex?'

He hadn't thought about her using his name, especially in such a familiar way, as if she had known him a long time. It caught him unawares, uncertain and he felt annoyed with himself. He hesitated.

'No, no not long.'

She smiled again, knowing he was lying and for a second it could have been Rachel looking at him, behind the heavy make-up, with that same knowing look, all those years ago and he felt his face tighten, and weirdly his ear lobe ached.

'Thank you for meeting me.'

'I tried you know.'

She sat back in her chair, surprised. Moved her hands to the safety of her lap.

'I knew about you and Jak, knew that Rachel was pregnant – well, didn't know about twins of course – but she, but your mother, didn't tell me. Not about you. When you were born I mean. Somebody else told me and the hospital of course. She could get so angry… so angry at times, that she seemed to lose all reason, and the hospital wouldn't let me in. I tried. I really, really, tried. They took over. Just took over.'

Alex looked nervously around the pub, afraid that others could hear him, but it was still almost empty, except for the barmaid now cooing and smiling at the young baby in the pram, with its mother looking on. Nobody seemed interested in an old man with a younger woman. He suddenly wondered if the baby had a father or if the young mother was even bothered.

'So, where were you? I always presumed you would be by her side. I never really understood that bit.'

'I was away. Rachel knew where I was. I left a number of course. She was in good hands.' He omitted the blazing argument before he left. Rachel's fear. His ambition. 'She went into premature labour. That was completely unexpected. I got back as quickly as I could, but it was too late. I was told she wouldn't see me and the hospital wouldn't let me in.'

Georgia watched him, unblinking, reached for her glass, looked into it and swilled the ice around with a tiny tinkling sound.

'I am so sorry. It was quite terrible.' His voice broke slightly.

'That's what happens I guess when you break the rules.'

Alex smarted inwardly but said nothing.

Georgia picked up her glass and finished her drink in one long draught. The action reminded him for a moment of Rachel. Always with a drink in her hand, always looking for the next one. But this was different. He knew that.

'Were you together? I always hoped.'

'Together?'

'Yes. You and Jak, your brother. Were you?'

She gave him a little smile. 'No. We were separated at birth. I never even knew of his existence until my teens. A friend told me.'

'A friend.'

'No, not a friend. Of course not. My foster mother. Yes, my foster mother told me. It was strange.'

'So you never met? Found out what he was doing?'

'No. Afraid not.'

The conversation faltered and stopped. Alex felt perspiration prickling on his brow.

'But they did look after you? You were alright?'

'My foster parents? Oh yes. As if… you know.'

Georgia sat back and looked directly at him. She waggled her empty glass.

'Oh… can I get you another?'

'Oh no. I'll get it.' She paused. 'You haven't touched yours.'

'No, not yet.'

'I don't normally drink at this time of day but…'

'I understand. I really do. Please let me pay for it Georgia.' It was the first time he had spoken her name, his daughter's name and the word caught in his mouth. He wondered how many times he could have used it by now, written it, heard it in her lifetime. Others, her friends and colleagues, even complete strangers, would have done so thousands upon thousands of times; but for him it was the very first, face to face. He felt totally wretched.

'Thank you Alex. You are very generous.'

She stood and made her way to the bar. Alex watched her and noticed that the hem of her long black coat was frayed and felt the urge to trim it, mend it, replace it, maybe even as a birthday present. *Oh my God. Her birthday. I have never ever sent her a card or given her a present. I know the date, of course I do, and it has passed now what – forty-eight times – and I have never done anything about it, and all the time, this woman, my daughter, has wondered.*

He got up and made his way to the toilets. Georgia was engaged in a conversation with the barmaid but looked up as he passed and waved his intentions. She nodded. Inside, he leant his head against the cool tiles and tried to take stock of the thoughts and emotions that were reeling inside him. The toilet was not that clean and the pungent smell of urine assaulted his nose. For a moment, he was back in that cold, damp alleyway and for a moment, he felt that that was what he deserved.

They spent the afternoon talking and exchanging stories, not noticing that the pub had slowly filled up and at last become alive. Eventually as the evening approached, they headed for the street again; Georgia declined a lift, shook Alex by the hand and disappeared into the crowds, promising to contact him shortly.

*

It was late when an exhausted Alex returned to Samantha and slumped into an armchair, a glass of white wine at a perilous angle in his hand.

'So, what happened? How did it go? What is she like? Was it OK?'

'Yes, it was OK.'

'Oh Alex. I've been so worried about you all day.'

'Sorry but I'm so weary and confused and… oh I don't know.'

'It must have been very difficult for you… for you both.'

'Yes. And I had to wear new shoes.' He grinned wearily to himself, placed the glass on the marble table and heaved himself into an upright position. 'Well she certainly reminds me of Rachel.'

'You did have the photo that she sent.'

'Yes, I know. But photos can be deceiving, can't they? Different when you meet people face to face. There was something about her look.'

'Her look?'

'Yes.'

'But? Is there a "but" coming?'

'It's more about expectations I guess.'

'Expectations?'

'Well, this is the baby, the little girl in lace and pigtails who I took to the park and taught how to ride her first bike and sat on my lap. Except of course I didn't. Instead a slightly run-down mature woman approaching fifty arrives full of her own thoughts and ideas and experiences. Yeah. Expectations.'

'But she is your daughter?'

'I think so. Yes, she must be.'

'You think so? Doesn't she have any papers? Any official documents?'

'Apparently they are very difficult to get hold of. But she did have a number of photos including this one, which she let me have rather reluctantly, and a letter, or at least part of one.'

Alex took a small, battered, black-and-white photo from the wallet beside him and offered it to Samantha.

'That's Georgia. When she was about fourteen or fifteen.'

The photo showed her grinning at the camera, with an adult standing behind her, hands on her shoulders, top half cropped away by inexpert handling.

'And the letter?'

'She gave me this copy. But I saw the original.'

'This is only part of a letter. The final page. Nothing before that.'

'No. She never had the envelope, that would have been thrown away and she could only find this page.'

'So, we don't know who it was sent to or when?'

'No but it *was* from Rachel. I recognise the handwriting and signature and look at the bottom there, see those little drawings. She always did that. Drew all over everything. Even me sometimes.'

Samantha missed his final words, reduced by his weary tone, as she quickly read to herself.

… have finally come up trumps. Strangely it has drawn us even closer and I'm so grateful for that. I still have this vast, gaping void full of pain which I hope will heal as time goes by. What a cruel world. But now in the cool light of day I feel much calmer and realise that blame is so negative. I have also decided to abandon my career in art. I was never very good anyway (as you know). Just a game really. Hope you get this OK.

Looking forward to seeing you very soon. All my love.
Rachel xxx

'So, we don't know who it was written to.'

'No. Her parents I guess. Or maybe her brother. God, I'm knackered.'

'Oh Alex. I'm sorry. You must be exhausted. Come on, a nice hot shower. Have you eaten? Then let me tuck you up in bed.'

They lay together, naked as always, facing each other. Samantha kissed him lightly but fully on his mouth and reached down to hold him, as she always did. Tonight, for comfort.

'Goodnight Alex.'

'Goodnight Sam.'

He fell asleep almost immediately. Samantha eventually turned away from his embrace and stared at the ceiling for a long time. *How did Georgia get hold of that letter?*

12

—

Sad News and a General

'GEORGIA PHONED.'
She stood before him, hands uncertain as to what to do. Concern clouding her eyes.

'Oh yes. Is she OK?'

'She wants you to phone her back.'

'Is everything alright Sam?'

'She sounded quite upset.'

'Oh dear. I'd better phone her right away.'

'Come and sit down first. You've only just got in.'

'Yes, but if she's in trouble…'

'Sit down Alex. Come on.' She walked towards the settee and sat down. 'Come on.' She patted the space next to her. 'We need to talk.'

'I've been on the common. Did some flower sketches. I'll show you.'

'Later darling. Later.'

'We should visit the coast really. Find some interesting stuff. Did I tell you I was thinking of doing some landscapes? Maybe semi-abstract. Bit like Paul Nash or Eric Ravilious. You know the exhibition has given me such enthusiasm.'

'Yes, of course. Alex. Alex, we need to talk.'

He bent forward and rubbed his face with both hands down to the point of his chin, as if that would rub the anxiety away. He sat up.

'I know.'

'This has been worrying you, hasn't it? I hear you walking about at night.'

'Just going for a pee.'

'We need to discuss this Alex. Your so-called daughter.'

'So-called? What do you mean so-called?'

'This woman turns up, out of the blue, about the right age—'

'She is the right age.'

'You don't know that. Just because she tells you. Have you seen a birth certificate?'

'No. She said she had lost it and was applying for a copy.'

'That's very convenient, don't you think?'

'No, not necessarily and anyway there's her eyes and hair. She reminds me so much of Rachel and of course there are the photographs.'

'Well of course, I've never met her…'

'No, but you will Sam, you will. You'll like her I'm sure.'

They both paused. Samantha leaned across and placed her hand on his thigh and rubbed gently.

'I don't want to upset you. That's the last thing I want to do. It's just…'

Tears filled his eyes and threatened to run down his face. He tried hastily to wipe them away.

'Oh Alex, darling, sweetie, come here.'

His voice was muffled against her shoulder.

'I'm so confused, Sam. Confused and guilty and angry and lost and… pathetic.'

'You're *not* pathetic. You're *never* pathetic.'

He sat up. 'Then why can't I think straight? Why don't I know what to do? It was the same then… exactly the same. I let them down, all of them and then walked away.'

He stood and walked to the window, his back to her.

'I deserve this, I really do.'

She went to him and placed her arms around him.

'Come on Alex. There was little you could have done. The system was stacked against you. You must see that. As soon as Rachel became pregnant, neither of you had a chance. Not a chance. She wasn't going to marry you and the state simply took over to protect the children. At least that's what they thought. Your feelings and needs were simply irrelevant. No wonder she was angry. She lost her son and her daughter. Snatched away. I can barely imagine what that must have been like. If I had lost my girls… She must have been distraught. She simply took it out on the only person she could. And that, my sweet, was you. What a tragedy.'

'You know, in the middle of all the fun and parties and booze and drunkenness, I think I really loved her. Loved Rachel.'

'I know. I've seen the drawings.'

'Really? Does it show?'

'Oh, it does. You know that.'

'You're not jealous, Sam.'

'Think I am a bit.'

'It's only a drawing you know.'

'It's a lot more than that.'

'Samantha Reagan, you are *full* of surprises.' He smiled. 'So, what about the drawing I did of you? What do you see in that?'

'More than I'm prepared to say. Come on, *you* are going to have something to eat.'

'What about Georgia?'

'Georgia can wait. I told her you wouldn't be in until late. Gives us a breathing space to decide our tactics.'

'Tactics. Now you sound like a general.'

'Perhaps I am. Come on you. Eat. That's an order.'

They moved to the kitchen and Alex sat quietly, watching her bustling around.

'Pizza OK? I've made some extra topping and a nice glass of white wine.'

'Perfect thanks.'

She watched as he ate.

'I think she is going to ask for money.'

'Money? What makes you think that, Sam?'

'She apologised for not getting back to you sooner, but she had a small problem. Nothing too serious she said. Just a domestic problem. When I asked her what it was, she was reluctant to say. Quite hesitant. Just asked you to phone her back.'

'OK. So, what do we do?'

'Well, let's see what we have. Georgia knows about you and Rachel and claims to be your daughter. How does she know all that?'

'Through her foster parents or the adoption society or maybe the Salvation Army? Or maybe she is a beneficiary in Rachel's will and somebody tracked her down.'

'OK. What about the photo?'

'Comes from her life with her foster parents.'

'And the letter. How did she have a copy of a letter that Rachel sent to someone else?'

'Don't know. Kept in her effects again, I guess.'

'Why didn't she tell you all this when you met?'

'It was hardly the right time for such detail. It was a pretty emotional time.'

'Yes, of course.'

'*And* she looks like Rachel.'

'Does she really or is it that you want her to?'

'Oh Sam, you make me sound desperate.'

'Sorry. I just don't want you to be hurt.'

They both sat quietly for a moment.

'Shall I wash up?'

'No leave it. Think you'd better make that call. Do you want to be on your own?'

'No, of course not. Come on, I'll make it in the lounge.'

Alex sat in one corner of the large room, picked up the phone and dialled, all the time looking at Samantha sitting opposite him. Georgia answered almost immediately. For a moment he didn't quite recognise her voice, which sounded quite breathless.

'Hallo. Georgia? Is that you? Oh good. Hallo. Yes, it's… er… Alex. Yes. Are you alright? You sound as if you've been running. No, nor me, well not anymore. Thank you for phoning. Yes, me too. Hallo, you still there? Oh good. Must be a bad line. Yes. I'm fine thanks and you? Samantha tells me you have a problem. Nothing serious I… Oh good. Nothing to worry about then? Good. Sam? Yes, for some time now. Yes, I suppose we are. Well it's a bit complicated. No. No that's alright. Hallo. You… Oh… er… yes of course. I'd love to. No, I understand, let me just write that down. And that's near Covent Garden. Yes, OK. Yes, got that. Oh OK. Yes of course. Yes, I will, thank you. Look forward to it. OK. Bye. Bye.' He put the phone down and looked at Samantha.

'That was odd. I had the strange feeling that she wasn't alone. Then, why should she be. Anyway, no money. Meeting her at a hotel. She wanted just me to go but I want you to come. Is that alright?'

Samantha nodded firmly.

*

They stepped into the empty reception hand in hand. The lone receptionist looked up briefly and then back to her computer. In front of them, a few steps led them up into a small lounge area with a bar and several seats and small settees. Alex looked quickly around and gestured towards one. They both sank into its low softness. 'Guess we're a bit early.'

The lounge had a slightly drab, well-worn feel, with table lamps balancing uncertainly on spindly stems, offering most of the soft, mute light. In the background, a machine hummed loudly, together with the low buzz of voices and the occasional laugh from somewhere unseen. In front of them, a large television screen silently mouthed some American daytime drama above a decorative carved wooden fireplace, long since cold and empty.

Alex picked up a menu from the round table in front of them. It was advertising Christmas. He put it back and stretched his legs.

'Can I get you anything sir? Madam?'

'Coffee Sam? Filter?'

She nodded.

'Two filter coffees. Cream on the side please.'

'Anything to eat?'

'No thanks. Too soon after lunch.'

'Of course sir.'

The afternoon moved on slowly with Alex frequently consulting his watch. Occasionally he got up to peruse the various framed paintings and photographs around the bar and reception and eventually went to talk to the receptionist before disappearing into the car park.

'No messages. Nothing.'

'Can't you phone her?'

'Tried. No answer. Hope she's OK.'

'And no mobile.'

'No mobile.'

'What do we do?'

'Just wait I guess.'

Dusk was beginning to creep around the hotel when they finally left. There had been no sign of Georgia.

*

Alex had said very little after their fruitless visit to the hotel and had spent a lot of time in his studio, only appearing when Samantha insisted that he eat something. Later, when he was out, she went to the studio and found it locked. Using the spare key, she let herself in and immediately saw his easel on which was a white canvas, blank, except for the word 'Georgia' brushed on several times, in different sizes, in grey paint and then scribbled over. The paint had sprayed over the easel and onto the floor. She had said nothing to him but waited, concerned.

'I think I'll go back to my flat. Just for a while.'

'OK.' She looked up slowly from her book, hoping she wouldn't give herself away.

'Just for a day or two. Just make sure everything's alright. Been a while.'

'Yes, it has. And it'll give me the chance to tidy a bit, stock up maybe, even have a go at the garden.'

'Am I that messy? That much of a nuisance?'

'No, no, of course not. We just both need a bit of space from time to time.'

She slowly placed a marker in her book and stood up.

'Come here.'

She placed her arms around his neck and shoulders and they stood together for a long time, saying nothing.

*

The old Volvo halted in the small car park. Alex turned off the engine, got out of the car, and locked it. He looked up at the building that housed his flat and was strangely reassured that nothing appeared to have changed in his absence except that it appeared to have shrunk slightly and if he was honest was not very attractive. *Postmodern ugly,* he mused.

He decided to enter by the side entrance thus avoiding any curious fellow residents, but also because he was anxious to see how Dionysus was faring. He opened and closed the side gate with the usual tussle and walked around to the small inner courtyard and garden. To his relief, the statue appeared, looking somewhat darker and greener then he remembered and largely covered by a shrub, whose leaves and branches had grown noticeably since the last time he had spoken to him. He stood for a moment, then gave a polite nod. *See you later.*

The flat was dark and small and stale. *I really need to clean its teeth and take it for a long walk.* A few books were still piled in corners and a dark-blue dressing gown was draped over his old armchair on which stood a mug, some papers, two magazines, a single sock and a screwdriver. In the sink stood a dish still full of water, with a spoon in it and an empty milk carton. He moved to the window, pulled the blinds open, moved the items from the chair to the floor – together with a handful of assorted letters and circulars that had almost blocked the entrance – sat down and shivered. *It'll be alright. Once it's heated up again and I've cooked something. Had a hot cup of tea.* He looked around.

For some reason, the phone was also on the floor, its green light winking with a message or two or more. Had been, all the while he'd been away, like a faithful pet waiting patiently for his master to return. He picked it up, balanced it on his lap and looked at it. *You will phone me won't you, when you arrive? Just so I know you're safe.* He could hear her voice; see the concern in her eyes. *That used to irritate me? Although it's not really much to ask. I used to think that she wanted to control me when I was away. How daft was that. We have come a long way.*

There was, without doubt, an energy that sizzled between them, even when involved in the most ordinary activities. A look across a breakfast table; a brush of hands in the supermarket; an exchange of glances in the post office; a tiny thank-you smile for opening the door for her; all would provoke an inner desire and the real prospect of later consummation. They seemed to have wall-to-wall foreplay crackling in their minds. It had nothing at all to do with age or having a young, smooth body. It was like being in the middle of a permanent Cole Porter song laced with liberal doses of Viagra. There was without doubt some sort of connection, some sort of energy, a chemistry between them. He smiled at the word. *Chemistry.* It was often used to describe that strange and powerful link between people, but he realised that he didn't really know what it meant or how it worked and of course nor did most others. Just some tacit understanding that something deep and mysterious was happening. Something that made people smile. Other people. And it was other people who smiled at them. They seemed to be able to recognise intuitively something bubbling away between them, even if they were unable to articulate it. It simply made them smile.

They would end up naked in bed. Always. That had become their default position. Nakedness made them close, both physically and spiritually. Sometimes, weary after a long day, they would sleep arms wrapped around each other, until the heat of the bed and their bodies pushed them apart. Often, they would talk. For hour after hour. About their day, their worries, their ambitions, their needs, their fantasies. Nothing was off the agenda. There were no secrets. Not anymore. And now, they were also committed students to the desires and secrets of their bodies; a joy all the more powerful as they realised, even at their age, how much more there was to understand and experience. They were not at the end. They were at a new beginning. How ironic that the controls and restrictions and denials imposed on them as young people, and the inevitable conditioning of guilt, should now become such a powerful aphrodisiac and consumer of wasted time.

He looked at his watch, wondered what she was doing and smiled. He knew he would miss her but at the same time he also knew how much he would relish his time away and the freedom that it gave him. A freedom that was all the more potent because she had given it to him, like a gift, and he to her. He picked up the phone and dialled.

Later, he sat thinking to himself as the evening slowly arrived through his open window, until its growing coolness forced him to close it. He picked up a writing pad and began to write in large letters, with a thick black pen; one word per page. Rummaging through a kitchen drawer he found an old reel of tape and began to stick each word separately to a wall. *RACHEL. ALEX. GEORGIA. JAK. SAMANTHA.* He sat back and studied them, like some crime scene, hoping for inspiration but none came. He wasn't even sure what he was looking for except something was missing. Something didn't quite add up.

*

Somewhere, there was a piercing noise that insisted on interrupting the dream that was percolating through his dishevelled mind. At first, he considered it part *of* the dream except its regularity was at odds with the haphazard sleep world that he was drifting through. He slowly emerged and half opened his eyes. The phone seemed to grow louder and then ceased abruptly, almost petulantly.

'Alright. Alright.'

He sat on the edge of the bed and yawned. Looking down, he realised he was still wearing socks as well as his T-shirt. He ran one hand over his stubble and hair, before walking uncertainly towards the lounge and telephone. The call listing showed that the last caller had been Samantha.

'Hi Sam. You called?'

She wanted to ask if he had slept well and had managed a decent breakfast and what he was doing that day and that she missed him in bed – but she resisted.

'Did I wake you?'

'A bit. What time is it?'

'Eight-thirty.'

'Really? God, I didn't realise. Must have been tired.'

'Sorry. It's just that I've had a phone call and thought you would want to know.'

'That's OK. Sounds intriguing. Who was it? Not Georgia?'

'No. It was from Edmund.'

'Edmund?'

'Yes. About a friend of yours, and his. Stephanie?'

'Stephanie?'

'Yes. Bad news I'm afraid. She died. Heart attack.' There was no reply from Alex.

'Did you hear?'

'Yes. Yes. Stephanie.'

'Sorry Alex. Were you close at all? Don't think you ever mentioned her.'

'No, not close.'

'Anyway, Edmund has left the funeral details for you, just in case…'

'OK. Thanks.'

'Anyway, must go. I'm off to the garden centre today. Have a good day.'

'OK. Thanks for letting me know.'

'OK. Bye.'

'Bye.'

Alex sat silently in his battered armchair. A sudden frisson of fear plucked at him, nudged him in the ribs, whispered into his ear. He felt slow beating wings fly silently over him and away. *First Rachel. Now Stephanie.* He reached and picked up the pad from the floor where it had fallen, found the pen, wrote two more names, stood and taped them to the wall. STEPHANIE. EDMUND.

*

'Well good to see you again. How are you? Stuck in your leafy straitjacket, except of course you can fly away whenever you want. You know, being a god.'

Alex gently cut the stems and leaves away from the statue's head and face like a hairdresser with a special client.

'There, that's better.'

He stood back to admire his work. 'You need a good wash. Are you allowed to wash a god? Seems a bit parochial. Can't you get some of your female followers to bathe you in asses' milk or something?'

He turned and moved to the nearby bench and sat down. From where he sat, the statue looked away from him. *Maybe he's turned away in dismay because I should know the answer; it's that obvious. Or if I really do know it, being brave enough to do something about it. Except I can't think straight. My mind is full of sharp memories and regret and pain and confusion, all mixed together into some sour stew. It is so frustrating.*

He stretched his legs and looked again towards Dionysus. *God, what am I doing, talking to a lump of plaster?*

He looked up at the clouds covering the dead sky like a painful bruise, grimly intent on reaching him. Then he heard the first splats of rain hitting leaves, making them dance, the sound enlarged by the tense silence that always precedes a storm. He stood up, pulled his collar up to protect him, quickly walked and then stepped inside the corridor that ran the length of the building and from where he could see the garden. As he did so, rain suddenly lashed across his vision, tearing into the flowers and plants, bending branches and flooding the window before him. Leaves were torn away and spat across the garden in a violent outburst, like angry, thoughtless words. Alex looked towards the statue, now hazy in the driving rain and a thought crossed his mind. *Had he just summoned this, just because I stopped talking to him, began to doubt him? No, that's crazy, but is it? The flower wasn't. The flower worked. That must have been him. Without the flower, well… who knows. And now this. Can't just be to make me wet, that would be beneath him. Why would he do something as trivial as that?* He shivered. Breathed in deeply. Outside, the rain stopped abruptly, as if at the command of a conductor's baton. The silence was only broken by large drips smacking into the sodden ground.

Alex spent the rest of the morning cleaning and tidying his flat. He found a large box, placed it in the middle of each successive room and threw away unwanted, broken and useless objects with a ruthlessness and energy that surprised him. By early afternoon he felt exhausted, made himself a cup of coffee, sat in his armchair and promptly fell asleep again. He awoke with a pounding headache, as the last light was beginning to drain from the sky. 'Damn. I meant to get this all done.'

He made his way to a chest of drawers and rummaged through it, eventually finding a battered shoe box. 'There it is.' The elastic band holding on the lid, long perished, snapped painfully as he attempted to remove it, leaving him sucking a finger. From inside came the aroma of must and years passed.

'Hi Sam. On my way. Pardon? Can't remember. OK. See you soon.'

*

'I thought this might be useful. My disgraceful history.' He sat on a stool in the kitchen, a half-eaten sandwich beside him and began to empty the box onto the marble top. The contents seemed to be largely old letters, still in their ragged envelopes, some postcards, a few photographs and a collection of odd but apparently meaningful objects. He removed the letters and put them to one side. 'Don't remember that,' selecting an old champagne cork. 'Remember that,' picking up a large brass belt buckle. Beside him, Samantha peered curiously into his past.

'What is that?' She pointed at what appeared to her to be a ring of small textile flowers. 'Bit large to fit a finger, isn't it?'

'Ah. Well. Wasn't actually meant to fit a finger. No. DH Lawrence has a lot to answer for. Wonder if it still fits?'

'Alex.'

He grinned. 'Look at this Sam.' He passed her a faded colour photograph. She paused to put on her glasses.

'Is that you?'

'Certainly is.'

Before her stood Alex, long, dark, curly hair to the shoulders of an open Afghan coat, sheepskin around the long collar and cuffs. She noticed a long tear in one sleeve. Beneath the coat he wore a dark T-shirt and tight jeans apparently covered in splashes of paint and held up by a thick leather belt and heavy buckle. That buckle. He was laughing at the person to his right, and although the joke bent her body into an inelegant position, Samantha could see she was stunningly attractive. She appeared to be laughing helplessly, eyes half closed, long hair and beaded necklace flying outwards, long, tanned legs wrapped in gladiator sandals, below a very short floral dress with long flared sleeves. To the far right of the photo stood another man. His Indian style patterned tunic came to just below his waist and was buttoned high at the neck. Around that neck he wore a slim metal chain with some sort of medallion attached. Below the tunic he wore tight, dark trousers. His neat moustache and goatee beard together with his general tidy appearance were at odds with the more flamboyant nature of the others. He had his arm around the shoulders of the fourth person, standing close to him, to his right; a young woman, quite short and stocky, who wore very distinctive black eye shadow, which descended onto her cheeks in tear-like drops. She appeared to have beads in her hair and wore a long, patterned skirt to her ankles and a tight top that showed off an impressive bust, between which hung an intricate necklace. Her right hand, covered in rings, held his fingers at her shoulder. They were both grinning at the joke unfolding before them. Samantha pointed.

'That must be Rachel.'

Alex nodded.

'She was very beautiful.'

He said nothing.

'And who is this?'

'That. Oh, that's Lord Edmund.'

'Lord?'

'Not really. Well not as far as I know. We just ribbed him over his posh voice and public-school background. Although he did come from a very well-connected family, which of course was a great advantage to him in the beginning.'

'Advantage?'

'Where do you think all those early portrait commissions came from?'

'Oh, I see. And who is she?'

'That. That's Stephanie. Poor Stephanie.'

Samantha turned to face him. Face a little uncertain. 'I presumed that Edmund is gay.'

'Yes. Probably is now. Not sure what he was back then. We never spoke about it. Too dangerous.' Alex had a sudden memory of Edmund, holding a glass of champagne, spilling it liberally over everybody, roaring and dancing wildly with men and women, wearing just a silk robe, which rapidly became undone.

'Dangerous?'

'Yeah. Remember the Sexual Offences Act only came into effect in 1967. Before that, men who had sex together, even with consent and in private, were committing a criminal offence. So, not only the prospect of prison but also blackmail, and Edmund and his family would have been perfect targets for a blackmailer.'

'Oh, how sad.'

Samantha returned to the photograph. 'But nonetheless, they are together. Look.'

Alex took the photo. 'Together?'

'Yes. Just look at them. They are a couple.'

'No. We were all good friends. That's all.' He put the photo back into the box.

'By the way, did it rain heavily here this morning?'

'No. Not a drop. Why?'

'Oh, doesn't matter.'

13

Funeral and Suspicion

S AMANTHA DROVE SLOWLY, even respectfully over the loose gravel and came slowly to a halt. She switched the engine off, looked across at Alex and then sat with him in silence.

'We're late.' He sounded sulky but she knew he was simply covering his feelings, hiding them away, afraid they might bubble to the surface and escape. They made no attempt to move but sat looking across the cemetery. In his mind, he knew it had been long ago, but despite the years, it was a time he still remembered *so* clearly. She hadn't been very nice to him, back then, when he had needed help, when he'd been lost. Maybe he had deserved it, but despite that, he still felt the need to be here. He also felt the urge to flee.

'Maybe they've all gone home?'

'No, the service has only just started. What do you want to do darling? Do you want to join them?'

He sighed. It had been a shock to hear of Stephanie's death. He could still see her; her round, sensual face smiling at him, large red lips and black painted eyes that offered. And of course, he *had* taken. They had been so young back then, younger than they knew, but full of laughter and hope and invincibility. False invincibility. Somehow, fifty years had passed like the turning of a page and now… she was gone. He struggled to equate the two. In front of him, four people were walking towards the chapel, the men sombre suited and the women dressed in black, one with a pink splash in her hair. They moved at a pace so much slower than normal life and said nothing. *Is that out of respect or is it an attempt to slow down what they were walking towards, what we are all walking towards?* Alex shivered involuntarily.

'Are you alright? Not cold?' Samantha placed a gentle hand on his thigh.

'No, I'm OK. Shall we get out. Have a look?'

He took Samantha's hand and held it tightly.

'What an extraordinary place.'

They paused on the rough roadway and looked around. Before them a jumbled mass of graves, headstones and crosses of all shapes and sizes were bent and twisted at every angle, as the ground had moved and turned and sunk. Suddenly, Alex had this macabre thought of the dead. Unable to lie on their backs, hands clasped, eyes staring towards heaven, they were being forced to hang on grimly to prevent themselves sliding towards each other in an undignified heap of bones. *No wonder they'd want a resurrection. Maybe death is as much a jumble as life.* He allowed himself a tiny smile, looked towards Samantha with the idea of sharing his irreverent thoughts but she looked too serious, too concerned. *Maybe not.* Nearby, vast willows spread their clipped foliage sideways, casting shade for the graves nestling beneath and the huge trunks of chestnut trees twisted upwards to where large fingers of leaves, now spotted with rust, held bright green leathery conkers, some of which had thudded disrespectfully onto the tombs below. Close by, a pair of crows strutted, completely unconcerned.

'Shall we sit for a while? We can see the chapel from here.'

They sat on a battered wooden bench.

'Did you notice the design of the back of the bench, Sam?'

'You mean the sunrise motif?'

'Or sunset.'

'Oh Alex. You are cheerful.' She smiled at him, squeezed his hand and then continued studying his face. 'Did you know her very well?'

'Stephanie? No, not really. We certainly weren't the best of friends.'

'Best? Sounds as though you didn't like each other?'

'Maybe closest is a better word. Not the closest of friends.'

'So, was she a friend of Rachel?'

'Goodness no.' He laughed. 'No, they certainly didn't really get on. Always sniping.'

'Because of you?'

'Me!' He turned to face her, panic rising as if she knew and then turned away, placed his arms on his thighs, clenched his hands and looked away into the distance.

'We were young and naïve and rather daft at times. We had no idea what we were doing or the consequences. Not like today when the young are so much more worldly wise and experienced. We didn't really have a clue.' He wanted to tell her more. Of Stephanie's plump, white body that he had wallowed in, of her cracked nails on his back, but he couldn't. He sat up. 'It's a bit odd sitting here, looking at your own inevitability. Shall we go on?'

They stood and slowly walked along, stopping to point out inscriptions as they went.

'Look Alex. Missing in… where? What does that say?'

'Why don't you wear your glasses?'

'Not in public. Couldn't do that. So, what does it say?'

'Missing in France. 1916. Aged twenty-one.'

'*Oh*, how awful. They never found him. In their minds, they must have spent the rest of their lives looking. We've been so lucky. Really. Haven't we?'

He pulled her towards him and gently kissed her cold cheek, knowing that she was trying to ease this for him. They walked hand in hand until suddenly, they arrived at a part of the cemetery where the landscape changed, where the large headstones and plots were replaced by a mass of small objects and faded colour. They both stopped and looked at the scene before them with some astonishment.

'It's children. Small children. Sam.' He turned towards her, his face pale.

'Come on Alex.' She pulled at his arm, but he moved further towards the tiny graves.

'Look at this.'

They moved past a mass of toys and teddy bears, dolls, lamps and toy furniture, windmills, footballs and football pitches, even tiny spectators. A sombre nursery room of lost joy, frozen in time and still trembling with silent pain.

Alex stood. Bowed. The years suddenly piled on him, etching into his face.

'I can't do this Sam.'

'It's OK my darling. It's OK.'

'I think we should go home. Sorry.'

They turned back towards the car park next to the chapel. As they did so, people began to emerge from the building and stood outside in a dark mass. Some shivered in the chill air, looked at the floral tributes, uncertain of words, turning to a desperate cigarette. Some men shook hands with each other, and a few women embraced. Alex suddenly stopped dead and put his hand to his mouth.

'There Sam. There.'

'What is it?'

'There. Getting into that car. It's Georgia.'

'Georgia?'

'Yes. I don't understand. What's she doing here?'

Samantha looked in the direction that Alex had pointed but only saw a large black car driving slowly away.

'Are you sure?'

'Yes. Of course I'm sure.'

'Wait here.' She strode off towards the group of mourners nearest to the point where the car had left from. Alex could see her smiling and pointing before walking back towards him, serious faced.

'Well, what did they say?'

'It wasn't her.'

'What? Of course it was her. I saw her plain as day. It was Georgia.'

'Nobody knew of any Georgia even when I described her red hair, exactly as you had told me. But they knew who had got into that car and driven off.'

'So, who was it then?'

'It was Stephanie's daughter.'

*

They drove back home in silence, each tangled in their own thoughts. Alex sat with his hands knotted in his lap, occasionally looking out of the side window as if hoping the answer would pass by.

'So, there must be something missing. Why would Stephanie's daughter pretend to be yours?'

She sat next to him, holding his hand but looking directly at him. Alex turned away from her gaze and put down his teacup. It rattled slightly. He looked down at the floor and began to speak in a low staccato fashion, occasionally glancing at her to gauge her reaction.

'Stephanie and I had a fling. It was nothing. She had most of the men in college at some time and maybe a woman or two. Who knows? That was it.'

'OK, and was this while you were with Rachel?'

'Yes, I'm afraid so.' There was a long silence. Alex spread his hands apart as if this gesture meant some sort of justification. 'She was very experienced. Did things I only dreamed about. Wasn't even sure existed. And I didn't want to be left out. I know. It's pathetic.'

'But Stephanie wanted more?'

'I'm not sure. Either that or she wanted to hurt Rachel.'

'Why would she want to do that?'

'Rachel was very beautiful. And clever. Stephanie wasn't.'

'And Rachel had you.'

'Yes.'

'Stephanie sounds very insecure.'

'Yes. Guess she was, behind that body of hers.'

'Did Rachel ever find out?'

'No, not really.'

'Not really?'

'Well every woman was suspicious of Stephanie. She made it quite clear what she was after.' He paused for a moment and then looked at Sam, gauging whether he should continue. She gently squeezed his hand.

'Alex, sweet Alex. Look, we all have loads of baggage and I don't want to pry but I do want to help you. You know that, don't you?' She saw his eyes moisten again and realised how hard this was for him.

'I just feel so foolish.'

'It was a long time ago. We were all foolish.'

He took a deep breath and smiled at her.

'So, do you think Stephanie is behind this?'

'Looks like it. Some sort of revenge.'

'And involving your own daughter like that. Seems a bit extreme. I mean after me, she simply moved on to the next. God knows what's happening in heaven. She's probably been kicked out already for trying to screw an Archangel.'

That night they lay side by side, holding hands, each full of their own thoughts. Waves of exhaustion shackled Alex's limbs and body and slowly his eyes.

'I need to turn over. Goodnight Sam.'

'Goodnight Alex. Sleep well.'

There was no answer.

*

'Do you believe in omens?' Alex spoke through the window, touching the cold glass with the tip of one finger. The image of the old woman in the coffee shop had pursued him, appearing whenever his restless mind relaxed.

'The ides of March you mean?'

'Thoughts that won't go away I suppose.'

'Are they omens?'

'Not sure.'

He continued to look through the tall Victorian windows. Outside, the garden was still and crouched uncertainly. Dark-clad people walked past briskly, turned inwards against the cold. Flattened against the outside glass were four small ochre-coloured leaves, carried there by wind and rain. They each displayed their shape perfectly against the flat pane, except for a tiny tail that had remained upright and quivered in the breeze, like some strange breathing creature. He studied them, pleased at the aesthetic they made, these four shapes, wondering how nature managed that or was it sheer serendipity? He knew where the leaves had come from. Facing him was an old silver birch tree. Once, it had been tall and slender, wrapped in dazzling white parchment, but now, it had thickened and twisted, its white now streaked with grey patches.

His eye caught a sudden movement. A thin branch quivered like a bow string as a small bird flew into the frozen air, from the cover of a thicket. Why had it done that? *Why not stay where you are, safe and concealed?*

Fiona was ill. Her mind was slowly shutting down and he knew he had to visit her, whatever the outcome, rather than stay here, safe in his bosky thicket. Beyond the garden, the watery sun summoned enough rays to catch a window or the metal of a greenhouse in a brief twinkle of light. A hopeful twinkle.

'I need to visit Fiona.'

Samantha looked up at his silhouette. 'Yes, I know.'

'Will that be alright?'

'Of course Alex. You know that.'

He wanted to say thank you but knew that wouldn't be appropriate. There was no need.

'When will you go?'

'Well, if I can get a ticket and a hotel room, I was thinking tomorrow.'

The drama of Georgia seemed to have settled down. There was no more contact and their phone calls to her remained unanswered. She seemed to have vanished. The phone rang.

'Not again.' Alex walked briskly towards the sound. 'Hallo. Hallo. Hallo. Anybody there?' He put it down noisily. 'No answer. Yet again. You sure you don't have another lover. Some young hunk?'

'Don't need one.'

They stood together, her arms around his neck, his hands on her flanks.

*

The cab was five minutes late, leaving Alex watching anxiously from a front window.

'I could always take you. It's only to the station.'

'It's OK. Be here in a moment. You do enough for me as it is Sam.'

She shook her head.

'Here he is.'

There was a mad flurry, a snatched kiss, a final wave from the roadway and suddenly, he was gone. Samantha watched the cab disappear from view, slowly closed the front door and stood in the silence that now replaced him.

It was about twenty minutes later that there was a rapid knocking on the front door. Samantha's immediate thought was that Alex had returned. Forgotten his ticket or something and she smiled at the thought of his bustle and colourful language and realised that she missed him already. But it was not him. The woman who faced her wore a black bobble hat, beneath which her face, made paler by the cold air, appeared round and white, punctuated by red lips and heavy black eye make-up. She was wrapped in a thick grey coat and over one shoulder was carrying a large red leather bag.

'You must be Samantha.'

Samantha tried not to shiver and cursed her decision to wear slippers. She pulled the door to behind her and stood, denying entry.

'He's not here.'

For a moment, the other woman looked surprised.

'You are clever.' A faint smile. 'I know. I saw him leave. Overnight bag. In a cab. Headed for the station I guess.'

'What do you want Georgia?' She could feel a chill catching her face and fingertips and another her stomach.

'I just want to talk. Woman to woman. That's all. Can I come in? I need to explain. Please.'

Two doors down, a neighbour, reaching for his house keys, stopped to take in the situation on the doorstep. He looked towards Samantha queryingly. She nodded back. *Everything was OK. Thanks.* He looked away as Samantha opened the front door, allowing Georgia into the long hallway.

'In here.' Samantha walked briskly into the lounge, not looking behind her and stood in front of the Twombly, arms folded.

Georgia stood facing her, looking around as she slipped off her coat, dropping it casually onto the settee. Her woollen hat followed, allowing her red hair to fall out. She shook it. Samantha could see it was dyed. 'What a lovely room. Lovely house. You are *so* lucky. I live in a small bedsit and it's damp.' She coughed lightly as if to prove the point, then sat down, crossed her legs, displaying plump thighs above black knee boots and pulled the leather bag towards her. 'Is it OK to sit here? You didn't say.'

'Why are you here Georgia? What do you want?'

Georgia looked slowly around the room again. 'I can see why he would be attracted to you. All this.'

'All what?'

'This.' Her voice rose. 'This. Dear Alex was always out for what he could get. Mind he doesn't dump you when he gets bored, like he did my mother.' Samantha ignored the taunt. *Until you see the whites of their eyes.*

'Your mother?'

'Yes. My mother. Rachel.'

She doesn't know.

'So, what is this? Revenge? Is that what you're after?'

'Revenge?' Her face gleamed, then she realised she had shown too much. Drew back. 'No, of course not. This, dear Samantha, is about the truth. This is about how that bastard ruined lives. Destroyed my mother, killed my brother and abandoned me.'

'Killed your brother?'

'What?'

'You said killed your brother.'

Georgia ignored her and pulled the red leather bag towards her, struggling to open it. The bag was old and scratched and heavy and for a moment Samantha felt a pang of alarm as she reached inside, afraid she might be reaching for a weapon. She looked around for something to defend herself with and then watched helplessly as Georgia withdrew a large battered book.

'It's here. All here.' She waved the book at Samantha with both hands and then drew it back into her bosom. 'You can see. You can't touch,' and she opened the book with the reverence of a priest at evensong. She looked up at Samantha now standing before her, anger filling her black-lined eyes. 'This.' She stabbed at a page. 'And this.' Each page was filled with violent words, press cuttings featuring Alex slashed through, drawn images of a man being crucified, photos with heads pierced by daggers, a colour photo of Rachel, but with dark tears drawn on her smiling face, a baby's identification tag that once fitted around a tiny ankle. Some of the papers had become yellowed and curled and brittle with age. Samantha turned away, deeply alarmed, wondering what to do.

'Yes. You might well be shocked. The evil bastard.' Georgia now dabbed her eyes with a tissue but just managed to spread the blackness further, until another wave of emotion swept over her and she sobbed aloud.

Samantha looked at the figure hunched before her, felt sadness but also anger. Increasing anger.

'How dare you come into my house with this rubbish.'

Georgia looked up. The sobbing ceased abruptly. She snorted. Face dry. 'What!' She struggled to stand up but Samantha stood over her, face set. *Rapid fire!*

'I know Rachel was not your mother. We saw you at Stephanie's funeral. Stephanie. Your real mother. You are nothing but a sad, pathetic hoax.' Her words slapped home, red across pale cheeks.

Georgia sat, open mouthed, eyes wide. Then leapt up, words suddenly vomiting from her.

'You cow. You fucking dried-up… fucking… old… *cow*.' Georgia screamed the last word. Samantha felt spittle on her face. Georgia stood defiant. Eyes wide. There was a trembling silence. Samantha faced her. Unflinching but inside she felt afraid. But there was no time for that.

'Now. Get out of my house.'

Georgia gently slid the book into its bag. She said nothing, but picked up her coat. She turned to face Samantha again, a strange smile now appearing on her face, eyes still black-smudged.

'What is so funny Georgia or whatever your name is?'

'Wouldn't you just like to know.'

She put on her coat, took a small compact from one pocket and proceeded to repair the damage to her make-up and check her hair. She did so quite leisurely as if Samantha was not present, as if she had simply called into a rest room. She snapped the compact shut and then looked at her, the same little smile still playing around her lips.

'She had no interest in him you know. None at all.' Her voice contained quiet venom. 'He was just a bit of fun that went wrong. A bit of necessary fun. She was always in love with somebody else. Madly in love. You know I'm talking about Rachel, don't you?'

'Go on.'

'All these years and he thought the great love of his life, the mother of his children, had deserted him. All these years. Such delicious pain.' She laughed.

'What do you mean?'

She turned to put on her hat, tucking her hair under, just leaving a few strands showing.

'Don't you have a mirror?' She looked around. 'You must have a mirror.'

'What do you mean?'

She smiled again. 'Haven't you guessed? Rachel was *never* in love with Alex or any man for that matter.' She leaned forward into Samantha's face. 'She was in love with Stephanie. Yes. Stephanie. My mother. They fooled you all. Now, are *you* going to tell him that, or am I?'

'I don't believe you.'

She began to walk towards the front door, bag over one shoulder. When she reached it, she stopped and turned. 'Who do you think the letter was for? The other half you don't have. That I have. Didn't you wonder?' Her laughter echoed in the empty hallway. 'Don't think this is over. It's far from over.' Suddenly she held out her hand. 'Nice to meet you Sam. Is that what he calls you?' She shrugged at the icy response, opened the door, looked up at the weather, pulled up her collar and slipped away. Samantha pushed the door shut and then leaned heavily against it.

*

Alex had initially phoned to let her know that he had arrived safely. He phoned again, later that evening to say he would be leaving Dumfries on the late morning train and then the Tube from Euston and a cab on to her. That would be easier. Yes, he had visited Fiona. Yes, she was OK. Yes, he would tell her everything when he returned. He had sounded very tired. She had put down the phone, pondering about how to tell him about Georgia's visit. Dare she tell him everything? How would he react? He might be devastated. Before her, the settee on which Georgia had sat now felt like a crime scene, a toxic spill and she felt an illogical need to scrub it.

Alex had enjoyed the landscape from the train window and the cool freshness of the Scottish air. He had been tempted to linger in the town, watch the river roll past, maybe old memories also but instead he had made his way directly to the care home. *Never look back mate.*

The home was crisp and starched and surprisingly bustling, considering the mainly static nature of the residents. A cheerful nurse had directed him. 'Fiona? Oh aye. She's fine. She'll be in the lounge, in her favourite chair. Straight ahead.' *Favourite chair? She never had a favourite chair. My mother always deferred to my father. He had a favourite chair. His chair. We had what was left over. No, not quite true. She had second choice; I had what was left over. Still, maybe now, after all this time, she deserves a favourite chair.*

He found her, gazing intently through a large window into a neat, well cared for garden, a serene smile on her face and despite the excessive heating, a plaid rug over her knees. He took off his coat, already feeling his forehead dampen. She did not turn towards him as he sat beside her, did not blink but continued to soak up some continuing wonder before her, in a garden that sat empty, waiting for the spring.

'Hallo Fiona. It's me, Alex.' He could not remember when Mum had changed to Fiona. She turned towards him but did not speak. The same smile on her face, regarding him intently, through pale eyes. Then turned back.

'How are you? I've brought you some flowers. Look, pink cyclamen. In a pot. You like them. Do you remember? In our garden? Fiona?'

He placed the pot before her. She looked down with the same expression, pulled it towards her, and then returned to the unknown appeal of the garden.

Alex sighed, placed his hand on hers and together, they sat silently for a long time, he full of memories, she full of the unknown, until eventually the light began to slip away. He stood, put on his coat, bent and kissed her on her cheek. She turned towards him, the same serene look, eyes searching for something, then turned away again. He left.

Alex was surprised by the level of clamour and the taste of pollution as he arrived back in North London. He felt weary and travel stained and looked forward to a long, hot bath, maybe with Sam. That would be nice, although he probably only had enough energy left to wash her back.

'Alex. Welcome back.' She flung her arms around him.

'Hi Sam.' He moved to kiss her. It was a long, lingering kiss. Searching. Questioning. Reassuring.

He declined her offer of a meal.

'Had a sandwich on the train. Dying for a cup of tea though. Any news? Anything happened?'

She hesitated.

'Nothing that can't wait. I'll get you that cup of tea.' *Her* own mouth also felt dry.

*

Later, she sat with him in the bathroom, the same bathroom where he had drawn her, only now *he* lay in the large roll-top bath, unshaven and with his wet hair flattened darkly to his head, arms resting on each side as if it were a throne.

'Georgia turned up.'

'She did? Where?'

'She came here. Just after you left.'

'Here?'

'Yes. She obviously watched the house and waited until you had left.'

'No. Sam. What happened?'

Samantha related the story. Of her strange behaviour. Of the book of hate. Of how she had confronted her and her violent reaction.

'She also told me something else. Something that might upset you.'

'Tell me Sam. I need to know. I need to know everything.'

'She told me that Rachel and Stephanie were together.'

'Together? What do you mean, together?'

'Oh dear. That they were in a long-term relationship. Always had been. They were lovers, I suppose. Everything else was a front. I'm so sorry Alex.'

Alex sat quite still. Looking straight ahead. Samantha reached for one damp hand. He didn't seem to notice.

'Are you OK? Alex, are you?'

He shook his head slowly. 'Yes. Yes. That sort of makes sense. When I tried to get to the hospital, it was Stephanie who tried to stop me, put me off. And I thought they didn't like each other. All that time. But they both had children, so was that a charade or a mistake? Did they not like men at all? No, surely not, Stephanie had just about everybody or at least that's what we thought. Maybe we all got it so wrong.' *So why did she want me, that Christmas time?* 'Although I must admit, Rachel always complained about my performance.'

'Really?'

'Afraid so. Ejaculation City. Frequent visits but never stayed long.'

'Oh dear, but maybe they were in the same position as Edmund. Not totally certain of their sexuality but certainly afraid to make it public. Surely that would have been disastrous for them and the end of *any* career back then. And they would have been stigmatised, maybe forever. How awful. How unfair.'

Alex nodded. 'Poor Georgia, if that's her real name. Obviously schooled by her mother to take revenge on men. On me. And I was so gullible.'

'No Alex. You thought she *was* your daughter. She *was* convincing and you were just…'

'Desperate?'

'Just wanted to do the right thing.'

'S'pose so.' He sat and thought. 'Also begs another question Sam. Who is Georgia's father?'

'Oh yes. And of course, have we seen the last of Georgia? She didn't seem very stable.'

'And another thing.'

'Yes darling. What is it?'

'This water is bloody freezing now. I hope nothing's dropped off.'

Samantha moved to fetch a warm towel, held it out to him.

'Are you alright, sweet man?'

He nodded.

'Are you sure?'

'Yes. I've only ever wanted to know the truth, and now I do.'

14

Clues and Confession at Last

SOME WEEKS AND then months passed and nothing further was heard from Georgia. However, they both still felt besieged, avoiding phone calls, tensely opening letters, wondering what might be left on the doorstep, turning to see if they were being followed in the street, waking in the night to suspicious noises in the darkness. Alex never left Samantha's side.

'This is ridiculous, Alex.'

'Yes. I know. But what do we do?'

'Let's look at all your photos and relics from the past again. Perhaps we missed something.'

'Relics?'

'You know what I mean.'

They spread the contents of the old shoe box across the floor.

'What are we looking for Sam?'

'Don't know. Anything.'

She picked up the photos one at a time. The four friends together.

'Seems different now Sam. Even more complicated. Are you still sure that Edmund and Steph are together in this photo?'

'Maybe.' She picked up the second photo. 'How old is Georgia here?'

'About thirteen I think.'

'And it is her?'

'Oh, without doubt. You must know that.'

'Yes. And who is that standing behind her?'

'Don't know, except it's a woman with half of her missing.'

'And where is it taken?'

'No idea. In the middle of a field by the looks of it.'

'Pretty manicured field wouldn't you say? And that building in the background or part of a building. Where is that?'

'What building? Let's have a look… Oh yes. So it is.' He looked up, hunting for a memory. 'Oh my God.'

'What Alex? What is it?'

'That. That's Edmund's place.' He looked again. 'Yes. I'm sure of it.'

'Edmund's?'

'Well, not his. His parents. We all went there once. Couldn't believe it. It was huge. His parents were away so Edmund took us. Head of Security or whatever he was called, Adolf I suspect, kicked us all out, including Mr Edmund. Don't think they appreciated hippy art students invading their fiefdom. Very powerful. Very protective.'

'Are you sure?'

'We were certainly asked to leave.'

'No. That this is the home of Edmund's parents.'

'Pretty certain.'

Samantha sat back, gently waving the photograph.

'In that case dear Alex, what is a young Georgia doing there, who is the woman standing behind her; could it be her mother with her hands on her shoulders like that; and *who* is taking the photograph?'

'Edmund?'

'Edmund. Must be. Who else?'

'Oh, my dear God. Now what do we do?'

*

It was a few days later when fate took a hand. Alex clearly heard the letterbox rattle and the letter strike the tiled hallway floor. He waited, listening for the pop of ignition or for an echoing explosion or the stench of canine excrement or some other awful miasma. The letter simply lay there, gleaming white. He picked it up and read the address. *Mister A R N James? Nobody has ever called me that. Nobody knows that… probably not even poor Fiona now.* He turned it over, but there was nothing on the back. He opened it with some trepidation.

> *Dear Mr A R N James,*
>
> *I am writing to you on behalf of your dearest friend Mr Edmund who I know you appreciate greatly. He has talked about you consistently. I have melancholic news. Mr Edmund has become very ill. I am hoping that you forgive my temerity, but I do believe that a visit by yourself would be very efficacious.*
>
> *Your sincerely,*
> *Vihaan Lal.*

*

They stepped from the shade of the Tube station into the confident bustle of a sunny Sloane Square. Samantha dropped her sunglasses down from their perch in her hair.

'Look Alex.'

He followed her gaze.

'So pretty.'

Before them stood a row of young magnolia trees, their flowers like plump purple tulips, inviting a squeeze, and contrasting delicately against the stone and plate glass of the surrounding buildings.

Alex had phoned Edmund. His voice had sounded weak and tired.

'Hallo you old bastard. How are you?'

'Alex. Is that you dear boy? What a lovely surprise.' Alex could hear the warmth returning to his voice.

'Thought it was about time we visited you.'

'We? Does that mean the lovely lady as well? That would be delightful. God knows what she sees in you though.' The warmth deepened into mischievousness.

'No. Well. Thanks. So… anyway, how about next Saturday. About two? After lunch?'

'That would be perfect. I'll have the bubbly ready old mate.'

'Mate? That's a bit lowbrow for you, isn't it?'

'Well. I do accept that it is normally associated with commoners but…' Alex heard his voice break, just slightly. '…but I'll make an exception for you.' His voice faded, then returned. 'Don't be late will you, old chum?'

'I'll be there. Bye.'

They walked hand in hand into the Kings Road, negotiating the Saturday crowds, occasionally stopping and waiting patiently, sometimes squeezing through gaps in the moving human wall. Around them came the eclectic mix of many languages and from a cluster of small street stalls flowed a flurry of cooking aromas, catching their nostrils. Nearby, people sat on low walls and steps, happily devouring their culinary choice in the sunshine. Normally, Alex would have stopped to join in and soak up the air of contentment, particularly as they were now opposite a major art gallery, but he pressed on, anxious about his friend.

'Is it very far?' Samantha's feet were already beginning to ache. Perhaps she should have worn something flatter, more comfortable but she had wanted to look good for Alex.

'Not now. Straight on until Oakley Street and then left over the bridge.'

The bridge, when it arrived, ornately spanned the sparkling Thames like some confection in its coat of pink, blue, green and grey.

'Have you been here before Sam?'

'Henry had some business contacts in Battersea I think. Anyway, I do remember crossing at night, when it was all lit up, like a fairy tale.'

'Not far now.'

They stopped in front of a row of red-brick buildings.

'This is it.'

Alex pushed open a wrought-iron gate and they climbed steps to the front door, where he pressed the intercom.

'Hi Edmund. It's us.'

There was a very long pause.

'Hallo darlings. First floor. Door's open,' the reply crackled back abruptly.

They entered a long, dim, musty hallway, within which were traces of coffee mixed together with a dash of oil paint or turps. On the floor, patterned lino, made indistinct by generations of footsteps, shone from the light creeping around a partly opened door at the far end. The tall walls were divided by an old dado rail, above and below which embossed paper, once painted bright white, had now faded to a comfortable cream and here and there, small pieces had torn or become unattached. As they approached the door, their steps echoing on the lino, they passed numerous framed paintings and prints hanging on the wall. Normally, Alex would have stopped with a smile to study each one but now he resolutely ignored them.

'You there Edmund?'

'In here my dears. Come right in.'

The room was dominated by light pouring through windows that stretched almost floor to ceiling and looked out onto a small walled garden. Edmund was sitting in a tall bamboo chair, which fanned out dramatically behind his head. He was wearing a red spotted cravat within a black silk robe, which seemed to swamp his bony frame. His hair, pulled back into his small pony tail, was now white.

'Edmund, you old bugger.'

The two men shook hands.

'I'm so sorry lovely lady. Can't stand at the moment you know. Do take a seat.'

Samantha bent and kissed him on one cheek.

'How are you Edmund? We hear you've not been too well?'

'Not well? Was that Vihaan? Oh, what a naughty boy. I told him… Anyway, I'm fine thank you. Nothing serious.'

'Is he here? Vihaan?'

'No. The sweet boy has gone out. Left us oldies together. What a gift he is. Looks after me *so* well.' He reached across to pat Samantha's hand. 'Thank you so much for coming Samantha *and* for bringing him,' he nodded towards Alex, then sat back. 'And I must say, you look as lovely as ever. Right, the bubbly. Should be chilled by now. Vihaan has put a couple of bottles in the fridge for us. Alex, be a dear. In the kitchen. Next door. Would you?'

Alex left them, entered the small kitchen and leaned against a worktop, head bowed. He felt saddened to see his old friend looking so frail and Edmund's reluctance to talk about his illness simply fuelled his fears. And yet, there were also other issues, suspicions, to tackle. He felt sick. He opened the fridge.

'Sorry mate. No champagne.'

'Oh no. I distinctly told him. I'm *so* sorry.'

'Don't worry Edmund.'

'No, it's simply not good enough, when your chums visit. Look, Alex, be a sweetie. In the storeroom, there is a case. Can you put a couple of bottles in the fridge for me? Thanks so much.'

Alex found himself back in the long hallway. Through the slightly opened door he could hear Edmund's voice and Samantha's occasional laughter. He moved past the kitchen to the first room, opened the door and looked inside. It was a narrow bathroom. Over the edge of a large bath were draped a pair of white towels, monogrammed but with their softness worn down, looking a little threadbare. Next to them, a large chrome tap dripped slowly into a white basin, leaving a green trace. He closed the door gently. *Apart from champagne, what exactly am I looking for?* His mouth had become dry and he listened acutely for any sound that might expose him.

The storeroom was next door and he relaxed, knowing that this was where he was supposed to be. The room was full of packages and boxes and in one corner stood an old hoover and various mops and brooms and a black bucket full of cleaning materials. It was quite dark and he felt for the light switch. It failed but on the floor near the doorway stood the crate he was looking for and he quickly withdrew two bottles. *My goodness Edmund. Nothing but the best for you.* He left them in the doorway, stepped outside and listened. The comfortable drone of voices continued. That left two rooms. The next was a bedroom. *Not there.* That left just one.

As they had entered the flat, they had passed a room on their right, which he now realised would have been overlooking the road and the park opposite and so would be full of light. *That would be his room. Where he worked. Had to be.* He stood outside and turned the door handle. It was locked. He looked fearfully along the hallway. He felt a long way from safety but the key was still in the lock. He turned it slowly and as quietly as possible. *It's OK. I'll just say I couldn't find the right room. Didn't see the crate of champagne. The light wasn't working.* He stepped inside, aware that his heart was now pounding. It was the right room. To one side stood a small table with a chair pushed under. On it were a pile of sketchbooks, drawings on paper and pieces of charcoal. Nearby stood jugs and vases full of pencils and a variety of brushes and the adjacent floor was covered in pencil shavings and black charcoal dust. Around three walls were shelves, full of books of all shapes and sizes, boxes of materials and in between, odd artefacts, including a piece of blue and green abstract glass, a pine cone and a small bronze of a male nude. Next to the large curtain-free windows stood an easel covered in splashes of paint of every colour and along the walls were stacked dozens of canvasses. Alex began to swiftly sift through them. Many were unfinished. All were portraits or figures. He picked one up to look at in more detail. *My God Edmund. You are good.* He turned to the final stack and halfway through, he found it. The naked female figure stared out almost belligerently at the viewer. She was seated on the very bamboo chair that Edmund now sat on and was obviously heavily pregnant. It was Stephanie.

'Are you alright Alex? You got lost?'

'Sorry. Just coming.'

Alex realised that the atmosphere had changed in his absence. Samantha was sitting very upright and had uncrossed her legs, hands in her lap. Edmund looked silently at him, as if he was waiting for something. He seemed paler.

'Sorry. Couldn't find the storeroom and when I did the bloody bulb had blown. Anyway, they're in the fridge.'

'Thank you Alex. Thank you very much.'

Edmund and Samantha exchanged glances.

'Everything OK?' Alex's mouth felt dry again and he tried not to lick his lips.

'Well.' It was Edmund who spoke. 'Well, Samantha has been telling me about Georgia. How awful for you. Just awful.'

Alex flicked a look at Samantha, trying to gauge how much she had told him.

'Why didn't you tell me? I'm not sure what I could have done old friend, but at least we could have shared it, the three of us. Couldn't we?'

Samantha reached for her handbag. 'Well, you might be able to help Edmund,' and she took out the two photos.

Alex felt an icy chill strike him and he looked on helplessly, aware of the collision about to happen, needing the truth but afraid that his frail friend might now snap into a million pieces. *Please don't, Sam.*

'This is of the four of you.'

'Oh, my goodness. I remember this. Look at that. Look at us. I've got this photo somewhere. Oh my. All that time ago, and yet it only seems…' He looked at Alex with a broad grin. 'And you, wearing that disgusting fleece.'

Alex saw his grin, suddenly saw his teeth connected to his jaw bone, to empty eye sockets, to his skull and wanted to weep.

'And then, there's this one.'

'Who's that?'

'That's Georgia. A young Georgia.'

'Where did you get this?'

'Do you recognise the person standing behind her?'

'No.' He made to hand the photograph back.

'And what about the building you can just see in the background?'

'Sorry. No idea.'

Samantha looked across at Alex. Alex leant forward, arms resting on his knees, looking directly at Edmund. He wanted to extend his hands, to hold Edmund.

'It's your parents' place.'

'No.' Edmund shook his head slowly. Alex wasn't sure if the 'no' was a denial or a request to stop this horror. 'No.'

'Did you take it mate? Did you?' Alex spoke so softly as if he was talking to a lover or a small child. Edmund said nothing but looked at the floor.

'I found it.'

Edmund looked up. His face drained. He waited, almost expectantly.

'I found it. The painting.'

'I was hoping you might.'

Alex placed one reassuring hand onto Edmund's bony knee, then sat back.

'What painting? What painting, Alex?'

Edmund faced Samantha. Eyes glistening. 'I painted Stephanie, here, in this very chair in fact. A nude. When she was very pregnant. Never could resist a good subject.' He gave a wry smile.

Samantha paused and then leaned towards him. Face set. Eyes unblinking.

'So, you.' Alex felt the pain descending. 'You are Georgia's father?'

'Yes. Yes I am.'

There was absolute silence.

Edmund began to explain. He seemed relieved to finally unburden himself. It had happened after their abortive visit to his parents. 'You remember Alex? Remember that miserable arsehole who kicked us out. Threatened to set the dogs on us. And me, son and heir.'

'Dogs. Don't remember any dogs.'

'They were metaphorical dogs mate.'

'Go on. Edmund. Please.'

Sometimes Stephanie would join him and a few others for some heavy drinking.

'You never liked that, Alex?'

'Made me puke a great deal.'

Edmund was the only one who could afford this and that attracted hangers-on, but Stephanie was a friend and that plus Edmund's uncertain sexuality made them perfect drinking partners. The emphasis would be on the serious business of alcohol and not sex.

'And my God could she put it away, but Steph spent a lot of time asking about my background and my family and their position.'

Eventually, very drunk, he invited her back to his flat, something he rarely did, where there was a rare malt, only to be shared with another aficionado. She refused and took him instead to a dark, unpleasant and rather public alley nearby. Alex gasped.

'I was so surprised, but she grabbed me, and I think the idea of being seen excited her plus maybe the power of reducing me to this level. Anyway, against the wall, drunk, in the dark was not only physically demanding and as you well know Alex, things that physical were never an interest of mine, but also quite unsatisfactory. Later when she told me she was pregnant, I was amazed.'

It had been necessary to inform the family, who immediately began to make arrangements.

'They must have been horrified Edmund!'

'Oh no. They were delighted.'

'Delighted?'

'Oh yes dear girl. Their errant queer son had managed to sire a bastard. Things *were* looking up. There was, after all, a long tradition of children from the wrong side of the blanket. That, they knew exactly how to deal with. A homo for a son was a complete disaster. Not just criminally and because of the possibility of blackmail – although they would have dealt with that – but more importantly because of the slur on the family name. I was supposed to leave a long trail of weeping servant wenches.'

Samantha looked across at Alex. Said nothing. Knew what he was thinking. Edmund continued. So, there was a paternity test, Stephanie was offered an abortion, which she refused and then an income for life in return for her silence. She was also threatened with the consequences of not maintaining that silence.

'So, you see, that should have been that. I had no idea she was schooling her daughter against you. None at all. You didn't say anything.' He looked pleadingly from one to the other. There was a long silence. It was Edmund who broke it.

'Why Steph should want to do that, I have no idea. Because of poor Rachel I suppose. Despite appearances, they were quite close.'

Alex looked across to Samantha and shook his head.

'Anyway, dear friends, I will sort it out. It's the least I can do. I will tell the family and I'm sure a heavy will arrive on her doorstep with an offer she also simply cannot refuse.'

'Surely you don't mean…?'

'Oh no. Not at all. We will offer her an income for life. Should have done it before really. You won't be bothered by her again.'

'Oh Edmund. Have you never wanted to be a normal father to her? She is your daughter after all.'

'I would have loved that, Samantha, but unfortunately it simply was not possible. Maybe today in more enlightened times but not then and in any case, I would have been a terrible father. No, better Steph took that responsibility. I did meet her occasionally. Just to make sure everything was OK. You know, I was devastated when I heard of her death. Wanted to go to the funeral, but simply couldn't.'

'And what was she called? Steph's daughter?'

'Georgia of course. Same as Rachel's.'

All three sat, lost in their own thoughts. It was Alex who eventually spoke.

'So, what now? For you Edmund?'

He smiled at Alex. 'I need a holiday mate. Need to feel the sun on my back and young, smooth, tanned flesh under my fingertips. Sorry Samantha. A little graphic.'

She shook her head with a little smile.

'We'll fly east. Vihaan will look after me. He is such a joy.'

They sat in silence again, each full of their own memories, hopes and dreams. Edmund stood shakily; Alex shook his hand and hugged him for a long time like a lover, reluctant to let go. 'Look after yourself, you old bugger.'

'I will mate.'

He kissed Samantha on both cheeks and held her hands. 'Look after him.' He paused thoughtfully. 'Do you think I could have that photo? The one of young Georgia. I did take it after all.'

Soon they stood once again in the street. The sunshine had died away now into a warm evening. Alex looked up at the flat in the hope of seeing Edmund at a window, but he wasn't there. He felt that he would never see him again.

The champagne had remained in the fridge.

15

The Secret Garden

'WE COULD ALWAYS go into the garden.'
They both lay naked on top of the bed, fingertips just touching, windows open, curtains moving slightly as the last breeze of the day brushed against them. But now, night was arriving rapidly and sucking up the heat into a thick blanket and covering them. Outside, there was a heavy stillness and the land panted.

'It certainly might be cooler Sam.'

There was no immediate reply. Alex felt her fingers gently stroking his.

'I didn't mean that.'

He turned his head slightly to look at her, but her gaze remained upwards.

'Bit late for gardening Sam.'

She smiled to herself. Spoke quietly.

'I want you to fuck me in the garden.'

She turned herself towards him, watching his eyes, excited by her proposal, but part of her still waited for the reproach, waited to be stood in the corner in disgrace and with no tea.

He turned and raised himself onto one elbow.

'Fuck you? In the garden?'

'Yes. Yes. That's the right word. FUCK.' She pronounced it strongly, accentuating the sound. 'Absolutely the right word. You taught me that. Describes what I need exactly.' She paused. 'What do you call a word which describes itself?'

'Onomatopoeic?'

'That's it. Like cock.'

'Cock?'

'When he's big and hard and rampant, that sounds exactly like what he is. Doesn't it? He's certainly not a willy. Too childlike. Not a penis. Too biological. He's a… cock.'

'Samantha Reagan. I don't know what's got…' He stopped, realising that for the first time, he had spoken her married name and that it didn't matter. She didn't appear to notice.

'I don't know what the fuss is all about. I want to feel the grass soft under my sore feet and the hot breeze stroking my weary body. I want to hear the sounds of the night pouring into my ears and smell the night. I want to wallow – yes wallow – in the darkness and not make a single sound and feel my senses running sharp and wild. That's not lovemaking. Lovemaking sounds more like making cupcakes for someone. I want to feel the danger, the passion, the rawness, the urgency. I want to fly.'

He felt himself becoming aroused by her words.

'In the garden?'

She turned to face him, eyes sparkling. 'We've come so far Alex. You've made that possible and I want to be this woman who is capable of such pleasure. Such self-awareness. I know it's there. I know it. I've felt it and I want to break the rules. Other's rules. I'm tired of people seeing this creased old body and thinking that's me. That's all I am. I want to have this delicious secret. A secret that will make me smile. Make us both smile forever. I want to be naked with you in the garden. Not unclothed but naked. You're right Alex, naked is so completely different. I was unclothed before… except for skin-cream and self-consciousness, except for fear and doubt. Now I want to be fulfilled. Make me fulfilled Alex. Make me powerful before it's too late. Before the aches and pains eventually take over. Can we?'

'Wow. What a speech.'

'So… are we going into the garden? Can we? That thought makes me feel so… alive… and well… horny.'

He lifted his hands from his lap. 'Me too.'

'Oh my God Alex.'

The house watched them move silently through the darkness, heard the patter of naked feet on the kitchen flagstones and the door opening slowly. Outside, the air was no cooler and they stood for a moment holding hot hands and listening. In the far distance a car drove past, its engine note quickly disappearing into a pinprick of noise and from nearby came the relentless drone of a television, its muffled voice rising and falling. Only the slightest breeze rustled the parched grass and limp leaves but so faintly as to exist mainly in their imagination. The world was hot and still and rubbed up against their bodies. Alex resisted the temptation to giggle aloud at their boldness.

They moved together slowly and silently, like shadows, hearts pummelling and laid a quilt onto the grass. No sound. Not a word was whispered. In silence, Samantha laid down. In the dim light, she could only see his pale outline above her and imagined his hot eyes, watching her.

He lay down beside her, on his side, his flesh brushing her skin, a sensation so normal but now like that of soft needles rippling over her. One hand cupped her shoulder and then moved. In her mind, she imagined its travel until it finally rested on her breast. Above her, she sensed the pressure and heat of his mouth coming towards her and she met it. A crushing, sliding collision, scalding and frantic, until breathless. She felt him move, saw him dimly, knew that he now knelt, knees pushing through the quilt and dry grass into the hard soil far beneath him. He leaned forward and placed his mouth on her, hot and wet, as he had done before, hearing her tiny sound, running his hands upwards along her hot body, searching, recognising, finding her alert, knowing that even in the darkness, her eyes would be closed and her head would begin to move slowly, from side to side. Suddenly, loud applause broke out from the muffled television. Startled, he stopped. Even in the darkness he knew she was grinning. The applause died away, back to its vague babble.

He felt her hands on his head, pulling at his hair, then feeling for him as he moved upwards, guiding him until suddenly and with no sound, they were one.

'Don't move,' she whispered.

They lay together, motionless, feeling each other's heat, feeling their own longing growing stronger and stronger, now accentuated by different senses. They became aware of the powerful silence, of the intense softness of their bodies where they touched – thigh to thigh, belly to belly – like never before. They 'saw' their heartbeats and the blood flowing through them, heard their lungs pumping, sensed their nerve ends flickering, felt the damp heat of each other's breath. She closed her eyes again for a moment, feeling whole and complete and safe, feeling him tremble, feeling his inert power like a stallion waiting for the off, somewhere deep within her.

Alex felt her simmering beneath him, a rounded, soft warmth that dissolved softly at its edges. Somehow, it seemed divorced from her body but at the same time, emanated from her and within which he appeared to be floating. Was this magic, or simply the darkness denying some senses and insisting on others more mystical? His knew that her hands were moving slowly on his back, but now they were different hands. Now, they were the hands that once had held her babies, stroked her favourite dog, slipped over her young body in a long mirror. Now he felt those experiences soaking into his skin.

Within her, not moving, he found himself in a soft, velvet heat; that surprised him and removed his sense of place. His mind told him, could even draw a diagram and yet his body, this most sensitive part of his body, had become disconnected, drifting. He tried to understand but again knew the futility of conscious thought. This was indeed a strange magic, understood by the body but where the brain was a stranger, even an interloper. He tried hard to switch off the machinery, but it wasn't easy. It had been switched on for most of his life and still reminded him that he was aching, that he was still conditioned by a lifetime of superficial need, of local gratification, of rapid physical release. Now, however, he felt as if he was learning again, learning to swim again. Not convinced he wouldn't drown. Still needing to hang on to the pool side. But for now, he simply floated somewhere within both of them, welcoming sensations and wonder. An extraordinary energy seemed to flow back and forth between them, like warm waves, lapping against his conscious mind, slowly eroding it. Then, suddenly, he remembered his knees and they instantly began to ache.

Samantha opened her eyes, saw a handful of stars struggling in the polluted night sky, wanted to call out to them, encourage them, tell them that there was no need to worry, that despite pre-conceived assumptions, they could still burst into light, burn brightly like she now was. Alex's forehead lay on her shoulder and she moved her head seeking his hot cheek. He sensed the movement, felt the intention and moved his mouth to meet hers.

Above them, the same stars looked down on this man and woman, two incongruous bodies, creased and roughened, their bones and blood worn and weakened by time, learning at last to be themselves.

They lay silently side by side for a long time, holding hands, relishing their nakedness, ignoring the urge to retreat to the cover of the house, luxuriating in their behaviour, body and mind now buzzing with a sort of beautiful understanding and rebellion.

Samantha felt her eyes begin to moisten. Her past had held her so tight, dammed her juices, switched her to neutral, betrayed her. She knew that. Now the inner dam that had choked her for so many years had burst and the black fetid waters that had lapped against its side had flooded away. No more secret cities, no more dark fortresses, no more locked doors. Now they both had a new direction. The old had been limited and careful, part of their conditioning, leading them along false trails, through dark alleyways, often to dead-ends. Many had tried to stop them, sending them in the wrong direction with an incomplete map and no compass, but finally they had arrived. She felt safe and secure. The barriers had fallen. Worn away by words. Crumbled by conversation. Demolished by dialogue. Undone by understanding. Shattered by self-belief. Suddenly, she thought about her hands and held one up in the darkness. She knew it was tiny and tired, skeletal and stained like a tombstone; thick veined and rippled like sand when the tide is going out – and she knew it was going out. There was no stopping it. Before, she thought they had served their purpose and should be tucked away, out of sight, quietly lost in her lap, that her fingers had become hard and empty-tipped, switched off, inert. But instead they had become flushed with the touch of his body, the closeness of his hand, alive now and rippling with power and joy – defiant and gripping like a new-born in a new world.

Above them, the lights of an aircraft moved across the sky, left to right, heading east. Alex watched it move silently across the dark sky. *Maybe Edmund is on that plane. With Vihaan. And even Georgia. His Georgia. Looking down at us.* He watched until the lights disappeared and even then, continued watching. Eventually he sat up, turned onto his knees, gasped quietly and stood, unsteadily. He held out his hand in the darkness and whispered, 'Come on Sam.'

Carefully they made their way back to the kitchen and stood in its centre, leaving a small trail of grass cuttings and held each other in the darkness.

'I can't stop trembling Alex.'

'I can feel you.'

They stood together for a while, quietly, minds replaying, feeling each other's closeness. She spoke against his chest.

'That was… immense, Alex. Really immense. Like nothing… I can't explain.'

She looked up at him. 'Are you alright? I don't know. You didn't…? The darkness…'

'Extraordinary. Quite extraordinary.' He could feel the dampness on his brow and upper lip and across his body. The flagstones were beginning to feel welcomingly cool under his feet.

'Come on. Let's have a warm bath.'

'A bath? OK. Don't turn the light on just yet. Need to find something to put on.'

'Put on? You've just been rolling about in the garden stark naked.'

'I know. Silly isn't it.'

*

They sat facing each other, saying nothing, Samantha smiling at him continually, hair loose. Alex swept his hand slowly and absently over the hot suds, deep in thought. At how easy it had been to get lost, to follow the stony path trodden by so many other elderly feet, not to query, simply to accept. He had wanted to move, heard the old stallion whinnying desperately but had ignored it. That had not been easy, but the outcome had been a closeness and a strange magic that he had never known before. She lay back and watched him. He had given her so much. Yes, his sensitive fingers and eyes exploring her. His heat and energy within her but more than that. His unashamed touch in front of the world, his help for her to emerge and grow. But his greatest gift? He had shed his armour and sword, laid down his cloak and revealed a soft underbelly, so vulnerable, so easy to slice into and he had trusted her with that. Now for the first time ever she felt complete.

She slipped down the bath and rested one hidden foot high between his thighs. He looked up suddenly, grinned at her. 'Samantha Reagan. How come, a repressed statistician with a degree in tidy logical minds can become so outrageous in bed *and apparently* increasingly out of it?'

'Don't complain. It's you who opened the flood gates.'

'So, am I in danger of drowning then?'

'Only in pleasure, sweet man.'

16

Revelation

IT WAS SAMANTHA who answered the front door. In front of her stood a young man, quite short, wearing an open-neck white shirt and dark jacket. He smiled broadly at her, the whiteness of his teeth contrasting with his brown face. She noticed curiously that his hairstyle was unusually traditional, almost old fashioned with a side parting, and that the short black moustache and beard around his chin struggled slightly. The man raised both hands together in front of him and bowed. 'Good morning.' He continued smiling broadly, as if he had known her forever, his brown eyes fixed directly on hers.

She might have felt a pang of alarm at the intensity of the stare but instead felt a smile appearing which had the potential of becoming a laugh for no reason.

'Good morning.'

'Are you Miss Samantha?'

'I am.'

'Oh, I am so pleased to meet you,' and he reached forward with both hands and shook one of hers vigorously. 'And is Mr Alex in the house?'

'He is.'

'Oh, again I am so pleased. I have something for you. Please can you help me?' He half turned and pointed towards a large van parked nearby.

'Of course. What is it?'

'It is from Mr Edmund.'

'Edmund?'

'Oh yes.'

Samantha paused for a moment. 'So… are you Vihaan?'

The young man bowed again and the smile slipped away, for a moment of respect. 'I am Vihaan.' Then returned as broad as before. 'Come Miss Samantha, it is not heavy, but it is quite large.' His eyes never left hers. He opened the iron gate for her, moved to the back of the van, opened it and began to pull at a package wrapped in thick brown paper, secured with wide adhesive tape and containing a number of official-looking labels. Together, they carried it into the hallway, just as Alex appeared.

'Alex, this is Vihaan. He has brought us a mysterious package. From Edmund.'

Vihaan raised his hands in greeting as Alex did the same. 'Namaste.'

The young man's eyes shone. 'Namaste Mr Alex.'

'So how is Edmund? We haven't had a word.'

'He is quite unwell. Too ill to write or phone at the moment.'

'Poor Edmund.' They all looked from one to the other, rather helplessly.

'Vihaan, you must stay for a meal. Stay the night. You must be tired.'

'Thank you for your kindness. But I must get back to the airport to return the van and catch my flight home. I don't want to leave him so long, but I promise I will write to you. Mr Edmund says nothing but good words about you.'

He waved cheerily from the van, his smile as broad and infectious as before and then he was gone. Alex and Samantha stood watching the van disappear, reluctant to move, feeling a cocktail of emotions, as if a very close friend or relative was leaving them, maybe never to be seen again. Samantha shivered.

'Suppose we had better undo it Sam?'

'I feel quite nervous.'

'Me too.'

Soon the floor was strewn with brown paper, heavy cardboard and balls of sticky tape. They withdrew the contents, placed it against the settee arms and stood back, together. They found themselves looking at a large painting.

'Oh, it is so beautiful. Is it by Edmund?'

'Oh yes, but like nothing I have ever seen before.'

'Is there a note with it? A letter?'

'Can't find one. Think this might be it.'

Samantha pointed. 'This is the letter?'

Alex nodded.

'My goodness.' She began to look more closely. 'And that's you? And that's Rachel and Stephanie. So that must be Edmund?'

'Yes. You remember your portrait Sam? You remember the symbolic bits he included? That beautiful blue stopper bottle and the ivy? Yes? Well, this is the same.'

'So, what does it all mean?'

'At the moment, I have no idea. Except it is a thing of extreme beauty. My goodness Edmund. What a tour de force.'

The painting was long and rectangular and produced on canvas, stretched over battens. Thick cardboard corner pieces had protected it, together with a substantial cardboard casing. The air smelled of oil paint. They both stood in silence, overwhelmed and trying to make sense of it.

'Why has he done this Alex? So much time and effort but why?'

'Think he is telling us something, or asking us maybe. Maybe his last opportunity.'

'Oh Alex. Don't.'

They stood closer, looking at the detail, Alex shaking his head from time to time in sheer admiration.

The four main figures stood in a row in pairs, facing the viewer, each having an arm outstretched towards their partner. They were dressed as they had been all that time ago in the old photo they had shown Edmund. *He must have found his copy.*

'Have you noticed he has put Stephanie and Rachel together, looking towards each other and almost holding hands? Not quite. Fingertips stretched and almost touching and you and Edmund the same, except Edmund is glancing across at Stephanie, you're looking outwards and it's your fists that are touching. Like friends do.'

'And she's ignoring him. She's looking the other way. At Rachel.'

'So, he knew after all. About the two of them.'

'Looks like it, which is sad for Georgia. No wonder she's so mixed up.'

'Unless of course, he is accepting them, maybe even wanting to protect them.'

'Why?'

'Because they were also on the margins. You know, gay or bisexual or whatever they were. Doesn't really matter what they were, they were still excluded, shunned by society, even criminalised.'

'Maybe. Difficult to tell from their expressions, because they don't really have any. Quite deadpan.' She looked closer, from one to the other. 'No, nothing really. Oh my God.'

'What? What have you seen?'

'It's you Alex. You. You have eyes and a nose, but you don't have a mouth. It's been left blank.'

'Yes, I noticed.'

'So, what does *that* mean?'

'Again. I don't know.'

He continued to silently scour the painting, lost in appreciation but also seeking clues and understanding. Behind the four figures stretched a long landscape, whose style reminded him of the background landscapes of Da Vinci, based on reality but inherently strange and mysterious. Villages tucked into towering mountains, winding roads going nowhere, empty lakes, rocky outcrops, drifting clouds and a complete absence of people. He knew that Edmund had done this for him on purpose, but why? Was this a comment on his profession, that it was empty and unreal? Or on his own lack of ability, relying instead on the genius of others? Would he be that cruel? Or maybe that life really was strange and unpredictable, closer in reality to Da Vinci's imagination?

'Have you noticed the flowers Sam?'

'All over the ground?'

'Yes, but they are each holding them, in some form or other. The girls have a bunch in their arms, Edmund is wearing a flower and I have a pot of them beside me. So, how's your flower recognition?'

'Not bad and I have gardening books of course.'

'Do they include meanings?'

'What, the meanings of flowers?'

'Exactly. That's why he has included them. Even the different colours of the same flower make a difference.'

'Well, I'll fetch it, shall I, my book? But that and that and that and that,' she pointed towards each figure, 'is white lilac. That I do know and you each have one.'

Samantha left Alex to study the painting. From above Rachel's head, he could see two silver white doves soaring upwards towards one of the two suns placed at either end of the painting. The edges of their wings were painted gold. It reminded him of a Byzantine panel, and he was sure it also occurred in Psalms somewhere. Above Stephanie, another gold-tipped dove flew to meet them. Wasn't the dove a symbol of peace and innocence? The peace and innocence of little children. The thought shook him.

'Here it is.' Samantha appeared with a large book, whose dust jacket was torn and bent over in places. 'It means youthful innocence and memories.'

'What's that?'

'White lilac. You all have that.'

Alex huffed through his nostrils.

'And what's that? Growing between Edmund and myself. Looks like a fir tree.'

'Don't know, except look, he's written words, here and there, between the plants, some of them, along the ground, in perspective. You can just see them. Isn't that clever? Arborvitae. Yes, that's a type of cypress, I think. Means… let's have a look. Means… everlasting friendship.'

Alex smiled.

'Don't think they are all so positive I'm afraid. Look, you and Rachel are carrying marigolds. That means pain and grief and that yellow tulip means hopeless love. What about the rue?' She turned the pages quickly. 'There. Regret, sorrow, repentance. Oh dear.' She looked at Alex. 'And there's a lot more. Carnations of all colours – red, pink, yellow, purple, mauve. You're right, they'll all mean something different. There's a dandelion, an acacia, yellow roses, pink roses and that's a morning glory.' She closed the book, too concerned to continue. 'Not to mention the objects in the grass. Look, there, a serpent. Think we know what that means. And the odd apple, there and there and why has Rachel got a key hanging around her neck?'

'I know that one Sam. Seen it before. Means lost love. Death of a lover. Question is, does it literally mean death or just loss and of course which lover did she lose, which lover is she mourning for?'

'Please don't get upset darling.'

'Don't think I am. Rather overwhelmed that Edmund would do all of this for us.'

'For you. His everlasting friend.'

'Think you are in there somewhere, Sam.'

'Maybe.'

*

Alex woke up very early the next morning. He looked across at Samantha, sleeping peacefully, carefully got out of bed and tiptoed out of the room, taking his robe which hung on the back of the bedroom door. It was just after dawn, the day had barely awoken and waited fresh and quiet, pondering what was to come. Alex suddenly thought about Dionysus, and how he witnessed this magic every morning. *Lucky him.* He had lain awake for a long time, thinking about the painting downstairs, imagining the four figures talking to each other throughout the night; laughing, arguing, joking, complaining, remembering, experiencing. He had even considered getting up again. Wanting to sit quietly in front of it. Eyes wandering. Needing to soak up its meaning. They had even followed him into his sleep, the four figures, talking incessantly to a very young Alexander, who stood mute between them, rooted to the spot, looking quickly from one to the other, trying to grasp their words and meanings, aware that although their faces and bodies were still so youthful and hopeful and beautiful, their eyes and minds and mouths were full of the years that had passed. Sometimes they laughed, sometimes they were sad, sometimes they turned away, denying him answers.

He pulled the heavy curtains apart, allowing the morning light to slip in and then sat, with some difficulty, cross-legged in front of the painting. The colours had changed. They now seemed more brilliant, deeper, and as he immersed himself, the rest of the room around him slowly disappeared. He imagined himself sitting on top of a mountain, looking across a valley, into a landscape. Was that blush of colour a vague rainbow, in the distance? Could he feel a tiny breeze tugging at his hair, gently ruffling the grass and flowers and clouds before him? He looked at himself, standing there, one fist touching that of his friend, the other extended outwards, away. He hadn't really noticed before. Had missed it. It must have been there. He saw that *this* hand was open, as if he was offering it and he knew at that moment that she was there, that Samantha would slip her hand into his and that the picture would then almost be complete.

He moved onto his knees and with some difficulty pushed himself upright. Edmund had offered him his story. It stood before him, flowing with pain and sadness and joy and uncertainties and success and failure but now at last, he could see it all, grasp it, own it. Knew that it couldn't hurt him anymore.

He moved to a writing desk, opened a drawer and took out a pencil. He held it up, inspected its point and moved before the painting.

Very carefully, he drew a smile onto the missing space on Alex's face.